ENDURANCE

FADE INTO YOU BOOK 3

DAKOTA WILLINK

DRAGONFLY INK PUBLISHING

DAKOTA WILLINK, LLC

This book is an original publication of Dakota Willink, LLC

Library of Congress Cataloging-in-Publication Data
Paperback ISBN: 978-1-954817-06-7
Endurance | Copyright © 2021 by Dakota Willink | Pending

Cover Design by: Dragonfly Ink Publishing
Cover Image by: Deposit Photos
Editing by: Tamara Grisanti
Formatting by: Dragonfly Ink Publishing

Published in the United States of America

PREFACE

Dear Reader,

Thank you for reading *Endurance*! This book was previously published in K. Bromberg's *Driven* World Project. It is the same story, but some characters and places have been modified for copyright protections.

Thanks again, and I hope you enjoy the book!

Dakota Willink

"Like shining stars, every one of us has the potential to light up the darkness with our own particular brilliance."

— UNKNOWN

PROLOGUE

Kallie

Bright neon lights lit up the starless night and excited chatter echoed across the extensive field covered with carnival tents, rides, and games. The smell of popcorn and fried dough filled the air as eager kids dragged their parents from one location to the next. The Arlington County Fair had always been one of the most extraordinary weeks of the year for me, where I'd made countless memories with my mother. But this year, things were different. It was no longer just the two of us parading in and out of funhouses and craft tents, sampling fried Oreos and gorging on kettle corn. Our family of two was now a family of four—and soon to be five.

I glanced at my semi-blended family as we waited in line for funnel cakes loaded with powdered sugar and cinnamon. My father was staring adoringly down at my mother as if she were the only person in the world. He was smiling with his hand resting on the slight curve of her belly. As tiny as she was, my mother couldn't disguise the baby bump swelling at her middle for much longer. She thought I didn't notice, but I did. I wondered how much longer they would wait to tell Austin and me.

My gaze traveled to my half-brother. Austin, completely oblivious to the new sibling on the way, was being a typical eighteen-year-old male. His eyes were glued to the ass of a brunette who'd just passed by us. I could almost see the wheels spinning in his head, wondering if he'd be able to sneak away from the family to chat it up with her. I shook my head and snorted a laugh.

"You're a little too obvious, Austin."

He glanced at me and grinned sheepishly.

"I have no idea what you're talking about," he denied.

"Kallie, leave him alone," my mother chimed in. "It's only normal—especially when they're that pretty." She chuckled and winked at Austin. It didn't surprise me that she'd noticed his wandering eye. She rarely missed a trick with me while I was growing up. Austin, even though she was still getting to know him, was no different.

After we got our funnel cakes, the four of us aimlessly roamed across the fairgrounds, taking in the sounds and sights of the night. Eventually, we ended up in front of a giant purple tent with gold lettering boasting gypsy psychic readings. Smoke machines had been strategically placed around the temporary structure to give it a creepy yet mysterious aura, seeming deliberately over-the-top by hitting all the classic stereotypes. It was Madame Lavinia's tent—my least favorite place at the county fair.

"This is new," my father observed.

"Nah, it was here last year," Austin said. "Don't you remember Kallie freaking out about Gabby's broken arm?"

I gasped upon recalling with happened to my friend.

"Freaking out? That gypsy predicted Gabby would have a

tragic accident. The next day, she broke her arm. I was right to freak out!"

"Oh, yeah. I kind of remember that happening," my mother mused. "Fell off a diving board, right?"

"Yes," I confirmed. "I warned Gabby not to go into that tent, but she didn't listen, and look what happened."

"Don't forget about Charlie-Charlie," Austin reminded me.

"There was that too! The Charlie-Charlie game said Gabby would injure herself in 2013, and the gypsy predicted the same!"

I gulped, thinking about the game my Aunt Joy taught me. Gabby and I used to play the paranormal game all the time, spending many of our nights calling on a Mexican demon named Charlie to answer all of our questions. It was a simple game consisting of two pencils crisscrossed perpendicularly to form four sections on a piece of paper labeled with words like yes and no, or years and months. We'd then press the ends of the pencils until they started moving without our control—something Austin regularly mocked us for believing. He insisted that someone was always controlling the game by pushing a pencil one way or another to get the desired answer to the questions asked.

"Charlie also predicted that the guy who kisses Kallie during a sunset would be her soulmate," Austin added with a smirk. I huffed out an impatient breath and slapped his arm.

"I'm serious about this."

My pragmatic mother shook her head and rolled her eyes. She could think I was acting silly all she wanted. It wasn't just about the Charlie-Charlie game. My mother hadn't been there to see the ominous eyes of Madam Lavinia when she whispered the warning to Gabby.

"Kallie, I'm sure it was just a coincidence. Games and psychic gypsies can't tell your future any more than the origami fortunetellers I used to make when I was younger could."

"I don't know about that," my father said. "The origami you made for me once upon a time was pretty accurate."

"Oh, don't give Kallie any more reasons to believe in this nonsense, Fitz. Besides, I was the one who made the origami and asked all the questions. Therefore, I controlled the outcome." She paused then, giving in to a yawn, before looking at my father. "I'm getting tired. Ready to call it a night?"

"I'm ready if you are," he replied.

"But we still need to ride on the Zipper," Austin complained.

My gaze traveled to the opposite end of the carnival, where the Zipper's oval frame rotated like a Ferris wheel with free-spinning cars suspended from the sides of the boom. It was one of my favorite rides.

"Why don't you two head home?" I suggested to my parents. "Austin and I can catch an Uber."

"What's an Uber?" my mother asked.

Now it was my turn to roll my eyes. "You see, Mom. There's this little app you can put on your phone that makes cars just magically appear to take you wherever you want to go."

"Okay, smarty pants. I might not be up on all the—"

"Cadence, don't get yourself all wound up," my father interjected. "We can leave if you want to. If these two want to stay and have their brains rattled around in that Zipper contraption, so be it. Besides, we haven't had the house to ourselves in quite some time." He flashed her a crooked smile and waggled his eyebrows.

"Ewww, gross!" Austin and I yelled in unison.

My mother laughed and slipped her arm around my father's waist.

"Kallie, don't stay too late. You have to start packing in the morning."

I groaned, not needing the reminder. As excited as I was to start my freshman year at the University of San Diego in a few weeks, I was dreading all the work that went into packing for a cross-country move.

After my parents walked away, I turned to Austin.

"Alright, let's go get zipped!"

"Not yet," he said and took hold of my arm. "Let's go see the gypsy first."

My eyes widened as he began to pull me toward the tent.

"I'm not going in there," I said with a vehement shake of my head.

"Chicken," he taunted.

"So what if I am?"

"Come on, Kallie. We're both leaving for college in a few weeks. Who knows when we'll be able to go to the county fair together again?"

"Um...next year, when we're home for summer break," I pointed out sardonically.

"Maybe—assuming neither of us gets a job and decides to stay on campus. Come on. Stop being a baby and do something memorable this year."

"Do you honestly think a chat with a crazy fortuneteller is going to make today more memorable somehow?"

"I do," he said with a curt, all-knowing nod before pulling harder on my sleeve.

"Austin, I said no!"

"You're acting like a scaredy-cat. It'll be fine, you'll see."

Before I could protest further, Austin shoved me through the opening of the purple tent. I blinked as my eyes adjusted to the dim lighting.

When my gaze landed on Madame Lavinia, I froze. She stood next to a round table covered in an intricately embroidered tablecloth. Incense and candles burned in every corner of the tent, causing a smokey haze to billow around her. Her clothing was exactly as I remembered it from the year before. Her puffed-sleeve blouse with a low neckline flowed over the waistline of a long, colorfully pleated skirt of bright chiffon. Gold hoop earrings, bangle bracelets, and jewels weaved through her long black hair to complete her appearance, but it was her eyes—one ice blue and one brown —that stood out the most to me. They stared unblinkingly, and when her unwavering gaze darkened, I felt a shiver race down my spine.

It was like she could see straight into my soul.

Austin nudged me forward again, and I staggered as if I had two left feet. I was about to protest, but the gypsy spoke.

"Tarot cards or the crystal ball, my dear?" she asked in a deep, raspy voice that made her sound much older than she appeared.

"Oh, um...ne-neither," I stuttered. "We were just headed over to the Zipper. Sorry to have—"

"Tarot cards or the crystal ball?" she repeated.

"She wants the crystal ball. Right, sis?"

Austin bumped me again. I looked in his direction and noticed his mocking smirk. I scowled, wanting to do nothing more than smack him. My brother didn't believe in superstitions and had slept through the lesson in history class when Mrs. Beecher talked about Nostradamus. Predictions and prophecies were real and could be dangerous. I didn't know if this fortuneteller was the real deal or not, but after what happened with Gabby last year, I wasn't going to take any chances.

"No, really. I should go," I said with a weak smile as I turned toward the exit.

"You have heartache in your future," Madame Lavinia announced. Slowly, I turned back to face her. A pit formed in my gut, and I was afraid of what she might say next.

Damn you, Austin!

"Wha-what do you mean?" I hesitantly replied.

The gypsy took a few steps toward me until she was close

enough to reach out and take my hand. Her slender fingers turned my palm, so it was face up. Her grip was so cold; it caused goosebumps to rise on the surface of my skin.

"I see travel in your future. And the sun—the sun setting in the west."

I stifled a tiny gasp.

How does she know I will be traveling?

It had to be a coincidence.

"Last I checked, the sun always set in the west," I told her, trying my best to sound skeptical, even though my heart was starting to race.

"You're a Gemini?" she asked.

I frowned. She had a one-in-twelve chance of getting my zodiac sign right, but still...

"That's right. Lucky guess."

She smiled knowingly at my aloof reply, then looked down at my hand where she had begun tracing a red-painted fingernail along the creases in my palm. After a few moments, she clasped my hand between hers and led me over to the chair in front of a table supporting an eerie, glowing crystal ball. Smoke swirled inside the glass orb as it pulsed with multicolored light. I tried to remind myself that it was probably only trick magic.

But what if it wasn't?

"Sit," she ordered. My breath quickened, and my pulse pounded in my ears. I was suddenly too terrified to do anything other than comply as she rounded the table and took a seat across from me. "Now tell me, what fortune do you wish to hear from Madame Lavinia?"

I glanced back at Austin. He stood near the entrance to the tent, looking gleeful. I scowled at him before turning back to the gypsy.

"Well, just a basic fortunetelling, I guess. Just don't tell me anything bad."

"I can't guarantee that. Your destiny is your own." Her eyes narrowed, and I sat transfixed, unable to look away from her shrewd stare. She stayed silent for what seemed like hours, but it was probably only a few seconds before moving both hands to hover over the crystal ball.

"I see something—something that is very important to your future. Destructive and doomed love surrounds you. Remember the weaknesses of a Gemini, my dear, or you'll be destined for a life of heartbreak. Your eagerness to express your emotions will be your downfall," she warned.

My eyes widened, not sure what she was getting at.

"My downfall?"

Madame Lavinia slowly nodded her head but never took her eyes off the glowing sphere.

"You will fall in love under the bright sun in the west, giving someone the power to destroy you. And make no mistake—destroy you he will."

"What do you mean by...by destroy me?" I whispered.

The wind outside the tent picked up, rustling the thin walls and causing the candle flames to flicker. The gypsy inhaled sharply and snapped her head up to look at me. Her two different eyes turned black as night as she reached across the table to grip my hand tightly.

"The man who tastes your lips under a California sunset will be the one to break you."

1

Six Years Later

Kallie

"Good night to the old lady whispering hush. Good night, stars. Good night, air. Good night, noises everywhere." I slowly closed the *Goodnight Moon* cardboard book and looked down at my five-year-old little sister, Emma. Her eyes were closed, and her breathing even. I smiled at her sleeping, angelic little face. She had inherited my father's dark hair but had my mother's green eyes and creamy complexion. Although I was more than twenty years her senior, there was no denying the bond I shared with her. She had brought so much joy to our family and was the symbol of a long-awaited happily ever after for my parents.

As quietly as I could, I placed the book on her nightstand

and tiptoed out of her room to go back downstairs to the living room where my brother and best friend were waiting for me. Austin was lounging lazily on the couch, and Gabby sat with one leg draped over the arm of the chair across from him.

"She's out cold," I told them after I entered the room.

"Where did your parents go tonight, anyway?" Gabby asked.

"It's their anniversary, so I offered to keep Emma overnight for them."

"Gotcha. So, are you finally going to tell us why it was so important for us to come over tonight?"

"Yeah, what's the big news?" Austin pressed. Popping a few potato chips into his mouth, he frowned with his mouth full. "I rescheduled my Madden football tournament with the guys for this. Whatever it is, it better be good."

I waved him off.

"Football, shmootball. I promise you—this is important. And stop being a slob with those chips. You're getting crumbs all over the couch." I pushed Austin's long, muscular legs off the couch and brushed bits of potato chips from the cushions. Taking a seat next to him, I snagged a chip from his bowl, then looked meaningfully at each of them. "It's about Dean."

"What about him?" Gabby prompted.

"He proposed."

"Oh, my god! You're kidding me! I can't believe it!" Gabby gushed. "Tell me all about it. Did he get down on one knee?"

"Well, no. He just..." I glanced to my left, noting Austin's silence. He'd gone perfectly still, watching me curiously, as he waited for me to continue. Feeling uncharacteristically nervous, I leaned toward the coffee table and topped off my half-empty glass of wine from earlier. "Well, you know how Dean is. He's always so practical. He just explained how this was the natural next step. He probably didn't feel the need for all of that fancy wedding proposal fluff."

"Well, what do you expect from a doctor? As you said—he's practical," she agreed.

"Dean's not an actual doctor. He's a dentist. It doesn't get more boring than cleaning people's teeth for a living," Austin said with a smirk. His opinion mattered so much to me, and he was clearly not impressed. Taking a long swig of his beer, he gave me a pointed stare. "I hope you didn't expect skywriting or some shit like that."

"Oh, who really cares about that stuff?" Gabby chided. "Dean's a great catch—nobody can get it all. I'd rather have a nice practical guy over hearts and roses any day. So, did you set a date?"

"No. Not yet."

"What are you waiting for?" she admonished.

"Well, I haven't exactly said yes."

Gabby froze, with her wineglass halfway to her lips, then glanced down at my hand.

"Is that why you aren't wearing the ring? Wait." She stopped short, closed her eyes, and took a deep breath as if she were trying to find patience. "Please tell me you at least *have* a ring."

"Um..." I hesitated. "Not exactly. Dean thought it would be better for us to pick it out together and make sure it was the right size."

Austin audibly snorted. "Typical Dean. Such a dud."

"Dean's a sweetheart, Austin. You're just mad that he beat you at golf," I pointed out, rubbing salt in a wound that my brother refused to let heal.

"It's not that at all, Kallie. You two are just an extremely odd match. Dad says you're like the exclamation mark at the end of a sentence. I mean, look at you. You're all about flowy skirts, rainbow hair, free love, and world peace. Then there's Dean, my-middle-name-is-boring, rocking sweater vests and scraping plaque all day."

Taken aback, I unconsciously reached up to touch the clip-in rainbow extensions braided through my natural blonde hair.

"Gee, Austin. Say what you really feel, why don't you?" I snapped, then looked to Gabby for support. To my surprise, my best friend was frowning and nodding her head in agreement.

"He's got a point, Kals."

"Ugh, you guys. I'm serious! I want to make sure this is the right decision. I mean, I never want to get divorced, so I asked him to give me forty-eight hours to think about it."

"Think about what? Don't you love him?" Gabby asked.

"We've been dating for over two years. Of course I love him."

"So, why not give him an answer? We've been friends for as long as I can remember, Kallie. I know you always act first and think later. Why are you waiting this time?"

"I'm not waiting. I'm reflecting."

"Did your tarot cards tell you to do that?" Austin quipped.

"Shut up, Austin," I snapped in frustration. He wasn't helping. "I knew I shouldn't have invited you over. But if you must know, I haven't looked at my deck in over a month."

"I'm just teasing you. Come on, Kallie. I'm your brother. It's my job to razz you. You know I've always got your back. I just want to—"

My cell phone rang, cutting off whatever else Austin was about to say. I glanced down at the coffee table where the phone sat. My father's name showed up on the caller ID.

"Hold that thought. It's Dad. He's probably calling to check on Emma." Grabbing my phone, I headed into the kitchen and answered. "Hey, Dad! If you're calling about Emma, don't worry. She's tucked in for the night and fast asleep."

My father chuckled.

"No. I trust you have things handled with her. She loves sleepovers at your place. I'm actually calling about a business matter."

"Please don't tell me you're working during your anniversary dinner. Mom will kill you."

"I'm not," he assured. "We haven't even gone out yet. We had to push back our reservation time because your mother got an urgent call and had to go into the office."

My heart sank. My mother ran Dahlia's Dreamers, a non-profit organization that aided immigrants with a legal path to citizenship. Urgent calls usually meant someone was in jeopardy of being deported.

"Is everything okay?"

"Yeah, everything is fine for now. She just got back. But you know how it is around here—never a dull moment. We were about to head out when Devon called me about a new client in need of immediate assistance."

"Who's the client?" I asked.

"His name is Sloan Atwood."

"I've never heard of him."

"To make a long story short, he's a race car driver in Los Angeles whose career ended rather abruptly. I don't know all the details. All I know is that he's been on a bender. His agent, Milo Birx, called me to fix it. I was hoping you could help."

I thought about the long hours my father put in at his PR firm, Quinn & Wilkshire. While he always made plenty of time for our family, I'd seen first-hand how trying the job could be almost as soon as I started working for him. After receiving my MBA in public relations, I wanted to work for the best. My father's nationally known firm was precisely that—and people rarely came to him when things were going well. It wasn't until after something went wrong did clients want the firm to run damage control. Despite the perception, bad press was never good, and our job was to get people out of the negative spotlight with a positive public relations campaign. Quinn & Wilkshire did exactly that, and we did it well, no matter what time of the day it was.

"What do you need me to do?"

"Honey..." he hesitated. "I'll be honest. Since your sister was born, I've been trying to limit the hours I spend with clients to have more family time. But you know how it is—it's tough. Devon just got back from a thirty-day stint with an NBA player. Now he has a baby on the way. If he adds Sloan Atwood to his client list, his new wife just might kill him."

"And rightly so. He works like crazy," I said with a laugh.

"Well, considering that, Devon and I have been in discussions for the past month about lightening our workload in general. Do you remember how you mentioned one day becoming a partner at the firm?"

"Of course, but I figured that would be decades away."

"Yeah, well... This commission is huge—too big for the firm to pass up. If you can handle Atwood, we might be willing to speed up that timeline by a few years, so you don't have to wait decades. But, before you agree to anything, there are some things for you to consider."

"Such as?"

"Milo emailed me a file on Atwood. After looking it over, Milo and I both decided we can't manage this from the DC office. This is a major commitment. If you take Atwood on as a client, you'll have to go to California."

"That's not a big deal. After all, I lived there for four years, and I travel all the time for clients."

"Six months, Kallie. You'll need to be in LA for a full six months. There would be a bonus payout of twenty thousand dollars for you after the completion of the contract. Milo is serious about this and wants a solid commitment from someone who can be there daily. He won't get that with a long-distance rep, which is why I don't think Devon or I should take him on."

I blinked, pausing to soak in his words. Quinn & Wilkshire

never had a client who required that kind of time commitment, as far as I could recall.

"Why so long?"

"Milo worked out some deal with a charity out there called Safe Track. It involves working with foster kids over the span of a few months, and Milo is terrified Atwood will screw it up. I'll email you the file after we hang up so you can see why. You'll need to be Atwood's shadow. When he eats, you eat. When he sleeps, you sleep. When he shits—"

"I get the picture, Dad," I said and rolled my eyes. "Six months is a long time, though. I'll need to talk to Dean."

"Of course."

"When do you need to know by?"

He hesitated again.

"Tomorrow morning at the latest. If you say yes, I'll have our travel coordinator get you on plane by late afternoon or early evening."

I puffed out a breath. Twenty-four hours to decide on a cross-country move wasn't very long, even if it was temporary. However, I knew my father. Fitzgerald Quinn would never ask this of one of his associates if it wasn't necessary. There was also the big fat carrot he'd dangled. The bonus was a definite perk, but fast-track to partner was something Quinn & Wilkshire never offered—especially to anyone who was a friend or family member. Nepotism was frowned upon and taken very seriously. Considering his firm belief in starting at the bottom and working your way up, I knew this must be bigger than he was letting on.

Financially, this was huge for me. While my parents had paid for my undergrad, I was on the hook for graduate school. The twenty thousand dollar bonus would more than cover my remaining loans. Plus, if they made me a partner at the firm, the raise I'd receive would ease the financial burden I was currently facing with my hefty mortgage. The townhouse in I'd purchased in Georgetown didn't come cheap, and my bank account could prove it.

"Let me take the night to decide. I'll let you know in the morning," I eventually said.

After ending the call, I went back into the living room. Gabby was channel surfing, and Austin was, once again, sprawled across the entire couch. Rather than push his legs aside again, I took a seat on the floor and threw back the rest of my wine in one long swig.

Gabby eyed me curiously. "Everything okay?" she asked.

"I'm not sure yet. My dad wants me to go to California for six months."

"Kallie's going to Cali," Austin said with a laugh. "Nice."

"You're such a turd," I said and tossed a throw pillow at him. "Add this to the list of decisions I need to make. Adulting sucks. I miss our college days when my biggest decision was which class to register for."

"I'm assuming this is a work thing," Gabby absently remarked, and she continued to flip through the channels on the television.

"Yeah, some race car—oh, wait!" I sat up straight and pointed to the TV. "Back up to the last channel. I love that movie!"

Gabby clicked the remote until *Singin' In The Rain* was on the screen.

"Aww, come on! It's bad enough you fed me tofu for dinner. Don't make me sit through a chick flick," Austin complained.

"This is a classic, Austin. Besides, our parents fell in love at summer camp while putting on this production. You have to love it because of that."

"Yeah, I know the story. Dad loves to tell it every year on your birthday," he grumbled.

"Hush!" I waved him off. "This is my favorite part."

The three of us fell silent just in time to hear Don

Lockwood say, "You sure look lovely in the moonlight, Kathy." He'd just finished setting the stage—quite literally—to create a romantic atmosphere so he could profess his love to her in a song.

As he sang the romantic ballad and stared adoringly into the eyes of his beloved, a feeling of melancholy settled over me. Dean never looked at me the way Don Lockwood was looking at Kathy Seldon. I knew it was just a movie, and actors were supposed to be convincing, but still... The song lyrics came from somebody's real-life experience—an experience I wanted to have. If truth be told, I didn't have that kind of chemistry with Dean.

I thought back to Gabby's question.

"Do you love him?"

Undoubtedly, the answer was yes. However, what Dean and I shared wasn't anything like what I witnessed on the television screen. While I knew not everything could be like it was in the movies, I still knew what true, undying love looked like. I'd had a front-row seat to it for years with my parents. After a seventeen-year separation, their love never faded. My baby sister in the next room was proof of it. But with Dean, I'd always felt like something was missing between us. There were no gentle touches or furtive glances. The new relationship flutters of excitement had long since disappeared. There was no anticipation because Dean was always predictable. He was practical, and he was safe. I may have loved him, but I wasn't convinced I wanted to settle for safe.

That's why I told him I needed to think about his proposal. I didn't know what was more important to me—the relationship security Dean would surely provide or the idea of being swept up in song and dance with the person I loved. I wanted both, but I wasn't sure if that was asking for too much.

As I continued to listen to Don Lockwood sing about how

his beloved was meant for him, I asked myself if the same was true for me.

Were Dean and I meant for each other?

I didn't know the answer. Tears began to well in my eyes from the realization, and I quickly blinked them away. Perhaps the opportunity to go to California was fated. At the very least, it would give me time to work out these conflicting emotions and let destiny guide the way.

"Kals, you okay?" Austin asked, eyeing me curiously.

"Yeah, I'm good." I offered him a forced smile and turned my attention back to the television, wishing real life were like it was in the movies.

2

Kallie

After two hours of listening to me weigh the pros and cons of marriage and a temporary move to California, Austin and Gabby bid their farewells.

"I love you, sis. I'll keep my ringer turned up. If you need to call and hash out your thoughts in the middle of the night, I'm here for you," my brother said, pulling me into a fierce hug.

"Thanks, Austin." I squeezed my brother tight. Despite our constant teasing, I knew Austin would do anything for me. He understood the magnitude of the decisions I was facing and would support whichever choices I made.

"That's ditto for me," Gabby added.

I let go of Austin and embraced my friend. "Thanks, you guys. I love you both so much."

As they headed for their cars, I stood in the doorway of my townhouse, watching until their taillights disappeared. After closing and locking the door, I headed upstairs toward my bedroom. Along the way, I passed by the guest room to check on Emma. I smiled when I saw her tiny arms wrapped around the purple plush teddy bear that I'd given her on her fourth birthday. Her breathing was deep and even, assuring me she was still asleep.

Giving in to a yawn, I gingerly closed the door and went to my room. Austin's mention of my tarot deck had been on my mind ever since he'd said it, and I was looking forward to the quiet solitude and reflection they always seemed to bring.

Sitting on my bed, I opened my nightstand drawer and pulled out the cards. Settling in, I tapped the deck twice, then gave them a thorough shuffle before cutting the pile three times. I was fairly new to tarot reading by most standards. I'd dabbled in college but had recently become more serious with general readings for myself. They helped to give me perspective on the past, understanding of the present, and insight into future possibilities.

Focusing my intent and energy, I fanned the cards into an arc across my bedspread. After selecting the first eight that called to me, I placed them in formation face down. Flipping over the first one, the Judgement card lay before me. It was upright, symbolizing reflection and awakening, and would be the theme for today's reading. Reflection was fitting for my current situation, as I'd been doing a lot of that lately.

Leaving the card in place, I turned over the next card to reveal the reversed Moon, symbolizing confusion. I frowned. Tarot cards were always open to interpretation, but it was almost scary how much they were in tune with my energy.

Flipping over a third card, it revealed an upright Temperance card. I closed my eyes and called on my intuition, trying to see how the symbol of patience applied to my current situation. After turning over the first two cards, I'd felt anxious and found myself taking a few deep breaths. Perhaps that's exactly why the card presented itself. I needed to maintain a sense of calm and balance to better channel my energy.

Turning the fourth card, I let out a small gasp when I saw the upright Tower card—a symbol of disaster in my future. My heart began to race again, and I quickly flipped over a fifth card. It was the upright Devil, which meant addiction and materialism.

With only three cards left, I slowly reached to flip over the one that would give me insight into external influences. It was the reversed Lovers card. My stomach dropped, knowing this was more than just an omen. It was something I'd already been feeling—a sense of imbalance in my relationship with Dean. This card told me that a move to California could have a very negative impact on my relationship.

After talking with Austin and Gabby, and before taking out my tarot deck, I'd been almost certain of my path. I thought I would go to California, then return in six months to marry Dean. If our relationship was meant to be, we would get through the separation.

Now I wasn't so sure.

In all honesty, I'd been shocked by his proposal. Perhaps it was because I had a history of failed relationships. Everyone who came before Dean was either a cheater, a self-indulgent bad boy, or a suffocating control freak. I'd often thought back to the gypsy's warnings so many years ago when she told me I was cursed in romance and destined for a life of disappointment and heartache. When I met Dean, I had thought the curse was broken because he was the complete opposite of the other guys I'd dated.

"Did I settle too easily?" I wondered aloud to the empty room.

Reaching for the second to last card, I flipped it to see an upright High Priestess. Her appearance could signify that it was time for me to listen to my intuition rather than prioritizing my intellect and conscious mind. Considering that, I remembered what Dean had said about marriage being the next practical step. A part of me began to wonder if I was actually *in* love with Dean. I feared that I might only love him more as a friend but was simply falling in line with society's natural order of things.

I shifted my gaze to the final card. Considering that all of my cards so far had been Major Arcana, signifying impactful and life-changing events, I was almost afraid to turn it over. When I did, I found myself staring at the upright Fool. I sighed at the foregone conclusion and tapped my finger on the jester's face.

"You just had to show up today of all days, didn't you?"

In love, the Fool tarot card signaled that I needed to experience new things to find the romance I desired. It meant taking risks to find love in the most unlikely places. The card could also mean new beginnings in my career, and I should welcome the chance to be bold when starting a new journey.

As I stared at the imagery on the cards to determine the story they were trying to tell, my cell phone began to ring. Rattled by the sudden noise, I didn't even look at the name on the caller ID before answering.

"Hello," I said absently.

"Kallie, it's me," Dean replied, effectively snapping me to full attention.

"Dean! Hi...um, I didn't expect to hear from you tonight." I paused and glanced at the clock. It was nearing midnight. "You never stay up this late."

"I'm in bed, but I can't sleep. I started thinking about the plans to tell my mother we're engaged. I thought—"

"Tell your mother? But I haven't even said yes yet," I interrupted, trying to keep my voice light.

"Doll, you and I both know that's just a formality," he said with a chuckle. "After we get the ring, I thought we should take her out to a nice dinner and give her the good news."

A nice dinner?

I nearly scoffed. When Dean proposed, we'd been sitting at his kitchen table. He decided to pop the question over Thai take-out. Now here he was, saying he wanted to treat his mother to a nice dinner so we could tell her about our *non-*engagement when all I got was subpar vegetable pad thai in a cardboard container. I inhaled a deep, calming breath and forced myself not to sound petty with my reply.

"Look, Dean. We need to talk. My dad called earlier about a job in California. We picked up a client who lives in L.A. It's a lot of money and I think I'm going to take it, but I'd have to leave tomorrow."

"Well, that's great, doll! More money is always good and I know how much you like to travel, so—"

"It's for six months, Dean. I'd have to move there temporarily."

"Six months? But I have the American Dental Association dinner next week. I need you to be there."

"I'm sure you'll be fine without me."

"It's not about whether I'll be fine or not. It's about how it will look if I show up without a date. Everyone will be there with spouses or significant others. You can't expect me to go alone."

I pinched the bridge of my nose.

"Honestly, Dean. I don't know why you would want me to be there anyway. You know I hate those things because I can never be myself. The charade is exhausting."

"Kallie, we've been through this. It's not a charade. You just don't understand acceptable decorum."

I pursed my lips in annoyance. For Dean, acceptable decorum at formal events meant no colorful hair extensions, always remembering to place my napkin on my chair when I left the table, and only speaking when spoken to. Heaven forbid I say something that could embarrass him in front of his peers.

Feeling frustrated, I glanced down at the tarot cards spread out over my bed. I absently pushed them together until they were in a neat pile and placed them back inside my nightstand drawer. Regardless of what the cards were trying to tell me, I knew in my heart what needed to happen. I had to figure out if Dean and I were meant to be together—and this conversation was definitely not helping. Marriage should be forever. It wasn't fair for me to waste his time or his life if I was having doubts. I believed everything happened for a reason, and I did not doubt that California was fated.

"I'm not going to debate acceptable decorum with you. Our views on that will always be different. As for my move to California, I think it's a sign that we should put the wedding plans on hold. We can discuss it when I get back."

"That's not going to work for me, Kallie. I need you at that dinner," he stated matter-of-factly as if that settled the matter. An angry heat flooded my cheeks, and no matter how hard I tried to tamp it down, my temper began to simmer.

"Why do I feel like you're dismissing me—as if I'm no more than a woman on your arm for your stupid event?"

"Oh, stop it. You know you mean more to me than that."

"Do I? I mean, never once did you say you'd miss me if I were to be gone for six months. No. Instead, your first instinct was a black-tie dinner."

"You're not being fair. Of course I would miss you."

I sighed, knowing I was acting slightly irrational, even if my feelings were justified.

"Alright. Let's not fight. I don't want to leave with things on a bad note."

"So you're going? No discussion?"

I paused, unsure of how to respond. When my father called about the job opportunity, my first thought was to talk it over with Dean. However, at some point over the course of the night, I'd already made up my mind. I was going with or without Dean's approval. What did that say about me and my relationship with him? In a roundabout way, I was acting just as dismissive toward Dean as he was to me.

"Yes, I'm going. My father wouldn't have asked if it weren't important. We'll just have to work through the separation. What's six months? It will go by faster than you think."

He stayed silent for a long moment that seemed to stretch on forever. Just as I was about to ask him what he was thinking, he finally spoke.

"Fine," he said curtly, clearly unconvinced. "What time is your flight tomorrow?"

"I don't know yet. After I hang up with you, I'll shoot my father a text to let him know I'm in. He has a travel agent that will handle all of the arrangements for me. Once I know, I'll forward you the itinerary."

"My appointment schedule is full tomorrow, so I probably won't be able to see you off."

My heart sank—but not for the reason it should have. I was disappointed because, deep down, I knew Dean wouldn't have been there even if he didn't have a packed schedule. He was never a big believer in nonsensical, tear-filled goodbyes. I'd gone on numerous short business trips in the past, and rarely did he see me off. If I saw him at all, it was simply to give me a ride to the airport, and I never expected more than a quick peck on the lips before he drove off.

"Okay. I'll text you when I land then," I replied, desperately trying to keep the sadness out of my voice. "Goodnight, Dean."

"Night."

The line went dead. There were no I love you's or air kisses through the phone. Just silence.

I tossed my phone to the side. Shaking off feelings of melancholy, I stood from the bed, walked over to my closet, and tried to focus on something positive. Buried behind a plethora of shoes and handbags were a couple of suitcases. I pulled each one out and laid them on the bed.

Unintentionally, I found myself humming the tune of "Leaving on a Jet Plane" by Peter, Paul, and Mary as I began to pack my clothes. Was I still frustrated after my phone call with Dean? Yes. I was sad too. But I also couldn't help feeling a little excited about whatever possibilities lay ahead.

3

Sloan

There was a particular atmosphere that came with a good beach bar. It was more than just the music blaring from a jukebox loaded only with beach-vibe songs. With a fruity drink in hand and toes in the sand, people were able to leave their worries behind, lay back, and enjoy a carefree life—even if just for a few days. The Soggy Sand Dollar in Long Beach offered precisely that. It was the reason their crowd ranged from tourists showing off their new vacation clothes to local sea-drenched surfers with tanned cheeks. Everyone was happy. There was no misery—just an escape from everyday life.

And I loved it here.

Location was key, and a bustling boardwalk on a white sandy shoreline made for prime real estate. The front of my favorite hole-in-the-wall bar was wide open to the beach and always packed, day or night. Not only were the drinks cheap and readily flowing, but the cabanas out back were a convenient place to crash for the night after having a few too many. All I had to do was slip the bartender a fifty, and a cabana under the stars was all mine. It had become a regular thing for me, and today would probably be no different. I had arrived at three in the afternoon and managed to get a steady buzz going by five. With any luck, I'd be well past drunk in an hour. After all, it wasn't like I had any place to be.

The more beers I knocked back, the less I found myself caring that I had been served the cheap kind. I looked down at the silver can in my hand. Beach rules dictated that The Soggy Sand Dollar maintain a no-glass policy, making aluminum and plastic part of the official serving ware. Coors Light was watery and barely even beer, but it was getting the job done— especially when I poured it into a red Solo cup with a shot of Jack Daniels and chugged it as a boilermaker. Fortunately for me, that was on the menu today.

"Johnny!" I called out to the bartender. "I'm almost empty."

The aging, lifelong bartender glanced my way and grinned. His eyes crinkled in the corners, and I wasn't sure if it was because of too many late nights slinging whiskey or too much time in the sun. Perhaps it was a little of both.

"Almost is the keyword, my friend. Don't worry. I've got you covered," Johnny assured.

I returned his smile, then shifted on the barstool to gaze out at the beach. Waves crashed into the surf, and there was a slight breeze in the salty air, whispering just enough to make the blazing California sun more tolerable. I decided right then and there that my night would be spent in the cabana. Tonight, I planned on being lulled to sleep under the stars by the sounds of the ocean.

My cellphone vibrated in my pocket. Pulling it out, I glanced at the screen. The sun was so bright, and I couldn't read it. Turning back toward the bar, I leaned forward and balanced my elbows on the polished oak top. I blinked a few times, struggling to focus. The words were fuzzy, the letters seeming to blur together momentarily. I thought about the painkiller I took after I'd first arrived at The Soggy Sand Dollar. I probably shouldn't have popped prescription oxy on an empty stomach. I would need to order up a couple of the chef's famous fish tacos sooner rather than later. Combined with the booze, I was feeling the effects of the pill more than usual.

Forcing myself to focus on the cell phone screen, I groaned when I saw it was a text message from my agent, Milo Birx. He had an annoying habit of checking in on me daily. Not bothering to read his message, I switched over to my voicemail inbox. Scrolling down the list, I selected a voicemail I'd received a month earlier and brought the phone to my ear.

"Mr. Atwood. This is Dr. Haskell. After going over your test results with your physical therapist, I'm sorry to say this, but I can't clear you to race again. The risks are just too great. Please call the office at your earliest convenience. I'd like to schedule an appointment to go over the test results in more detail, as well as discuss alternate options for pain management."

Just as it had on the day when I first heard the message, my stomach sank. I'd had to replay it three times before I grasped the words. I squeezed my eyes shut, trying to will away the memories from over one year ago, but the effort was in vain. Flashbacks from the crash assaulted me, reminding me once again that my life was now permanently altered.

I could still hear the crunch of metal on concrete when I swerved to avoid a slowing car, spun out, and hit the wall—driver's side first—at high speed. The screeching tires and the scraping sound of the car along the wall until it finally slid to a complete stop would not be something I'd soon forget. I'd been conscious when my crew arrived to cut me from the wreckage but passed out before making it to the ambulance. I barely remembered the weeks and months that followed.

I raked my hands through my hair, painfully yanking at the roots in an attempt to drown out the sounds in my memory. I shouldn't have listened to the doctor's message again. I wasn't sure what compelled me to do it. I certainly didn't need a reminder of all that was lost—I'd spent every day of the past month trying to escape it.

I looked down at the drink in front of me, realizing I wasn't just buzzed—I was drunk—just like I wanted to be. A few more boilermakers and I could be out back, fast asleep in a cabana.

"Johnny!" I called out again.

"I hear ya. I'm coming."

As I waited for my refill, I let my gaze wander over the faces throughout the bar. I'd been all over the world, and if there was one thing I'd noticed, it was that everyone looked the same as they did everywhere else. Short, tall, thin, overweight. Blonde, brunette, old, young. They may have had different skin tones or worn different clothes, but they were still all very much the same.

Until now.

Out on the beach, a woman emerged from the water, sparkling in the sunlight where the surf kissed her skin. Rainbows flowed from her head and cascaded over her shoulders as she moved across the sand, stopping only to tie a turquoise-colored wrap around her shapely waist. She moved without purpose, defying gravity, and I wondered if her feet were even touching the ground. I couldn't be sure. It was as if I were staring at a mystical mermaid sent from the depths of the ocean straight to me. I didn't know where she'd been or where she was going—I only knew I wanted to go to wherever she was headed.

"Who is that?" I whispered to myself, her gravity pulling me until I was locked in. Everything around me seemed to disappear, and all sounds fell away until I could only focus on her. Gone was the boardwalk, the loud chatter of people, and the music from the jukebox—it was only me, the white sand, and my rainbow mermaid. She alluded grace and confidence, the sensual sway of her hips so fluid it was as if she were still moving in the water and not on land.

She looked up and seemed to catch my eye. Before I could think to wave or motion her over, she disappeared—gone, poof —as if she were no more than a mirage. The world came rushing back into focus. I blinked, then scanned the beach, wondering if I'd only imagined her.

Johnny appeared to set a new Solo cup and a can of Coors Light in front of me, then began pouring a shot of Jack Daniels. Turning my attention away from the surf, I looked at him.

"Did you see that woman?" I asked.

"Working here, I see a lot of women," Johnny said with a laugh.

"No, I mean the woman with the rainbow hair out on the beach. Bikini, all curves, walked like she was floating on air. She was like a... I don't know... a mermaid or something."

"A floating mermaid? I've seen many things in my years, but I ain't never seen a floating mermaid. You're seeing things, my man. Are you sure you can handle another shot of whiskey with this beer?"

Pursing my lips into a frown, I nodded.

"Yeah, give me the shot. I wouldn't be able to drink this piss you're serving any other way."

Johnny chuckled.

"Owner was trying to cut expenses, and the regulars aren't too happy. I'll be sure to pass on your complaints," he said as he poured the beer into the cup, then dropped in the shot of whiskey. "You take it easy now. I'll save a cabana for you, but you need to use your own two legs to get there. I don't care how famous you are, Atwood. I ain't goin' to carry your ass out there."

The sound of a hand slapping down hard on the top of the bar caused Johnny to startle. Both of us turned in the direction of the noise.

"I knew it was you!" said a man three stools down. He thumbed in the direction of a beefy man sitting beside him. "I just said to my friend, 'Hey, that's Sloan Atwood!' He didn't believe me, but sure as shit, I was right!"

I gave the two men a short, two-finger wave, then turned back to my drink.

"So what? I don't fucking care if it's Sloan Atwood," the beefy guy said.

"Dude, he was a god behind the wheel! Do you know how many championships he won?"

I tried to tune them out, not wanting to listen to their critique of my racing abilities as if I weren't sitting right there. Picking up my beer, I chugged it back, taking three long swigs until the cup was empty. Since my anonymity was now lost, it was time for me to pay my tab and leave.

Reaching into my pocket, I fished out my wallet and removed a one-hundred-dollar bill. Motioning with my chin, I signaled to Johnny, my sole focus being anything other than the discussion the two men were having about me.

"I'll ah... I'll take that cabana now," I said.

"Really? It's early, man."

"Yeah, well..." I trailed off when I realized I wasn't able to focus on the bartender's face. Everything was foggy, and the room seemed to tilt. "I just gotta get out of here, Johnny."

Moving to stand up, I swayed and grabbed the edge of the bar to steady myself. I knew I was feeling pretty good, but my struggle to stay upright made me realize I was drunker than I'd initially thought.

"See what I'm saying? Just look at him," the man down the

bar prattled on. "Atwood ain't no Tony Stewart. He's a washed-up has-been."

Slowly, I turned my head to look at man number two and gave myself a moment to focus. My initial impression was that he was beefy, but that implied muscular and powerful. This guy was anything but. He was overweight and out of shape, trying to hide his gut by puffing out his chest like a goddamned neanderthal.

"Who the fuck are you calling a has-been?" I challenged.

"Atwood," Johnny warned.

I ignored him and took a few unsteady steps toward the fat asshole. He stood up from his stool and glared at me.

"I'm talking about you, Atwood. You have a problem with that? It's a shame, really. You're not even thirty years old yet."

"Shut the fuck up," I snarled.

"Aww, poor baby. What's the matter?" he said in a cooing, mocking tone. "Don't like hearing you're all washed up?"

No matter how valid his words were, I reacted without thinking. Stepping toward him, I lunged at him and swung what I thought was a well-aimed punch.

It wasn't.

Completely missing my mark, my foot caught the edge of the step leading to the boardwalk. I stumbled forward and tried to regain my footing, but the effort was in vain. I twisted, grappling for something to hang on to, only to find fistfuls of air. Falling backward, everything in my line of sight passed in a blur as I went down. I heard the startled cries of the people around me.

Then, everything went dark.

———

Six hours later, I leaned my head back against the couch in my less-than-tidy living room in Beverly Grove. Milo had just dropped me off, but not before giving me a lecture about pulling my shit together.

Much like the months following the crash, today was a complete haze. Details about how I got into a bar fight were a blur in my memory. I knew what happened, yet I didn't. It was as if the essential scenes in my mind were veiled behind a thin gray curtain, where only distorted shapes and shadows could be seen. The combination of oxy and too much booze can do that. Synergism was what Milo had called it. One minute I was sitting at the bar, then the next minute, my drunk ass was in a jail cell.

According to Milo, my attempt at punching a man who'd been goading me had failed. When I pulled back to take a swing at him, I'd fallen over, smacked my head, and taken out a little girl in the process. She'd been walking on the boardwalk with her mom, and neither of them even saw it coming. I'd been too drunk and high to pay much attention to anything, let alone notice innocent bystanders. All I cared about was bloodying a man's face. As a result, a young girl ended up in the hospital with a broken arm and a bunch of cuts and scrapes that needed stitching—and I ended up behind bars.

Thankfully, Johnny knew to call Milo right away. My agent showed up at the holding center soon after, and I was lucky to have only spent a few hours in the slammer. Still, the damage was done. Milo had made it clear that the parents of the little girl would most likely sue me. There was no going back from tonight, just like there was no going back to before the crash.

Consequences. There are always consequences.

No matter which way I looked at it, my life was screwed.

I stood up and went to the living room credenza, where I kept my liquor stash. I was still more than just a little buzzed from earlier but not drunk enough to fall asleep—and I was fucking exhausted. I hadn't had a good night's sleep in what felt like forever. Every time I tried to rest, my mind would start to race. I was consumed with too much regret. If I had any hopes of sleeping tonight, I learned months ago that a nightcap or two was the only sure way. It would mean no dreams, no sounds of crunching metal, no ache in my hip. Jack Daniels was the only thing that seemed to quiet the noise and dull the pain. If I happened to combine it with a bit of oxycodone now and then, so be it. I knew I was on a collision course with no off-ramp. Yet, I couldn't find the energy to care in the least bit.

Bottle of Jack in hand, I went back to the couch and set it down on the coffee table. I eyed up the bottle of deep amber liquor, standing proud next to the prescription oxycodone. There were only two pills left in the little orange bottle, and I knew Dr. Haskell wouldn't prescribe more—especially after Milo told him what happened tonight.

I shifted my gaze to the clear plastic envelope sitting beside the bottle of amber-colored whiskey. It contained the personal effects returned to me by the police after Milo sprung me from my cell. The sight of it disgusted me, knowing that I—Sloan Atwood, race car driver extraordinaire—had been reduced to drug and alcohol-induced violence. That wasn't me—or at least, it wasn't who I *was*. I shook my head, knowing the old Sloan Atwood died on the track over a year ago. I'd never be the same again.

I poured a shot, then threw it back. I barely felt the burn as it went down, yet I still poured another and knocked that one back as well. Slamming the shot glass on the table, tiny droplets of brown liquid splattered over the surface. Finally feeling tired enough to go to sleep, I dragged myself out of the armchair and stumbled my way up the stairs. With any luck, I'd be pulled into a dreamless sleep within minutes.

Stripping out of my shirt and pants, I crawled into bed naked. I didn't bother to set the alarm. After all, it wasn't like I had anything to do in the morning.

I fought off the sensation of the room spinning, closed my

eyes, and welcomed the weight of sleep. My alcohol-clouded mind thought about the past year, the physical rehab, and time spent going to countless doctor appointments. Every minute had been filled with a hollow emptiness. I had nothing anymore.

Without racing, I was no one.

4

Sloan

Waking up after drinking too much was always a challenge. The pounding in my head was killing me. I peered at the clock to see it wasn't even eight o'clock in the morning yet. I didn't want to be awake. I'd been dreaming, and for once, it wasn't a nightmare. Mr. Sandman was kind last night, bringing me visions of a beautiful rainbow mermaid. I rolled over onto my stomach and groaned, determined to go back to sleep, and wondered why I'd woken up so damn early.

The answer to my unspoken question came in the form of a loud, intrusive knock on the front door. Then the doorbell rang, the sound piercing through my sensitive eardrums and causing my head to pound even harder. I opened my eyes again and squinted against the bright sunshine coming in through the balcony's glass doors off my bedroom. I silently cursed myself for forgetting to close the curtains before going to bed.

Another knock sounded on the door—this one louder than the last.

What. The. Fuck.

Dragging myself out of bed, I pulled on a pair of gray sweatpants and headed downstairs to see who the unwelcome guest was. I assumed it was a salesman or someone pushing religious literature. I was in no mood to listen to a vacuum sales pitch or hear why I needed salvation.

I yanked open the front door, my body tense from being pulled unwillingly from the comfort of my bed. I was ready to give an earful to whomever was standing on the other side but stopped short when I saw it was a beautiful blonde. Her bright green eyes were wide with surprise—probably from the way I practically ripped the door from the hinges when I opened it.

I was about to lash out but stopped short when I noticed her hair was pulled to the side in a loose braid. Multi-colored strands had been braided through it—rainbow strands. As if my dreams had come to fruition, I gaped at her in disbelief. She was my rainbow mermaid.

"It's you. What are you doing here?" I asked, unable to stop looking at the colorful braid cascading over her shoulder and breasts—and what a fine set of breasts they were. I couldn't help but notice the way they accentuated the tempting curves of her waist. What can I say? I was a man, and I loved tits, and when they were right in front of me, I was definitely going to look.

Clearing her throat, she angled her delicate face to the side.

"I'm sorry?" she asked, seeming confused.

"You're the woman from the beach. I saw you and thought..." I didn't finish the sentence, quickly realizing how ridiculous it would sound if I said I'd thought she was a mermaid.

"I'm not sure what you're referring to. I don't believe we know each other. Are you Mr. Atwood?"

"That's me. Who wants to know?"

"My name is Kalliope Benton Riley. I'm a public relations agent from Quinn & Wilkshire. Milo Birx sent me."

I scratched my head, feeling foggy from the rough night, and I wasn't sure if I'd heard her correctly.

"My agent sent me another agent?"

"Well, I suppose you could look at it like that, but he doesn't handle PR. I do."

I took a second look at her. She was slight of build and relatively short when compared to me. I estimated her to be no more than five feet two inches. My six-one frame towered over her, yet her small size still managed to have a commanding presence in my doorway. Her bohemian dress attire didn't suggest business professional in the least bit. The tribal-print blouse hung just low enough to see the swell of those breasts I'd been admiring. The shirt was knotted at the waist, where a long apricot-colored skirt flowed over her hips, stopping to skim the tops of her sandaled feet. Large silver hoops hung from her ears, with matching bangles on both wrists. She reached up to tuck a loose piece of hair behind her ear, revealing a certain amount of careless grace in her movements.

Her overall look had a hippie vibe to it, and as much as I wanted to punch Milo for sending a PR rep to my house so early in the morning, at least he had the sense to send someone who was sexy as sin. The fact that I'd spent the night dreaming about her made it even better, and I couldn't push away the intrigue I felt. She made a definitive impression, seeming small-town yet worldly, innocent yet cunning, and beautifully exotic in every sense of the word.

Feeling more than just a little bit curious, I cocked my head to the side and offered her a small smile.

"Okay. Despite the early hour, I'll play along, Ms... What did you say your name was?"

"Kalliope Benton Riley. But you can call me Kallie."

"Well, then you can call me Sloan. You might as well come on in." I stepped aside and allowed her to enter, noting the subtle mix of patchouli and vanilla that emanated from her as we made our way to the kitchen.

Holy hell, she smells damn good too.

I motioned for Kallie to sit at the kitchen table while I put on a pot of coffee. If I wanted to get through this with a clear head, I needed a boost to wake my ass up. So consumed with needing caffeine in my veins, I was barely conscious of the takeout containers littering the table and floor until I saw her disapproving stare. My house had an open floor plan, leaving the mess of clothes, empty bottles and cans, and car magazines scattered about the living room in plain sight. I tried to ignore her as my need for caffeine suddenly turned into a need for something much more substantial.

"Can I get you anything?" I offered. "Coffee? Soda?"

"I'm okay, but thanks," she replied.

"Suit yourself." I shrugged, scrapped the idea of making coffee, and grabbed a Pepsi from the refrigerator. Caffeine was caffeine, no matter what the form. Cracking it open, I casually leaned against the wall and took a long swig.

"Mr. Atwood, before we begin discussing business matters, I must insist that you put some clothes on."

Glancing down at my bare chest and tattered Formula One sweatpants hanging low on my hips, I grinned awkwardly. I hadn't looked in a mirror, but I must have been quite the sight. I absently brushed my fingers over the three-day-old stubble on my face. If the taste in my mouth was any inclination to how I must smell, I could only imagine what she was thinking. Her tone was light, but I could sense the condemnation. I reached up and smoothed out my hair as best as I could, slightly embarrassed to be seen this way. Still, I couldn't help but notice her furtive glances at my torso.

The side of my mouth quirked up. I couldn't say why, but

something about this woman made me want to toy with her. I wasn't naïve. I knew how women looked at me—and Kallie didn't seem to be immune. I took a step closer and leaned down, so one hand was pressing on the table.

"I would have dressed, but I wasn't expecting company. Does my naked chest make you uncomfortable?" I teased, deliberately lowering my voice to just above a whisper. She glanced at my chest again before quickly averting her eyes. My cock stiffened when I caught sight of a delicate blush sliding into her cheeks.

Fuck, is she ever gorgeous.

When she swallowed hard, blinked, then crossed and uncrossed her legs nervously, I half wondered who was actually toying with who. I barely knew her, yet all I could think about was spreading her out on my kitchen table so I could taste every inch of her creamy skin.

Seeming to catch herself, she frowned. Angling her chin in defiance, she gave me a cutting stare.

"If you had checked your messages, you would have known I was coming," she replied, effectively side-stepping my question. She tossed me a warning look, and the meaning couldn't have been any clearer. She was letting me know that my interest in her was duly noted, but it wasn't going to be reciprocated.

Standing upright, I returned to my position against the wall and shrugged. "Yeah, well... I've been preoccupied with a few things."

"Mr. Atwood—"

"Sloan," I reminded her.

"Sloan, why don't we get right down to the reason I'm here?"

I almost chuckled.

"Not one to waste time with idle chit-chat, are you?"

"Not particularly. You have a mess on your hands, and I'm here to fix it."

Taking another swig of Pepsi, I eyed her suspiciously over the rim of the can, still unsure what to think about her. "Your accent. It's not Californian. Where are you from?"

"I live just outside of Washington D.C."

I raised my eyebrows in surprise.

"You're a long way from home. PR firms are a dime a dozen in these parts. Why would Milo enlist the help of someone from across the country?"

"Because Quinn & Wilkshire is the best—and you're wasting my time. Can we please get down to business now?" she asked with an air of impatience, but it was nearly impossible to take her seriously. The multicolored strands intertwined with her golden blonde tresses made her look like a princess who just stepped out of a fantasy book—or in my experience, a rainbow mermaid emerging from the ocean. It was a stark contrast to the tightness of her jaw and determined expression, but it may have been the sexiest combination I'd ever seen.

"Fine. Have it your way," I conceded with a shrug. "We'll skip the small talk, but I'm going to take a shower first. Sit tight, Rainbow Brite. Give me ten minutes, and then we'll talk."

Without giving her a chance to respond, I set my empty pop can down on the table and headed toward the bathroom.

As promised, I finished showering and shaving in less than ten minutes. I brushed my teeth and exchanged the old sweatpants for a pair of jeans but deliberately skipped putting on a shirt. Instead, I slung a plain white t-shirt over my shoulder and made my way back into the kitchen. Perhaps it was a dick move, but I had rather enjoyed watching her squirm uncomfortably after the way I had caught her looking at me earlier.

However, when I entered the kitchen, she wasn't the one

squirming uncomfortably—I was. In the short time I'd been gone, she'd cleaned up the mess of Styrofoam containers and beer cans that had been lying around. The trash was now piled into the garbage can, and the aluminum cans were neatly lined up in the recycle bin outside the utility room near the kitchen.

Well, shit.

I really wished she hadn't taken it upon herself to clean up. Now I'd have to play nice—within reason, of course. Scrapping the plan to saunter in like I was James fucking Dean, I pulled the t-shirt off my shoulder, slipped it over my head, then grinned sheepishly at her.

"You didn't have to do that," I told her, motioning to the now tidy space.

"I know. I was just bored waiting for you to come back, so I made myself useful. Don't get used to it. I'm your PR rep, not your maid."

I cocked one eyebrow at her straightforward tone, then shook my head and smiled to myself. I was more than just a little captivated by the delectable woman sitting at my kitchen table. Her heart-shaped mouth, round emerald-colored eyes, and easy blush made my dick twitch. She was leaving herself wide open, and I couldn't resist another opportunity to see that delicate blush again.

"Oh, I have plenty of thoughts on what you could be for me, Miss Kallie. Maid wasn't one of them."

Just as I'd hoped, a flush began to creep up her neck again. I grinned as I took a seat in the chair across from her, knowing I was getting to her.

Mission accomplished.

She sighed, ran a hand over her colorful braids, and met my eyes again.

"Listen, Sloan. I'm not here to play cat and mouse. Your agent warned me about what I might find when I got here, but I didn't expect this." She paused, seeming to collect her thoughts.

"To put it bluntly, after being here for barely twenty minutes, it's plain to see that you're a train wreck. Enough beer cans and whiskey bottles are lying around this place to fill an entire dumpster. Drinking yourself into a stupor every day isn't going to get you very far."

I bristled at her condescending tone.

"What I do isn't any of your business."

"Everything about you is my business now. I know what you've been through. Milo sent me a file that outlined it all. It was a tough road, and I get that. I also know any man who was able to endure what you did is better than this. However, cleaning up your act is up to you. I can't force you to do anything. I can only work with people who have the will."

I scowled, pissed about the drastic turn in the conversation. I no longer wanted to casually flirt with this mermaid apparition who'd played a starring role in my dreams last night. Instead, I wanted to put her over my shoulder and toss her judgmental ass out the front door.

"Cleaning up my act, huh? I'm not sure what you think you know from my supposed file, but a few paragraphs aren't enough to even scratch the surface of what I've been through."

"I'm sure it doesn't. So, why don't I tell you what I do know, then you can fill in the blanks?" When I didn't respond, she held out a hand and began ticking things off on her fingers. "I know you were in a terrible accident just over a year ago. Your car hit a wall during a practice session. You fell unconscious, were airlifted to a hospital in critical condition. The doctors said you had less than a twenty percent chance of surviving your injuries."

"Yet, here I am," I interrupted, extending my arms as if to prove it.

"I'm not finished," she stated curtly before continuing. "The left side of your body was immobile, and your skull was fractured. You had a collapsed lung, several broken ribs, and a shattered hip. You spent three months on a ventilator in order to breathe. Despite the odds, you pulled through after nearly a year of intense therapy—but it wasn't enough. The damage to your hip was too great, and you were told you could never race again. After receiving the news, you fell into a depression, started drinking, and popping too many painkillers. The result? Milo phoned me this morning to tell me that a little girl named Tanya Griffin is in the hospital because of your drunken rage. This morning's newspapers have painted you as a monster, and I expect a lawsuit from the girl's family to be filed any day now."

I winced as I listened to her recap the traumatic events of the past year. She'd barely taken a breath as she listed everything in chronological order up until this moment. I wasn't sure what Milo sent her, but there had to be a bunch of HIPAA law violations somewhere in there. As for possible lawsuits, I couldn't care less about those—I deserved them and would forever be plagued with guilt over accidentally hurting an innocent child.

But while Kallie's summary was correct, I was still right about one thing. The file she read didn't even scratch the surface. Never once did she acknowledge what I'd truly lost in the crash that happened one year and three months ago. There were some things I'd never get back—the feel of the engine revving, the wind as it whipped around the car, the roaring of the tires, the adrenaline rush that always came when I got behind the wheel.

Or the euphoria felt during the victory lap after a big win.

"You think you know everything, but you know nothing about me or what I had to give up," I said through gritted teeth. "Milo's intentions were good, but I think it's time for you to leave. I had a late night, and a bottle of ibuprofen is calling my name."

Her stiff posture softened, and to my surprise, she reached across the table to cover my hand with hers. Her bright green eyes appeared concentrated as she stared back at me, and a strange sort of energy passed between us.

"I told you I was going to list the things I knew, and then you had to fill in the blanks. I'm not insensitive to how you might be feeling. You were in the prime of your life, only to have it all ripped away. I won't pretend to understand what that feels like, but I can try if you'll let me. The sooner I figure out who you are, the better I can do my job." She stopped, seeming to come to some sort of realization, then cocked her head to the side contemplatively. "Sloan, I'm a big believer in fate. The destiny of every single person on the planet is written in the stars. There's a reason I was sent across the country to help you. Maybe you can consider this a new beginning."

I stared back at her, soaking in her words. She wore a curious expression, and I had to wonder if her comment about fate was actually about her—not me. But it was her earnestness about a predetermined destiny that made me pause. As ludicrous as the idea was, she made me believe it. Something flashed in her deep pools of green. I wasn't given a chance to figure out what it was before she stiffened and pulled her hand away from mine.

"Kallie, I want to help you out here, but I don't even know where to begin. There are just some things that can't be explained on a piece of paper. Racing was everything. I don't know who I am without it," I admitted with total sincerity. "I'm not sure how a fancy PR firm is going to help me get past that."

She pursed her lips as she considered me with inquisitive eyes.

"It won't, but it will help your less-than-savory reputation. Milo lined up a volunteer opportunity for you with Safe Track, a company sponsored by NASCAR that handles the fostering of young boys. He hopes to reverse the media spin that you somehow hate children. It's a good start, but I have a few other ideas up my sleeve as well. If you're willing to give this a go, let's start tomorrow at Motor Club Speedway in Fontana. A man by the name of Cooper Davis will be there tomorrow with a few of the boys from Safe Track. Meet me at ten o'clock."

"I'm familiar with the track, and I know Cooper. He's a friend of mine."

Her expression brightened, and I could almost see the wheels spinning in her head.

"Good. That should make things easier. I've put together an informal photoshoot and plan to invite the media."

"No," I stated firmly and adamantly shook my head. "No media. They spent years worshipping the ground I walked on, then turned on me in a hot minute after the accident. I haven't seen today's newspapers, but I'm sure it's even worse now. I don't trust them. They'll be looking for me to screw up."

"Well, then, Mr. Atwood, I guess you shouldn't screw anything up."

Kallie stood and swung her crocheted purse over her shoulder, signaling she was about to leave. When she turned and began walking toward the front door, I quickly followed her, overcome with a strong desire to ask her to stay. For what, I didn't know. It was odd considering that just fifteen minutes earlier I'd wanted to throw her out.

When we reached the door, she opened it, stopped just outside the threshold, then turned to face me. I stared down at her and our gazes locked. And there it was again—gravity, just like I'd felt when I saw her on the beach. She pulled me in, and I thought I might drown in the green sea of her eyes. I'd just met this woman, but there was something about her I couldn't quite place. She was familiar yet so unfamiliar at the same time. She was a stranger, yet I felt like we knew each other intimately, as if we were two infinitely magnetic souls.

I took a deep breath, attempting to get ahold of myself, but it didn't help. Her vanilla patchouli scent filled the air, and it was practically making me high—on her.

"Kallie, why did you agree to come all the way here?"

"It was a job assignment. I had no choice."

For some reason, her response pissed me off. Perhaps it was my ego, but I wanted her to be here for me and not just another job assignment. My feelings were ludicrous. From the way she spoke, she most likely never even heard of me until my agent hired her—yet that might be the most appealing thing about her. She didn't seem affected by my fame. She didn't have stars in her eyes or look at me as a meal ticket. There was no fangirling or gold-digging to worry about. I was a stranger to her in a way that I wasn't to so many other women.

I reached out and wrapped my fingers around her slender arm. Electricity seemed to sizzle under my palm, shocking me so much, I nearly pulled away. Yet, somehow, I held my grip firm as I stared down at her pink heart-shaped lips. My only thought was keeping her here—I didn't want her to disappear like she had yesterday. I wanted to make this rainbow mirage become a reality.

Without giving it further thought, I leaned in and planted my mouth on hers.

5

Kallie

I stiffened in protest as my mind grappled with this unexpected development.

Is this happening? Is he really kissing me right now?

I anchored my hands on his biceps, intending to push him away and end this madness—he was a stranger in almost every sense of the word. However, the heat I still felt from seeing him shirtless clouded my judgment, and my brain seemed to disconnect from my body. I was confused and didn't know what to do. I didn't want this...yet I did at the same time.

Without meaning to, I found myself kissing him back. My hands shifted from his shoulders to curl around his neck. My acceptance of his kiss encouraged him to press deeper into my mouth. Tasting. Claiming. His masculine scent of spice and earth sent my body reeling. I met every stroke of his tongue as he wrapped his arm around my waist, crushing my torso against his.

His fingers caressed the nape of my neck, gliding over the slope of my collarbone. I was drowning in sensation. I could hardly breathe as a wave of dizziness made my head swim. I knew it was wrong, but his possessive, animal touch made me feel powerfully female and profoundly desired. I felt it from the top of my head to the tips of my toes, and every molecule was consumed in molten heat. This was what I'd not even known I'd needed, and it felt so damn good. I finally knew what had been missing between Dean and me—it was chemistry and unbridled passion.

Oh my God. Dean.

Almost intrusively, thoughts of my potential fiancé popped into my head. I tore my mouth from Sloan's, shocked at myself and awash with feelings of guilt. I stepped back, only to see his heavy breathing matched my own. His short dark hair was mussed, and I half wondered if I'd been the one to do it or if it had just dried that way after the shower.

What in the world has come over me?

The kiss had only lasted a few seconds, but it still took me a moment to calm my racing heart. I tossed him an accusatory glare.

"Why did you do that?" I demanded.

"Do what?"

"Kiss me like that!"

Leaning against the door jamb, he looked me up and down. His piercing blue eyes seemed to say he had a secret only he knew, while the side of his mouth quirked up in the sexiest lopsided grin I'd ever seen.

"Would you have preferred me to kiss you in a different way?"

"No! You had no business kissing me at all!"

"Remind me again. Why did you agree to come to all the way to California?" he asked.

I puffed out an impatient breath, not sure why he wanted

me to repeat what I'd literally just said a minute earlier. "I said it was a job assignment. I had no choice."

"Well, then that's my answer too."

My brow furrowed in confusion. "What are you playing at, Sloan? That's your answer to what?"

"You wanted to know why I kissed you. The answer is, I had no choice. Your lips are just too irresistible." He shrugged, tossed me another crooked smile, then took a step back. "I'll be at Motor Club Speedway tomorrow morning at ten. I'll see you then, Kalliope Benton Riley."

Without another word, he closed the front door.

I stood there for a solid minute, completely shocked over what I'd allowed to happen with a total stranger. Too stunned to do much else, I slowly turned and walked down the driveway toward my rented BMW. As my astonishment began to dissipate, my fury began to mount. Once I was safely inside the confines of the car, I slammed my palms against the steering wheel and let out a scream of frustration.

"Argh! Of all the nerve! Who does he think he is?"

I glanced at my reflection in the rearview mirror. My cheeks were flushed pink, and I wasn't entirely sure if it was because I was mad or still turned on from Sloan's kiss. Knowing it was probably the latter only infuriated me further.

I took one last look at Sloan Atwood's contemporary-style home and wondered what I'd gotten myself into. With its oversized glass windows, sleek lines, and lack of any sort of feminine touch, the large Beverly Grove home was nothing more than an overpriced bachelor pad. Someone who lived in a place like this was probably used to getting their way with women without consequence.

I scowled at the house, then started the ignition and backed down the driveway. As I made my way toward the interstate that would take me back to my rental house in Santa Monica, I tried to force myself to keep my temper in check and focus on the road ahead. However, my effort was in vain. The I-10 was bumper to bumper. I'd nearly forgotten how bad California traffic could be, no matter what time of the day it was. What should have been a twenty-minute drive could turn into a two-hour drive in the blink of an eye. Crawling along at five miles per hour gave me plenty of idle time to get lost in my thoughts —and the more I stewed, the angrier I got.

People didn't just run around kissing other people without permission. The presumptuous jerk didn't even know me. Never mind that I'd kissed him back—he never should have advanced on me that way in the first place. He was a client, for crying out loud—not to mention that I was engaged.

Sort of.

I glanced down at my hand where an engagement ring should have been.

"Damn it!" I spat out. I angrily beeped the horn for no other reason than because everyone else was doing it. It felt good to vent some of my frustration. I cursed Dean for being practical —for not giving me a ring that I could use as a shield against unwanted advances. Perhaps if he'd given me one, I might have said yes to his proposal. But I also cursed myself for welcoming a stranger's kiss.

There was no doubt that Sloan was a man who knew what he wanted and took it. I could appreciate that because I was like that too in certain situations. It wasn't about wielding power and control. It was merely about being driven to achieve.

But what happened on his doorstep was none of the above.

Sloan emitted a kind of sexual energy I had never before encountered, and he managed to ignite every desire I hadn't known existed. With every look, every breath, and every word he spoke, my insides tightened with inexplicable arousal.

And I had loved every second of it.

I'd wanted Sloan to kiss me the minute he returned fresh from a shower wearing nothing but a pair of blue jeans. My stomach clenched as I recalled his appearance. His hair had been wet, the deep brown waves shedding tiny droplets of water onto his broad shoulders and chest. He had a face any male model would die for and a body to match. When he'd finally pulled on his white t-shirt, that only made my attraction to him even worse. His t-shirt had stretched tight around his arms, the sinewy muscle bulging from the sleeves. Seriously— the man's biceps could be considered arm porn. He hadn't just looked good, but he smelled good too—like the smell of the earth after a fresh rain, with just a hint of spiciness that made my toes curl.

The reaction he'd sparked in me was so out of character, and my response was unexpected. It had been near impossible to ignore the chemistry that threatened to knock me off my feet.

As a result, I was now a cheater.

I'd never cheated on anyone in my life. I knew what that betrayal felt like, and it sucked. It didn't matter if I'd already been questioning my relationship with Dean. I'd crossed a line by welcoming a kiss from Sloan.

While I had no intentions of repeating what happened in the doorway to his house, it didn't mean I could escape my guilt. I had to tell Dean the truth—and not just about the kiss. I needed to be honest with him about everything. One kiss with Sloan confirmed everything I already knew to be missing with Dean. What I'd felt with Sloan in just the briefest of moments was something I'd never experienced with the man who wanted to marry me. I now knew that Dean and I were not meant for each other, and I owed it to him—to both of us—to be truthful.

When I finally arrived at the house Quinn & Wilkshire arranged for me to stay at, I was a ball of nerves over the phone call I knew I had to make sooner rather than later. So, when I entered the quiet house, and my cellphone began to ring, I nearly jumped out of my skin. Fumbling through my purse, I pulled it out and saw Austin's name on the caller I.D. I sighed with relief. I wasn't ready to talk to Dean yet—at least not until I could get my thoughts together.

"Hey," I answered.

"Hey, Kals. I'm just calling to check in and see if you're all settled. Dad was telling me about the house he set you up in, and it sounds nice."

I looked around the spacious two-bedroom home. The owner was a financial advisor who had recently accepted a consulting contract working in Europe for a year. Rather than sell the house, she decided to rent the fully-furnished home. She'd been explicit in the rental agreement—she would only rent to a business professional, and no kids or pets were allowed. The minute I walked through the front door, I could understand why. The house impeccably maintained house had everything from custom drapes and luxury furnishings to an inground swimming pool in the back yard surrounded by immaculately manicured landscaping. Not a single detail had been missed, and it was easy to see why the home was the owner's pride and joy.

"The square footage is about the same as my townhouse in Georgetown, but it's all one level here, so it looks bigger. I like it a lot. It's very chic and a whole lot better than the hotel I was staying at. What a creep show that was!"

Austin laughed.

"You're so dramatic. I highly doubt your two-day stay at the Hilton was that bad."

"Trust me. You weren't there. The hotel itself was fine—it was the people in it. I went down to the gift shop my first night there to get myself a bottle of wine. I smacked right into someone wearing a lime green rubber bodysuit. Everyone else was decked out in weird garb too. You know me—I'm all about individual expression, but this was extreme on so many levels. I don't know if there was a costume event of sorts going on or what. All I know is that I felt like I was walking through the Capitol in *The Hunger Games*."

Austin laughed again, this time harder and longer, and I smiled. I missed him so much already, and I'd only been gone for a few days.

"Alright. I get the picture. L.A. is weird," he granted after he finally stopped laughing.

"Not weird. It's just different in a way I didn't expect. I mean, I was in Southern Cali for college for four years, but I never ventured north much. It's a whole different world here—the sounds, the smells, the air." I paused and looked out the large glass patio door. There had been an air quality alert today, and seeing the gray smog blocking the otherwise blue sky hurt my heart. "I guess I'll get used to it."

Austin fell quiet for a moment before speaking again.

"What's up, Kals? You alright?"

"I suppose so. Why?"

"Normally, you get excited to experience new things—even if they are weird. You seem hesitant right now... I don't know. Off, I guess you could say. I just want to make sure you're doing okay out there."

I sighed. Austin had the uncanny ability to read me—even from twenty-six hundred miles away.

"I met my client today."

"And?"

"He's an arrogant jerk, but nothing I can't handle."

"Is that it?"

"No..." I hesitated. "I have to call Dean later. I'm going to break things off with him."

"Oh, really?" He tried to sound surprised but had difficulty masking the glee in his voice.

"I know you aren't a big fan of his, but you could at least try not to sound so happy about it," I said dryly.

"I'll be honest. I can't say I'm disappointed, but I do wonder what brought this on."

My hand automatically moved to brush my fingertips over my lips. My mouth began to tingle as I remembered Sloan's kiss. I didn't understand my reaction to him, and I couldn't stop the rush of need that engulfed my senses as I recalled the memory. There was a reason I was drawn to Sloan in a way I'd never been to anyone else, and I was determined to find out what it was. But I couldn't tell my brother any of that for obvious reasons. Austin would think I'd lost my mind.

"There's always been something missing in our relationship. I just think it's the right thing to do. I feel like I'm being pulled—like my destiny is shifting by cosmic force. I just can't tell which direction I'm supposed to go."

"Here we go...the moon, stars, and planets are aligning," he teased.

"Oh, hush. I know better than to talk to you about this stuff. I should hang up now and call Gabby. She gets it."

"Speaking of Gabby, I ran into her at the grocery store this morning. She mentioned that she has some vacation time she needs to use and was thinking about coming out to see you."

I perked up, excited about a possible girls' weekend—or maybe a whole week—with my friend.

"Really? When?"

"She wasn't specific, but I got the impression it would be next month sometime. Call her and ask."

"I'll give her a buzz later after I talk to Dean. I'll probably need her ear after I make the call to him."

"I wish I could head out for a visit too, but my company recently picked up a project in Japan. I just found out I'll be crossing the globe a lot over the next three months. It will be hard planning anything in between."

Austin was an engineer who worked for a worldwide company that focused on everything from aerospace to defense systems. He frequently traveled for his job, but multiple trips to Japan were a lot—even for his company.

"What's in Japan?" I asked.

"It's an amusement park subdivision. The mouse is looking to expand again. Lots of new rides mean a shit-ton of hydraulics and motion control systems."

"Sounds boring."

Austin laughed but followed up with a sigh.

"Enough about me. Getting back to Dean—my feelings about him aside—I think you're making the right decision. You just...I don't know. You deserve better. I can't explain it."

"I hear you. And thank you."

"Alright, I've got to run. I leave in a few days, and I'm not sure if I'll talk to you before then. With the time difference and because I'm not sure where the hell I'm going to be on any given day, email is best if you need to reach me."

"Will do. Be safe. I love you, brother."

"Love you, too."

After I hung up the phone with Austin, I went into the living room and sat down on the couch with my laptop. It wasn't even noon yet, and I wanted to get a few hours of work in before calling Dean. I told myself it wasn't stalling but prioritizing. A call to him would only distract me from accomplishing much of anything today, and it was better to do it later. After all, I'd come to California for one reason—to fix a client's reputation. To do that, I needed to learn more about him.

Typing Sloan's name into the search engine, Atwood Racing Enterprise was the first thing to populate. After only a few minutes of reading, I learned that Sloan had once been an intimidating force in the world of racing. He'd won multiple championship races and was the youngest driver to win three consecutively. He was more than just a big deal. When he'd said racing was everything to him, my search results showed me that was the understatement of the year. It was almost hard to believe I hadn't heard of him until I was assigned as his rep.

After thirty minutes of reading, I found myself unable to stop staring at an image of Sloan on the screen. In the picture, he was decked out in his racing gear with his helmet at his hip. It was as if he were looking right back at me with those smoldering blue eyes. Desire burned hot in my belly, flipping and twisting like anxious butterflies.

Almost immediately, I felt guilty.

What am I doing?

I didn't know how I could have such a strong attraction to a man I'd literally just met when, just a week ago, I thought I was in love with Dean. Closing my eyes, I took a deep breath. When I opened them, I knew I couldn't put off the inevitable anymore.

Setting my laptop to the side, I picked up my cell phone from the coffee table and called Dean. As the phone rang, I began to feel the sting of tears. While I knew I was doing the right thing, it didn't make the call any easier. This deserved a face-to-face conversation—not a phone call from thousands of miles away. I should have been honest with myself long before coming to California and broke it off with Dean months ago when I first started having doubts.

But, as the phone rang, I reminded myself once again that everything happens for a reason. It was time to end this chapter because I knew in my heart that Dean wasn't meant to be my whole story. When he finally picked up after the fifth ring, I steeled myself for what I had to do.

"Dean, it's me. We need to talk."

6

Sloan

My head was still pounding. I should have gone back to bed after Kallie left, but there was no way I could sleep after what happened. I couldn't stop thinking about the taste of those pouty, heart-shaped lips or the power and energy that seemed to radiate from her when she submitted to my kiss. When she'd abruptly pulled away, I found myself feeling foolishly stunned. Catching me off guard was rare, yet I'd nearly been knocked on my ass by an eccentric goddess who could make my head spin with just one look.

I didn't know why I impulsively kissed her. I'd never done anything like that before in my life. In fact, I'd always considered guys who did things like that creepy. By doing what I did today, I'd officially crossed the line into the creeper zone. There had been nothing during our conversation that hinted she was interested in me at all, yet her body language told a different story, so I just acted on it without thinking.

While I knew I'd overstepped my bounds, I didn't regret it —not for a minute. My only regret was letting her walk away. We had only just met, but two people with a connection like that were not meant to stay strangers.

The crazy thing was, she wasn't my usual type at all. Tall brunettes, curvy in all of the right places, sultry with just the perfect amount of naughtiness, was the kind of woman I usually went for. Kallie, on the other hand, was the complete opposite. She had a wholesome vibe to her—and she was a total hippie. With her flowy skirt and rainbow-colored hair, she spoke of outlandish ideas about fate and predetermined destiny. It was ridiculous. Yet, for some reason, I couldn't turn away from her mesmerizing green eyes. And after just one taste of her lips, I knew she would be more than just another brunette pit stop. She would be a challenge, and that made me want to win her over all the more.

Resisting the urge to take a cold shower, I grabbed the keys to my Chevy Camaro and began driving to Motor Club Speedway in Fontana. As I navigated the highway, I couldn't help missing my Alfa Romeo Spider. It had been my favorite car over the years, but just like everything else, I'd been forced to give it up after my accident. I hated driving the Chevy. It just screamed douchebag with a mullet. If my hip injury didn't dictate the necessity for the custom paddle technology that only Chevy offered, I wouldn't have been caught dead in the car. I preferred the sweet and seductive features of the Alfa Romeo's unique design over the Chevy any day. Every time I complained about it, I forced myself to remember that I was lucky to have found something even remotely sporty. I could have been stuck with a Buick.

Just over an hour later, I arrived at Motor Club Speedway. I hadn't been to the track since before the doctor called and told me I couldn't race again. It was too painful, and I knew if I ever returned to any race track, it would have to be on my terms—

and preferably not under the watchful eye of Kalliope Benton Riley. With any luck, Cooper would be there, and I could talk to him about my current predicament with the girl who completely upended my morning.

When I walked through the main doors, I spotted Benjamin Dunn, the Crew Chief for Cooper's racing team, as I made my way through the main gates.

"Hey, Ben!" I called out to him. He glanced in my direction and smiled when he saw me.

"Atwood. Well, well! It's been a while. I didn't expect to see you here today," he drawled in a thick Southern accent.

"What can I say? I'm like a bad penny. I always turn up," I joked and clapped him on the shoulder. I was surprised by how good it felt to see him. "Man, you're a sight for sore eyes. How are things around here?"

"Same old since you were here last. You?"

"Eh, the same old for me too, I guess," I replied as casually as I could. Even though we both knew how drastically different things were in my life, there was no use talking about it. "I'm actually here to see Cooper. Is he kicking around?"

"Yes, sir. He's here—and his knickers are in a knot over something. Last I saw him, he was up in the box yelling at the newest pit crew member. I'm telling you... some of these kids coming in here lately have me shakin' my damn head. Porchlight is on, but no one's home."

I grinned, knowing exactly what Benjamin was referring to. Some new hires were better suited for selling team merch than holding a wrench.

"Got it. Thanks for the warning. I'll head that way."

I tossed Benjamin a quick wave, then walked down the corridor to the steps that would take me to the box seating area of the clubhouse. When I got there, I found Cooper with his arms crossed, staring down at the track. His shoulders were tense, and his jaw was set firm. He looked nothing short of furious.

"Rookie forget one of the lug nuts?" I asked as I approached.

Cooper glanced in my direction. Shock registered in his eyes before he quickly masked it and turned back to the track.

"No, but he could have if he'd been down with the rest of the crew."

"Why? What happened?"

"He was up here in the box, sleeping off a hangover. He's just lucky I got to him before Ben did."

"Oh, shit. Not good." I shook my head. Fatigue for any pit crew member was dangerous on a normal day—compounded by an alcohol-induced hangover, it could be deadly. "Did you cut him loose?"

"Nah, he's a good kid. He's been on the job for about six months and always brought his A-game—until today, that is. After I was through with him, he knows better than to come here hungover again. If he does, he's out. The crew is only as strong as its weakest link."

"No truer words have ever been spoken," I agreed. I looked down at the track and watched the crews bustling around as they prepped for a practice race. If just one of them missed a step, it could throw an entire race—or worse. I felt Cooper's eyes on me and turned my head to face him.

"How are you holding up, Sloan? You haven't been here in quite a while. I'm sure you didn't stop by to hear about a rookie fucking up."

"I'm fine."

"Now that's a whole load of bullshit, and you know it. I called Milo this morning after I heard about what happened in Long Beach. I'm worried about you. We all are."

I pursed my lips in annoyance. I could always count on Cooper for his no-bullshit way of getting straight to the point, but that's not what I needed now. I didn't want to talk about how fucked up my life was. I wanted to speak to him about Kallie and what I should do about her.

"What happened yesterday in Long Beach won't happen again. I'm more concerned about the little girl, Tanya. I can't tell you how bad I feel," I admitted.

"I'm sure you feel awful. If it's any consolation, from what I've heard, she's going to be fine."

"It doesn't matter," I retorted. "It shouldn't have happened."

"You're right on that front. It definitely shouldn't have happened. The Sloan Atwood I know is better than that. You've got to get your shit together. You're driving too fast on a dead-end road, brother. You need to change tracks completely."

I sighed, knowing how right he was.

"Milo hired a firm to help me out. The PR rep showed up at my house this morning. They lined up some shit to clean up my image—whatever that means. That's the reason I came here today. I haven't been here in quite a while, and I wasn't sure how it would feel coming back. Plus, the chick with the PR firm..." I trailed off, trying to find the words to describe what happened with Kallie. "After she came by the house this morning, I decided that I'm not sure if she's going to work out."

"Why not?"

Before I could respond, I heard a thunderous noise coming from the track. I drew in a sharp breath and turned to see the cars moving into their starting positions. The rumble of their engines caused a quiver deep in my bones. I was instantly overwhelmed with jealousy and desperate longing. I wanted to be down there—not up in a box talking about bullshit with Cooper. I craved the feeling of the tires roaring beneath my legs, the high that came during every turn, and the euphoric rush that was produced only when I hit top speed. I shifted my weight just enough to feel the dull ache in my hip—a reminder of why I'd never be behind the wheel of a race car again.

I bitterly tore my gaze from the track and turned back to

Cooper. I tried to ignore the pity in his eyes. He knew without explanation what I'd just been thinking about.

"She's not going to work out because I don't want her help," I told him as if the answer were really that simple and not about the consuming need I had for the mysterious rainbow mermaid who'd taken up residence in my psyche from the moment I first saw her.

"You never were one to ask for help," Cooper said warily and shook his head. "All I can say is to give this woman a chance. PR is her thing, after all. Maybe she can help you get around the bend."

"It isn't about not accepting the help—I'm open to it. God knows I need all the assistance I can get right now. I just don't want *her* as my rep." I paused and rubbed my thumb and index finger over my chin, thinking about all of the other ways I *did* want her. "She might not want to represent me anymore anyway. I may or may not have screwed things up with her this morning."

"How so?"

Lowering my hand, I looked squarely at my friend.

"I kissed her."

Cooper's eyes widened.

"You what? I mean, not that I'm one to throw stones, but didn't you just meet her?"

"I guess you could say that. I saw her on the beach yesterday, but we never actually met until this morning. I don't know what came over me. Hell, she isn't even my type. All I know is that she was on the beach, then I couldn't stop thinking about her. When that very same woman showed up at my house this morning, I was shocked to see her there. It felt like too much of a coincidence. We talked, and before she was about to leave, I realized I didn't want her to go. So, I went all caveman-like, grabbed her, and kissed her. I can only imagine what she thinks now."

Cooper started to laugh.

"Ballsy move. Did she kiss you back at least?"

A slow grin spread across my face as I recalled the memory of her petite hands curling around my neck.

"Oh, yeah. She definitely kissed me back—at first. Then she seemed to remember herself and pulled away. I think I caught her off guard. Supposedly, Milo gave her a file on me, and I'm pretty sure the file didn't list presuming playboy as a character description."

Cooper let out a low whistle.

"Fuck, man. Now what?"

"I told her I'd meet her here tomorrow morning. I guess I'll find out then. She's got something set up with Safe Track. I'm not sure if your wife has anything to do with it."

"Rochele mentioned she would be here tomorrow for a photoshoot with the boys. I didn't realize it had anything to do with you, though. What's the name of this PR agent?"

"Kallie."

Cooper scratched his chin contemplatively.

"Hang on. I have a better idea, one that might make things less awkward—you know, soften Kallie up, so she gets to know you a little better before tomorrow. I mean, I know how much you like your women, but you aren't a total dick."

I frowned.

"Okay. So... what's your idea?" I asked hesitantly. I wasn't sure where Cooper was going with this.

"It makes sense to get her and Rochele together since they'll be working together tomorrow. I think the four of us could all have dinner tonight—you, Kallie, me, and Ro."

"I don't think I can call her up and ask her to dinner at this point," I said with a laugh.

"You don't have to. I can ask Ro to set it up. Nothing fancy. We'll keep it casual with the goal of discussing the photoshoot. I don't know who Ro is planning to bring, but it's a good idea to brief you on each of the boy's situations. What do you say?"

I pursed my lips and considered his proposal. It wasn't a bad idea. I was familiar with Safe Track and knew they fostered boys from all backgrounds, many of which included extreme trauma with long-lasting effects. Having a better understanding of what I would be walking into would be a good thing. Plus, the idea of seeing Kallie again so soon was more than just a little bit appealing. The problem was, I wasn't sure how she would react to a night out with me after what happened this morning. Hell, I didn't even know if she still wanted to be my PR rep. A new agent might have already been assigned to me for all I knew, and she could be on a plane back to D.C.

My heart constricted at the thought of never seeing her again. It felt strange to be so affected by a woman—to want her so desperately despite barely knowing anything about her. My conscience nagged at me, telling me to rein things in before they went any further.

But I couldn't.

I'd had a taste of her, and I already knew I'd never get my fill.

"Alright. I'm in. Have Rochele set it up."

7

Sloan

F ive hours later, I pulled into a parking space in front of an eclectic sushi restaurant named The Lucky Koi. I'd never been there before and was surprised when Cooper texted me this as our dinner location. I wasn't a huge fan of sushi and hoped they had something mainstream on the menu. Still feeling slightly hungover, my body craved anything deep-fried and greasy over raw fish and seaweed.

When I stepped through the restaurant's doors, I was greeted by a formally-dressed Japanese woman standing behind a narrow podium.

"Welcome to The Lucky Koi," she said with a nod.

"Thank you. I'm meeting Cooper Davis, party of four. I'm not sure if they've arrived yet."

The woman looked down at her clipboard.

"Yes. I see two members of your party have arrived. Right this way, please."

Walking down a dimly lit hallway, I looked around. The place wasn't too fancy, but definitely more upscale than the local hamburger joint. When we reached the end of the hallway, the space opened up to reveal what looked like an Asian garden built into the Pacific coast. The walls were nothing but glass, giving a full view of the surf crashing into miles of sandy beach. Inside, slated stones, tall bamboo, and lanterns decorated the seating area.

I spotted Cooper and Rochele sitting at the far end. Cooper gave me a short nod when he saw me.

"I didn't take you for a sushi kind of guy, Cooper," I joked as I took the seat across from them. "Was there something wrong with the Crab Shack?"

"Not my choice. Blame Ro. She picked the place."

"I thought it would be better to cater to Kallie's tastes since this is supposed to be a business dinner," Rochele explained. "When I called to invite her, I asked about any dietary restrictions. She told me she was a vegetarian. I knew this place had plenty of vegetarian options, so here we are."

I shook my head.

"Of course Rainbow Brite is a vegetarian," I remarked, not bothering to suppress an eye roll.

"No rainbows tonight. Sorry to disappoint you," said a familiar voice.

Startled, I looked up to see Kallie had come up behind me. It had been less than ten hours since I'd last laid eyes on her, yet I felt as if I was seeing her for the first time. Gone were the rainbow streaks in her hair, replaced by purple strands that matched her dress. She wasn't wearing bohemian attire like she'd been this morning. Now she wore a thin-strapped, long bright orchid satin dress that whispered over her curves, giving me a glimpse at tiny details that I'd missed before. With her arms bare, I was able to see a delicate moon tattoo lacing over her right shoulder with little stars cascading halfway down her arm. There was writing as well, but I couldn't make out what the scrolling font said at a quick glance. The dark ink should have been too bold against her creamy skin, yet somehow it made her seem elegant and even more mysterious.

"Kallie, I didn't realize you...I, um..." I stuttered, uncharacteristically stumbling over my words as I quickly stood to pull out her chair. I was both surprised to see her standing there and amazed by how fucking gorgeous she looked. "I...ah, you look great—different. Please, have a seat."

Cooper attempted to laugh but had been mid-sip with his water and started choking. Once he caught his breath, he grinned from ear to ear.

"I never thought I'd see the day," he said with unmistakable humor in his voice.

"Shut up, asshole," I muttered.

Rochele pursed her lips and threw Cooper a scolding look, but she didn't comment. Instead, she stood and extended her hand to Kallie.

"I'm Rochele, but you can call me Ro. It's a pleasure to meet you, Kallie."

"Likewise. It's nice to put a face to the voice," Kallie graciously said as she returned Rochele's handshake.

Glancing back to where I stood waiting to push in her chair, Kallie smoothed her hands over her hips and sat down. She moved with devastating grace, her body wrapped in a satin dress meant for sin. Intense lust threatened to overtake me, so forceful it made me dizzy.

Shaking my head, I returned to my seat next to her, and an uncomfortable silence fell over the table—or perhaps I was the only one feeling awkward. I needed a minute to just fucking relax. I didn't know what the hell was wrong with me. It was as if Kallie had put some sort of weird voodoo spell on me. Thankfully, our waiter was efficient and came over to take our drink orders relatively quickly.

"What can I get for you, Miss?" he asked Kallie. She glanced at me, then placed a hand on my shoulder.

"Mr. Atwood and I will just stick with ice water. Thank you," she replied.

I blinked, not sure if I'd heard her correctly. I was about to speak up, but she squeezed my shoulder as if in warning. I looked at her curiously, and something about her expression compelled me to stay silent.

"And for you, Miss?" the waiter asked Rochele.

"I'll have a gin and tonic, extra lime."

"And I'll take a Sapporo," Cooper added. I eyed him questioningly, not realizing he was a fan of lighter Japanese beer. Cooper shrugged when he caught my eye. "When in Rome..."

When the waiter walked away, I rounded on Kallie.

"What was that all about? Is there a reason I couldn't order myself a damn drink?" I demanded a little too harshly. God only knew, the longer I sat at this table next to this spellbinding goddess, the more I felt like I needed one.

However, if Kallie was taken aback by my tone, she didn't seem upset by it. She simply picked up her water glass to take a sip of it. I noted how graceful the movement of her hand was, never hesitating but fluidly gliding as it would have if I hadn't just snapped at her. She raised one perfectly shaped eyebrow and eyed me knowingly.

"Do you see that guy sitting alone at the table over there?" She angled her head slightly, lifting her chin to the left. I turned to see who she was referring to.

"Yeah, I see him. What about him?"

"He's a reporter."

"How do you know that?"

"It's my job to know these things. Your every move is being scrutinized. If you want to fix your reputation, you'll take my advice and drink water tonight."

Cooper glanced in the direction Kallie had motioned. Turning back to face us, he released a low chuckle.

"Oh, she's good, Sloan. I recognize that guy. He's a reporter from the *Racing Beat*. I'd keep this girl around if I were you. She'll be able to clean up your image in no time."

Kallie smiled and nodded her head knowingly. She didn't look smug to be told she was correct but humbly confident in her ability to see things. I narrowed my eyes at her. A part of me wanted to signal the waiter back to the table and order a double scotch on the rocks just to spite her, but another part of me knew she was right. The newspapers were having a field day with headlines about me, many of them speculating why I fell into a bottle after the crash. The last thing I needed was to give them more ammunition.

Still, there was no way I was going to let Kallie win this power play. Leaning in closer so only she could hear me, I asked, "Are you trying to fight with me?"

"No, why?"

"Because if you are, you should know it's turning me on."

To my satisfaction, her eyes widened, and her face flushed ten shades of crimson. The way it crept up her neck and blossomed over her cheeks was like catnip for my soul—addictive and immensely satisfying. But even more rewarding was the unmistakable flash of desire in those endless pools of green. Sitting back in my chair, I crossed my arms and allowed myself a moment to enjoy her discomfort.

Rochele cleared her throat. She may not have heard what I said, but she was not oblivious to Kallie's recognizable blush.

"Yes. Well, speaking of your image, Sloan, let's talk about tomorrow," Rochele suggested.

"Fine. Let's talk about it," I agreed, choosing to accept the small victory over Kallie as I smugly—albeit begrudgingly—picked up my glass of ice water from the table and took a sip.

The two women dived right in. Cooper and I barely got a

word in edgewise. As I listened, I found out the two boys Rochele planned to bring to the track were new to The Residence, the place where the orphaned boys lived after losing their parents. While I'd met several of the boys staying at The Residence in the past, I was never introduced to the two who would be joining the photoshoot.

"Marcus has been with us for about six weeks," Rochele said. "He's ten years old and has been bouncing around in the system for years—that is until recently when a spot for him opened up at The Residence. His biological parents both died of drug overdoses."

"Oh, that's awful!" Kallie said regretfully with a shake of her head.

"I really hope we can bring him some stability. He desperately needs it. Eli is the other boy I'm going to bring. He's nine years old and has been with us for about a month longer than Marcus. He's been through a lot. His father is unknown, and his mother was a prostitute. She was murdered by one of her johns right in front of Eli."

I frowned, unable to mask the anger I felt from hearing the boys' stories. I'd been through my fair share of shit, but I couldn't imagine seeing my mother murdered in cold blood. A wound like that ran deep and would have long-lasting scars.

The waiter returned with Cooper and Rochele's drinks, then took our food orders. Cooper and Rochele decided to share a sushi sampler platter, and Kallie ordered something equivalent to rabbit food—edamame, avocado salad, and a vegetable sushi roll. I, on the other hand, managed to find the only thing that looked remotely edible on the menu—steak teriyaki.

The conversation continued to be about the two boys Rochele planned to bring to tomorrow's photoshoot, but I was only tuned in with half an ear. I was too preoccupied with the shades of purple twisted through in Kallie's braid. The two times I'd seen her before this, her hair had been rainbow-colored, and I wondered how or why she changed the colors. There was a lock of hair that always seemed to spring free near her left ear. She was forever tucking it back, and I couldn't tell if it was a nervous habit or if it was a hairstyle that refused to stay in place.

I had so many questions about her. She was like a riddle I had to find the answer to—but it was a riddle that certainly wasn't going to be solved over just one dinner.

When the food arrived, I shook my head as if to clear it, and I forced myself to focus on the conversation at hand.

"When Eli first came to The Residence, Ro said he wouldn't let anybody touch him," Cooper was saying. "I didn't realize how bad it actually was. I'm talking about full-on screaming fits. I saw it happen once when one of the younger boys at The Residence tried to be nice and hug him. It was brutal. My heart broke for the little guy, but they've made great progress with him."

"Thanks to Cooper," Rochele added. "Eli's love for race cars helped us break through some of his barriers."

"I was planning on keeping the photoshoot candid—nothing staged," Kallie said. "I just want everyone to relax and have a good time while the camera clicks away. Considering Eli's issues, that's probably a good thing. From what you've described, I don't want a photographer to accidentally trigger him when trying to get a group pose."

Rochele nodded her head in agreement.

"Eli's therapist, Dr. Dellaneve, assured me that he would be okay for tomorrow. Just remember that there can be no physical contact with him, and all should be good," she warned. My ears perked up upon hearing this.

"And if he's not?" I asked. "Kallie is insisting on having the press there. What if something goes wrong?"

"Let me handle that," Kallie said. "There are plenty of other things you need to focus on, including getting me a list of other possible problems that could arise."

"Such as?"

"Crazy ex-girlfriends, a falling out with a friend, bad blood with a family member—stuff like that."

"Right!" Cooper scoffed. "Like Sloan has kept any woman around long enough for her to collect dirt on him."

"Well, there was Skylar," Rochele reminded with a teasing wink. "I think she lasted, oh... maybe two weeks? Then there was Erica. How long did you keep her around for, Sloan?"

"Alright you two. Enough. What can I say? I'm a busy guy. I don't have time for the latch-on types."

I glanced at Kallie, feeling slightly uneasy. I wasn't sure why I cared about her opinion so much—I just did. Sure, I'd been around the block more than a few times, but I didn't want her to think I was some kind of philandering skirt-chaser. Although, after my advance on her this morning, I'm pretty sure that's exactly what she thought.

"Two weeks or two months. It doesn't matter," Kallie waved off, then looked directly at me. "I need to know about any skeleton in your closet that could give you negative publicity. I've got six months to make it disappear. I also need to know about anything that could help you. What is your relationship with your parents like?"

I instantly stiffened and felt my jaw clench. An uncomfortable silence fell over the table.

"I'm sure that information is in the file you have on me," I responded coolly. Kallie's eyebrows pushed together in confusion.

"Actually, I don't recall reading anything about them."

"Well, Miss Know-It-All, I don't know what to tell you then. I guess Milo was slacking."

Kallie's head snapped back, and she blinked twice, her

expression showing that she was clearly offended by my words and tone.

"Sloan, is there something I need to know?"

Before I could respond, the waiter approached the table with the check. Taking advantage of the distraction, I signaled for him to hand it to me.

"I've got dinner covered," I told the group and reached into my back pocket for my wallet.

"Nah, man. You don't have to. I'll split it with you," Cooper said.

"I insist. You can get it the next time."

Kallie didn't say anything but continued to look perplexed. I could practically see the wheels turning in her head. It didn't matter. A basic Google search would tell her everything she needed to know.

"I'm going to use the ladies' room before we head out," Rochele announced with a pointed look at Kallie.

"I think I will, too," Kallie immediately replied, and both she and Rochele stood from their seats.

After they walked away, I turned to Cooper.

"Why do they always go to the bathroom in pairs? It's fucking weird."

Cooper laughed.

"Not weird at all. I'm pretty sure Ro planned that after the way you snapped at Kallie. My guess? She's in there explaining your shitty behavior."

"I didn't snap."

"Yeah, you did. I felt that arctic chill from across the table. Cut the girl some slack. How is she supposed to know about what happened?"

I looked in the direction of where the two women disappeared and blew out an aggravated sigh.

"I suppose I owe her an apology," I murmured more to myself than to Cooper.

My friend laughed again.

"An apology is a start. I mean, yeah. She's your PR rep, but it's more than that. You've got it bad for this girl. I've never seen you like this."

"No need to point out the obvious. I don't get it either. I barely know her—not that I knew any of the other women I was with all that well either. But Kallie is different somehow." I paused and pursed my lips together, trying to find the words to explain the unexplainable. "I know what you're thinking, and you can say it. I'm fucked up."

"Nope. I think it's voodoo pussy."

"Jesus, Cooper. I haven't even been with her in that way. Yeah, it's like she put a spell on me, but there's no magical pussy taking hold of my dick—at least not yet."

"It doesn't matter. It was like that with Ro and me. I saw her and immediately wanted her. There was no rationalization for why I couldn't get her out of my head. It just was. I'm not saying what's going on with you and Kallie is anything like Rochele and me but trust me on this—if you want a chance to find out, you probably need to be a little nicer."

The waiter returned with my credit card, and as I put it back in my wallet, I considered Cooper's words. Before my accident, I was never a big drinker, and I never took drugs. Sex was my only vice. I'd had more than my fair share of women, but I wasn't a playboy. I merely appreciated the high that came with being buried deep inside a beautiful woman. It was an instant stress reliever.

After the accident, I'd felt more alone than ever before in my life. Cooper had been the only one dumb enough to stick around and put up with my miserable ass. When I found out I couldn't race again, I'd used alcohol and painkillers to dull the physical and mental ache no doctor could heal in an operating room. I shut out everyone and anything that reminded me of my previous life, including my ability to get laid with just a snap of my fingers. Depression took over, and I'd assumed no woman would want a broken has-been. In the process, I'd mastered the art of being an asshole.

Then Kallie showed up at my door.

A part of me wondered if the only reason I felt so drawn to her was that she was the first woman I'd allowed myself to be around for more than a passing minute since the crash. I wasn't certain, but I would have to heed Cooper's advice and start being a little nicer to Kallie if I wanted to find out.

8

Kallie

I stood in front of the restroom mirror and reapplied a thin layer of gloss to my lips. Rochele walked up next to me, leaned her hip against the counter, and gave me a small smile.

"I'm not sure what you're thinking, but I want you to know that Sloan isn't normally a complete jerk," she said.

"No. I don't think he's a total jerk. But I do think he's arrogant and assuming."

"Still mad about the kiss he planted on you this morning?"

"You know about that?" I asked, feeling shocked and embarrassed at the same time.

"Cooper might have mentioned it," she admitted with a knowing grin. "I have to say, I've never seen Sloan act like this before. You had him tongue-tied quite a few times over dinner."

"I don't know about that. He didn't seem to have any issue biting my head off just now."

"Don't hold it against him. There's a reason he turned cold

there at the end. Once you get to know the real Sloan, you'll understand why he reacts the way he sometimes does."

Dropping my gloss into my purse, I snapped it closed then turned to face her. "Help me out then. What am I missing?"

Rochele sighed and crossed her arms. "How far back into Sloan's past did you dig?"

"I didn't dig much at all yet. I haven't had the chance to. All I know is what was in the file Milo gave to me and what I pulled up in a quick internet search."

Her face hardened.

"Milo..." she trailed off and shook her head. There was no mistaking the element of disgust in her expression. "I've never been a fan of his, but it doesn't matter what I think. He did right by enlisting your help. Sloan doesn't deserve the headlines he's getting. He's been through enough."

"I read about it. The crash, the rehab—all of it is so traumatic."

"No, I'm talking about *before* the crash."

"What do you mean?"

She hesitated for a moment, seeming unsure if she should say more.

"Look, most of what happened right before Sloan's accident isn't anything that's not already publicly available on the internet. I just don't think you've come across it yet. If you dig a little deeper, it's all there. I don't think I'll betray any confidences by telling you about Sloan's parents and why he won't talk about them."

"What about them?"

"Sloan's father, Jeff Atwood, was a Formula One racer who died in a traffic accident on Ventura Freeway near Pasadena. It was a ten-car pileup about twenty years ago. From what I read about it, it was pretty awful. Six people died in total. Sloan was just a kid when it happened. He had always idolized his father, but after that day, he chose to continue his father's legacy and started racing."

"I didn't know his father raced too. I can understand why it must be hard for Sloan to talk about him."

A sad look spread over Rochele's pretty face, and she shook her head.

"No, that's not why he doesn't talk about him—or his mother for that matter. The morning before Sloan had the crash that pulled him from racing, he discovered a hard truth about his father. I was there when it all happened." She paused and seemed to be recalling the memory. "The song, "Ventura Highway," was playing from a Bluetooth speaker in the pit lane. It was just something Sloan did before every race, whether it be a practice lap or the real deal. It's a superstition he has. Cooper has superstitions too—in fact, most drivers do. Anyways, a reporter showed up and started asking him questions about his father, saying Jeff Atwood had been drunk and was responsible for the accident on the freeway all those years ago. Sloan shooed the guy away, and none of us paid much attention to what he was saying. However, Sloan must have been thinking about it. When his mother showed up right before the practice run, he asked her about it. It turned out to be true. His father had been drinking and driving—a fact his mother had kept hidden from him for years."

"Oh, no..."

"Sloan was furious to find out he'd idolized a man whose intoxication resulted in the death of five innocent people. He argued with his mother about it in front of everyone. There was a big shouting match in the pit lane, and Sloan ended up behind the wheel in a rage. Fifteen minutes later he spun out and crashed into the wall."

"Oh my gosh!" My eyes widened in shock as I tried to envision how the scene unfolded. Sloan had to have second-guessed every decision he made that day. Not to mention, his mother must have been beside herself with guilt. I knew I certainly would've been. "Does Sloan blame his mother for what happened?"

Rochele shrugged, the expression on her face letting me know I had yet to hear the worst of the story.

"I don't know. I never asked him because it was a touchy subject. His mother killed herself three days after the accident."

I gasped.

"She killed herself?"

"Yeah. That's why he snapped when you mentioned his parents. He's still furious about what she did. It's assumed that once Sloan's mother heard about his extensive injuries, she couldn't handle it. He was in really rough shape, and nobody expected him to live. With his mother gone, all he had was his friends to help him fight his way back. Being able to race again became his sole focus and the reason he fought so hard on his road to recovery."

I thought back to what Sloan had said to me. It felt like I'd heard the words a lifetime ago, not just that very morning.

"You think you know everything, but you know nothing about me or what I had to give up... Racing was everything. I don't know who I am without it."

Suddenly, the pieces started to fall into place.

"Then the doctor told him he could never race again..." I let my words linger in the air, not needing to complete the sentence.

Rochele nodded knowingly. "That's why I said not to be too hard on him. Just give him a chance, Kallie."

BEFORE LEAVING THE RESTROOM, I asked Rochele to say goodbye to Sloan and Cooper for me and left the restaurant alone. It was easier to make a quick exit rather than go back to the table to face Sloan. Now that I had a bit more insight into his past, I needed a moment to reflect on my newfound knowledge.

I was always a sucker for a sad story, and this was no exception. Considering how weak I was under Sloan's gaze, it would only make it worse at a time when I needed to focus on the job at hand. As much as I was a spontaneous kind of person, I'd never been a big risk-taker. I was methodical with any decision I considered life-altering, especially when it came to my career. I loved my job and was grateful for the opportunity to work for my father's firm. I'd worked way too hard to allow my hormones to mess it all up, and I didn't want to do anything that could jeopardize it—especially considering the money that was at stake. If I wanted to stop pinching pennies, I needed to keep my eyes on the prize.

I'd taken an Uber to the restaurant since parking near the Santa Monica Pier was so expensive. However, I was beginning to wish I'd taken my own car. Standing out there waiting for an Uber inevitably meant I'd see Sloan when he came out. Glancing back and forth between the door to the restaurant and the beach, I made a split-second decision to head toward the water and began walking across the sand until I reached the Pacific shoreline.

The large Ferris wheel on the Santa Monica Pier could be seen in the distance, and the setting sun cast an orange and red glow, making the people on the beach look like nothing more than dark shadows. Everything felt hushed as the water lapped at the sand. I'd spent a lot of time on the beaches of Southern California when I'd been in college, enjoying the tranquil setting the sand and sea offered. I'd nearly forgotten how much I loved it.

A young couple holding hands walked past me. They looked fresh out of high school, oblivious to everyone around them as they ducked their heads together and laughed at their private joke. I smiled to myself, appreciating their young and innocent love. But at the same time, seeing them also made me feel sad. It reminded me of the phone call I'd made to Dean earlier and all the failed relationships that came before him. Perhaps the gypsy was right—I was doomed when it came to love.

As if the mere thought of Madame Lavinia stirred something in the air, the hairs on the back of my neck stood on end. I felt something—like a presence—that caused goosebumps to rise on my arms despite the warm evening air. Instinctively, I slowly turned to look behind me.

Glancing in the direction of where I'd just come from, I saw Sloan standing on the edge of the restaurant's walkway. Wrapping my arms around myself, I shivered. It wasn't Madame Lavinia's presence I'd felt—it was Sloan's.

Even at this distance, I could see that he'd loosened the collar of his white dress shirt. It was now unbuttoned at the neck, and he had one thumb hooked into the right front pocket of his jeans. He stood tall and confident, oozing with power and an irresistible bad-boy vibe. The way he turned to look up and down the shoreline was almost as if he were searching for someone.

Is he looking for me?

I wasn't sure, but I knew the minute he spotted me. Turning away, I continued down the beach, suddenly feeling very self-conscious of the way I walked through the sand with my sling-back heeled sandals. Without skipping a step, I slipped off each shoe, looped the back straps around my index finger, and continued walking.

A moment later, I heard my name called, and my heart began to race. Resigning myself to the inevitable, I turned around to see Sloan standing directly behind me.

"It'll be dark soon. You shouldn't be down here alone," he said.

"I'm a big girl."

I expected a retort of some kind, but he didn't give one. Instead, he surprised me by reaching up to tuck a loose strand of hair behind my ear. His touch seemed to surge with electricity, causing my body to quiver from the brief contact.

"Do you like the beach, Kallie?"

"I do. But then again, I don't know anyone who doesn't. There's just something calming about the ocean."

"Very true," he said thoughtfully, then angled his head to the side curiously. "I saw you yesterday in Long Beach. At least, I'm pretty sure it was you."

I looked at him in surprise, suddenly remembering what he'd said on his doorstep that morning. He thought I was a woman he saw on the beach.

"That's right. I was there yesterday. I don't remember seeing you, though."

"It's probably good that you didn't. My head is still fuzzy about what happened, but I definitely remember seeing you. You looked like a mermaid coming out of the ocean. And the rainbows—there was no mistaking that when you showed up at my door. That's how I recognized you this morning. I really liked the rainbow weaves you'd had in your hair. Why did you change the color?"

I shrugged and thought about how much Dean despised the way I changed the color daily.

"I change the color based on how I feel that day. Some people wear clothes dictated by their mood. I swap out hair extensions. Ultimately, it's an expression of myself. Rainbow is for when I'm feeling optimistic—when I'm trusting destiny to take hold and make anything happen."

"Destiny, huh? And the purple? What does purple mean?"

I hesitated, unsure about how much I wanted to divulge. I couldn't tell him I wove purple through my French braid when I was getting ready for dinner because of how his kiss had turned me inside out—especially when I didn't understand it myself. Instead, I gave him the partial truth, but no less honest.

"Purple is when I'm confused or feeling conflicted over something. I also wear purple when I'm nervous."

He eyed me questioningly.

"Do you feel nervous?"

"No," I lied, albeit a little too quickly. In an attempt to recover, I brought the conversation back to business. "I'm conflicted about the right way to handle your PR strategy."

He nodded his head, but there was a glint of amusement in his eyes.

"I'm not so sure about that. I get the feeling there's more behind the purple today. Am I right?"

"Maybe."

Turning away, I continued my walk down the beach. Sloan fell into step beside me.

"Is that all you're going to give me? Come on, Kallie. We're going to be working together a lot over the next few months. At dinner, you wanted me to tell you everything about myself so that you can help me, but it's kind of hard to do that if I don't know anything about you. Give me something here."

Give him something? Why would I give up anything about myself when I know he is keeping things from me?

I stopped walking and turned to face him, the words on the tip of my tongue. I wanted to repeat what Rochele had told me, but instinct held me back. I knew Sloan would need to tell me his version of the story in his own time, not because I demanded it.

It's too personal.

Besides, it wasn't like he had the opportunity to share the story about his parents. It wasn't fair of me to accuse him of hiding things considering the length of time we'd known each other. Until he decided to open up about it, I'd just have to work with what I knew.

Shaking my head, I began walking again. "I'm not here because of me, Sloan. It's about you."

He fell quiet as he walked beside me, the only sounds coming from the waves crashing into the shore or the occasional laughter of people in the distance. "So... are you going to tell me the real story behind the purple hair?"

I pursed my lips, frustrated with his persistence.

"Since you insist on knowing, fine," I said with an exasperated sigh. "Before dinner tonight, I broke things off with Dean, my longtime boyfriend. He wanted to marry me, but I knew I couldn't go through with it for reasons I don't feel like explaining. Even so, my decision didn't come easy, and I have conflicting emotions about it."

"Oh. I didn't realize you were involved with someone."

"How could you? We literally just met this morning."

"Well, either way, the decision had to be tough. I'm sorry."

"Don't be. I mean, the breakup was inevitable. When I called him, he wasn't even shocked. He told me he'd expected it. He said pinning me down would be like trying to pin down a cloud."

"So you're a real-life Fraulein Maria, are you?"

I smiled. "You're familiar with *The Sound of Music*. I wouldn't have guessed that."

"It's not by choice," he admitted with a laugh. "My gram was into musicals and used to torture me with them when I was a kid."

"My mother loves them, too. It's in her blood. My grandmother, Claudine Benton-Riley, was a stage actress on Broadway. My mother grew up with show tunes all around her." I paused, feeling pensive as I thought back to what Dean had said. "I don't know. Maybe Dean is right. Maybe I'm too flighty."

"Do you want to know what I think?" he asked, and without waiting for an answer, he continued. "I think that bit about comparing you to pinning down a cloud was his ego talking. He probably just didn't want to admit rejection."

"No. You don't know him like I do. He's always so practical, right down to the engagement ring—or lack thereof." I let out a bitter laugh as I thought back to the other things Dean had said during our phone conversation. Even though I'd just told Sloan I didn't want to explain it all, I found myself divulging more than I should. "Dean originally told me he didn't propose with a ring because he wanted me to help him pick one out. I thought it was considerate of him, even if it wasn't very romantic, but I should have known there was a more logical reason behind it. The truth came out after I ended it. Apparently, he'd assumed I wouldn't say yes right away and didn't want to lose out on the interest he'd earn on the cash in his brokerage account while waiting for my answer."

Sloan stopped short, and I turned to see him looking at me with disbelief. "He actually told you that? The guy sounds like a real dick if you ask me."

I shrugged. "No. Not a dick. There wasn't any malice when he told me. It was just a statement of fact. At least now I know the truth. It's for the best."

Sloan cocked his head to the side with an expression of concern. "I hope that um... our kiss this morning. You have to know I don't normally do things like that. It sounds like things weren't too great with the two of you, but I hope what happened with us isn't the reason you broke up with him."

"No—yes. I mean, no. It wasn't the main reason. Our breakup was bound to happen. What happened between you and me, no matter how inappropriate, was eye-opening for me. But more importantly, I'm the PR agent representing you. That can't happen again."

"Hmm," was all he said, and I narrowed my eyes suspiciously. He had the most peculiar look on his face. He appeared both smug and elated at the same time.

"Why are you smilking at me like that?" I asked.

"Smilking?"

"It's like a smile and smirk at the same time," I explained. "Don't do that."

Sloan threw his head back and laughed long and hard.

When he eventually quieted, we stood looking at one another for the longest minute of my life, neither of us sure of what to say. It was as if my admission about breaking up with Dean suddenly left endless possibilities—none of which we could possibly explore. He was my client, after all. Not to mention, my father would have my head if I got romantically involved with Sloan.

But oh, how I wanted to—badly—and I couldn't understand why.

"I suppose you're right," he said.

"About what?"

"About us. It was rather presumptuous of me to kiss you like I did. Allow me to start over by properly introducing myself." Taking my hand, he brought it to his mouth and brushed his lips softly over my knuckles. Warmth spread throughout my body. "My name is Sloan Atwood, the audacious asshole who ravaged you without permission on his doorstep."

While his words were teasing, his gaze was intense. Energy crackled in the air, and I felt mesmerized by the sea-blue irises of his eyes. Unfortunately, the spell broke all too soon when the sound of a band began to play. I blinked to reclaim my focus, pulled my hand away, and looked up toward the street. A beachfront restaurant not far from the sushi place where we'd just had dinner had suddenly come to life. Twinkle lights crisscrossed above the patio like electric spaghetti, illuminating the guests circling on the dance floor. In the middle of the group there was no mistaking the white ball gown of a bride. She was in the arms of her groom, moving together to a smooth yet powerful stream of strumming guitar strings. A moment later, the lead singer began to sing a cover of "Marry Me" by Train.

"It's their first dance," I murmured.

Sloan followed my gaze. "That song is so cliché," he said.

Turning away from the dancing couple, I looked quizzically at Sloan. "I like that song. How is it cliché?"

"Just listen to the lyrics. They are cheesy as all hell."

I pressed my lips together and looked back at the couple. "I don't think so. Those lyrics were born out of somebody's experience. You can't write words like that without having felt them. It's about love and romance and dreams coming true."

"Nah, I don't buy it. Love songs are just a hoax designed to play on people's fantasies. It's all garbage. Romance and dreams are for fools."

I shook my head at his statement, unable to look away from the couple as they danced.

"Dreams aren't garbage—they define every one of our unforgettable moments. Everyone has them, and I'm sure you've had thousands. Those were all dreams that came true."

Sloan stayed quiet, and I wondered what he was thinking. Turning to face him, I saw that he wasn't watching the couple as I had been, but instead was looking out at the ocean.

"More often than not, my dreams turn into nightmares," he said quietly. His tone was so hushed, and I wasn't sure if he was talking to himself or me. If Rochele hadn't told me more about his past, I might not have understood the full implication of his statement—but I did, and my heart broke for him. Reaching out, I placed a gentle hand on his arm.

"Fate may have put you on a different path, but you owe it to yourself to forge ahead and make new extraordinary moments. Just look at where we are right now. The beach, the people, the sunset... this could be an unforgettable and extraordinary moment if you allow it to be."

He looked down into my eyes, his gaze penetrating. "I'm sorry for snapping at you earlier in the restaurant, Kallie."

I smiled. "It's okay. I forgive you."

Casting his gaze down to my extended arm, he raised a hand to run a finger over my shoulder, tracing the lines of my tattoo.

"What does this say?" he asked.

I automatically looked down at my exposed shoulder to where the tattooed stars and words swirled to disappear behind me. I angled my body so he could see the entire thing.

"It says, 'Loving in the moment is something luminous.' It's a song lyric by Alice and the Glass Lake."

"From what I know about you, it seems fitting. I... Kallie..." He hesitated and swiped a frustrated hand through his hair. He looked truly aggravated. For what reason, I had no idea. His eyes flashed with something unfamiliar before he turned my body until we were standing toe-to-toe. Heat clouded his expression, and my heart began to race. For a moment, I thought he was going to try to kiss me again, but then he spoke. "Ah, screw the rules and whatever you think about the level of appropriateness. Dance with me."

That was the last thing I expected him to say, and I couldn't stop the laugh that bubbled from my lips.

"What?"

"You heard me. I said dance with me."

Without giving me a chance to respond, he wrapped an arm around my waist and pulled me to him. Enveloped in his scent, I couldn't think straight. Before I knew it, he coaxed me into a gentle sway.

The slow melody changed only a short moment later when the band kicked it up with a cover of "I Want You To Want Me" by Cheap Trick. However, Sloan didn't increase his movements to match the tune. Instead, he continued to rock slowly, entirely out of sync with the music.

Then, to my astonishment, he began to sing.

It was quiet at first, almost a hum, until he began to form the words. I was completely enthralled—and not because of the quality of his voice. It was because of the way he said the actual words. It was as if he was trying to send me a message I knew I shouldn't want to hear. I half wondered if I was making more out of this moment than what it really was—as if I were fantasizing about the idea of sharing uninhibited passion with this man rather than acknowledging my reality. And the fact of the matter was, I barely knew Sloan. I was solely here to do a job.

I understood passion and chemistry could be like living, breathing things. When two people were cosmically compatible, one's existence could light up in life-altering ways. I believed destiny was written in the stars, and when the stars were perfectly aligned, things could seamlessly fall into place.

But I didn't believe in insta-love.

The pull I felt had to be imagined. It was the only thing that made sense. What was happening now was unadulterated lust and nothing short of pure insanity. I tried to resist the feelings, but it was like fighting a powerful undertow. The more I fought it, the quicker I'd drown. It was easier to float to wherever the tide took me, hoping that destiny would deliver me to solid ground.

When the song ended and transitioned into another, Sloan wrapped his hand around the base of my neck and tilted my head to look up at him. Emotion squeezed at my heart until I felt it might burst.

"You may be onto something with this whole romance thing. The sunset is so much prettier with you in it. You just might make me a believer," he murmured. "I'm glad you decided not to marry that guy."

"Why is that?"

"I might not know a lot about you, but I can easily see you

deserve somebody who will love you and leave you wild."

He leaned in, and I knew the kiss I so desperately wanted to feel again was coming, but his words jolted me back to reality. Untangling myself from his arms, I took two steps back and gazed out at the seemingly endless ocean and the setting sun. The gypsy's words from so long ago echoed off the crashing waves.

"The man who tastes your lips under a California sunset will be the one to break you."

I looked back at Sloan. His breathing was uneven, and his piercing blue eyes were dark pools of desire. His hair was slightly mussed by the gentle salt breeze that curled around us, which somehow made all of his rugged sexiness even sexier. My stomach clenched, my breath caught, and my heart seemed to still. God, how I wanted this man, but even though my body physically ached for him, I couldn't do this with him. Business relationship aside, nothing could happen here. Not in this place—not unless I wanted to risk a broken heart.

"I have to go," I said abruptly, then turned to walk away. If I hadn't been afraid of tripping over my own two feet in the soft sand, I would have run.

"Kallie, wait." He took hold of my arm and forced me to meet his gaze. He looked irritated, yet there was no mistaking the longing in his eyes.

"Sloan, please. Let me go. We can't."

"You can fight this all day long, but I say fuck this 'you're my client' bullshit. There's something unexplainable between us that you know you can't resist. Mark my words. One day, you'll be begging for it—begging for us—to happen."

"Don't be so arrogant. Believe it or not, my choice to not let this go any further has nothing to do with you."

"So what does it have to do with then?"

I glanced at the last sliver of the setting sun.

"A warning. You and I—we'll never work."

9

Sloan

When I walked onto the track the following day, I was exhausted, which was nothing new, but the reasons behind it were entirely different. Last night, I'd been consumed with images of Kallie.

Every time I tried to close my eyes, all I could see was her gorgeous face, shadowed by the fading rays of sunset behind her on the beach. The majestic picture she'd painted had haunted me all night long. And when I remembered how good she'd felt dancing in my arms, it took every ounce of control I had not to rub one out. She was a spellbinding, gorgeous beauty who made everything around her come to life with her mere presence.

I couldn't make sense of it, how a girl I hardly knew had gotten so far into my psyche I couldn't even sleep. At three in the morning, I'd considered getting out of bed and pouring myself a drink but ultimately decided against it because I knew

Kallie would disapprove. I didn't need the alcohol. It was just a bad habit I'd gotten into by telling myself it was the only way to make it through the night. Recognizing how quickly she had influenced my decision-making only served to keep me awake longer. Then there were her words about a warning. She was afraid of something. Of what, I didn't know, but I'd made a personal vow to find out.

Shaking off the concern that I'd done something to spook her, I shoved a hand through my hair and jogged my way toward the pit lane. A group of people was gathered near an open-wheel car. I spotted Rochele, Cooper, and two young boys who I assumed were Eli and Marcus next to a photographer assembling his gear. Milo was also there, off to the side and talking to Benjamin, but I didn't see Kallie anywhere.

Glancing at my watch, I noted that it was fifteen minutes past ten. I was a little late, and I'd expected her to beat me here.

"Sorry I'm late," I told the group. "Where's Kallie?"

"Don't look so worried, man. She's here," Cooper informed me with a laugh. "She just went inside to wash up. She touched something and got grease all over her hands."

Masking my relief, I simply nodded. "Gotcha. So, are you going to introduce me to the boys?"

"Sloan, this is Marcus," Rochele said, patting her hand on the shoulder of a young boy who looked to be no more than ten years old. Then she pointed to the other boy, a sandy-haired kid who was tracing an invisible circle on the ground with his foot. "And this is Eli."

I noticed she didn't place her hand on Eli's shoulder like she did when introducing Marcus. I recalled the conversation at dinner the night before and remembered Eli was the boy who didn't like to be touched.

"It's nice to meet you," I told them.

"Both of them just took turns with Cooper on the track, but now they are ready to work."

"That's right, boys," Cooper chimed in. "Races are won and lost in the pit lane. It's not all about driving a fast car, isn't that right, Sloan?"

"That's right," I agreed, trying to ignore the cameraman who was five feet away and snapping pictures. Doing my best to act casual, I squatted down a few feet in front of Eli. "What do you say, champ? Want me to teach you how to change a tire?"

Eli looked up from the ground with wide eyes. There was a hint of a smile on his face as he slowly nodded.

"Can I help too?" Marcus asked excitedly.

Instantly, Eli stiffened.

"We'll take turns, Marcus. I'll have you stand right over here," I said, pointing to a spot far enough away from the car so I didn't have to worry about him accidentally touching Eli. "After Eli changes a tire, you guys can switch places, and it will be your turn."

"Sweet!" Marcus said and jumped up in the air. Eli remained quiet but seemed to relax.

Taking the lead, I grabbed an impact wrench, then sat down on the ground next to the car. Patting the spot next to me, I motioned for Eli to sit down.

"The guys in the pit crew have an extremely tough job," I told him. "I used to work with a pit crew a long time ago before I started racing. It might not be quite as fun as driving a fast car, but it has its own kind of excitement. Guys in the pit have to work under pressure at lightning-fast speed, which is part of the reason they need to use these fancy tools."

"What is that?" Eli asked, pointing to the impact wrench.

"It's a kind of wrench that uses compressed air to remove and replace lug nuts as quickly as possible. But I have to warn you. It's loud. You might want to cover your ears."

Eli's eyes grew impossibly wide once again as he quickly held both hands over his ears. I mouthed the word 'ready,' and he nodded his head rapidly. I smiled, pleasantly surprised at how much I was already enjoying this, and pressed the wrench to one of the lug nuts. In five seconds, I had all but one of them removed, deliberately leaving it for Eli to practice.

"Who's making all the racket over here?" I heard Kallie say from behind me.

Feeling like I'd connected with a live wire, electricity sparked through my veins at the sound of her voice. I slowly turned to meet her gaze. She smiled brightly, and my breath caught. She was so goddamned beautiful—like a deity I secretly worshipped. Any thoughts about changing a tire were stolen right out of my head as I watched her with pure male appreciation. Bright green eyes sparkled back at me. I returned her smile, immediately noticing the rainbow hair was back. It wasn't braided today but pulled up into a high ponytail, allowing the Skittle-colored strands to flow with the golden blonde hair down past the base of her neck. All I could think of was the candy commercial, and it made me want to taste *her* rainbow.

Setting the impact wrench on the ground, I stood to greet her. Leaning against the hood of the car, I raked my gaze over her body. Clad in tight jeans and a wispy yellow tank, the sun glinted off her large gold hoop earrings, making her look like a sun-kissed gypsy.

"Why, hello there, Rainbow Brite."

"Hello, yourself."

"Feeling optimistic today?"

"Maybe," she replied coyly, and her face turned a pretty shade of pink. There was a hint of mischief in her voice, and I couldn't help but think she might be flirting with me. That was definitely a good sign. It meant she probably wasn't upset with me about last night.

"I heard you made a mess of yourself," I said, motioning toward her hands.

"Hardly. Just a bit of grease that washed off easily enough. What did I miss?"

"Nothing much. I'm just teaching the boys how to change a tire. Isn't that right, Eli?" I turned around only to find Eli picking up the impact wrench. "Eli, no. Don't touch—"

Before I could finish my sentence, Milo lunged forward to take the wrench out of the boy's hand. In the process, he grabbed hold of Eli's arm. I froze, immediately recognizing Milo's mistake. Instantly, Eli began to scream—but it wasn't just any scream. The sound from his mouth was the most gut-wrenching thing I'd ever heard. It was grief, fear, and hurt all rolled into one.

All at once, everyone scrambled to calm the screaming boy. Cooper roughly pushed Milo away from Eli to make room for Rochele. She was at Eli's side in two seconds flat, ensuring a safe distance as she whispered soothing words to him. Kallie stood wide-eyed, clearly in shock over the rapid shift of events, while I looked around for the photographer. Thankfully, he seemed just as stunned as the rest of us and had lowered his camera. However, the photographer was here on our dime and was the least of my concerns.

"Kallie, where's the press?" I asked frantically.

"They aren't here yet. I told them eleven o'clock. I figured that would give us time to get acquainted with the boys first."

I breathed a sigh of relief. The last thing I needed was a write-up about a kid who'd lost his mind while he was on my watch.

It seemed to take forever but was realistically only a few minutes before Eli quieted. Appearing satisfied that he was okay, Rochele turned to Kallie and me.

"Cooper and I are going to take Eli up to the box and get him something to eat and drink. He needs a break. Do you mind staying here with Marcus?"

I shrugged, not sure what other choice I had. I was just

thankful the screaming had finally stopped. Still, I couldn't help but feel for the kid. I'd never heard or seen such a display of anguish, and my heart broke for him.

Squatting down in front of Eli, I held up my hands. I wasn't sure why I raised them. I just didn't want to do anything to upset him further, and it seemed like the right thing to do—as if by letting him see my hands, he would find it reassuring and remain calm.

"Eli, are you cool with that?" I asked softly. "I'll let Marcus finish up your turn. Then you can come back to help when you're ready."

Eli nodded ever so slowly, the action somehow making him look hopelessly frail, before turning to walk away with Rochele and Cooper. Getting to my feet, I rubbed a hand over my face, grateful the crisis seemed to be over.

"Rochele shouldn't have brought him here," Milo barked after they were out of earshot. "He's got issues. That kid is all sorts of fucked up."

My head snapped back, shocked by the harshness in Milo's tone.

"Geez, Milo! Go easy on the little guy! If you hadn't touched him, none of this would have even happened," I pointed out.

Milo snorted.

"You think this is my fault? Maybe if you weren't too preoccupied with a piece of tail, the kid wouldn't have picked up the wrench in the first place."

"What the hell are you talking about?"

"I'm not blind, Atwood. I saw the way you looked at her," he said, motioning toward Kallie with a lift of his chin. "I hired her to help you, not to fuck you. I have half a mind to call her agency and have her replaced—unless screwing clients is part of her PR strategy."

"Hey! Who the fuck do you think you're talking to?" I

stepped up to him, ready to lay him flat, but Kallie moved between us.

"Gentleman, you have an audience," she reminded.

I glanced to my left and saw Marcus staring with apt curiosity.

Shit.

I took a deep breath and shook my head. Stepping away from Milo, I turned toward Marcus.

"Ignore the grownups. We can be dumb sometimes," I told him, annoyed that I'd lost my head so easily. "Come on over here, Marcus. We can't afford to lose focus when there's work to be done. And last I checked, we have tires that need changing."

I glanced at Kallie, and she gave me an approving smile. Milo, on the other hand, didn't say a word but simply walked away in a sulk.

Fuck him.

Milo was the best agent around, having mastered the art of obtaining endorsements and sponsorships for drivers all over the country. He was the most sought-after agent in the racing circuit—but he was also known to be a complete asshole. At the height of my career, I ignored the ugly rumors because I'd needed him, but there was no need for me to do that now. I wasn't entirely sure why I kept him around anymore. I should just fire him and be done.

But firing him would mean admitting your racing career is officially over.

Ignoring that thought, I sat down on the ground with Marcus and got to work.

10

Sloan

"I'm glad things ended better than they started," Kallie said as we walked along the long corridor circling Motor Club Speedway. "I was happy Eli calmed down enough to come back. The two of you working together was pure gold. The press ate it right up."

I shrugged.

"It wasn't hard. I mean, I'll admit I was nervous because so many eyes were on me. I just kept reminding myself that Eli is a good kid who was dealt a shitty hand. Focusing on that helped."

"Well, it worked. I've got to say, though, I didn't breathe for a full solid minute after you accidentally touched his hand when trying to maneuver the compressor."

I laughed, appreciating her sentiment.

"You and me both. Thankfully, he was so concentrated on the task he didn't seem to notice."

"Oh, I think he noticed. I just don't think he minded. He seemed comfortable around you." She stopped walking and placed a gentle hand on my arm. When she looked up at me, her eyes were soft and filled with pride. "Seriously, Sloan. You were really great with him. When you and Cooper were cleaning up, Rochele told me she was impressed with how you handled Eli. PR aside, you did a good thing today. You should be proud."

I looked past her toward the entrance to the track, unsure how to handle the gushing compliment. I didn't think I did anything special. At the end of the day, the sole reason I was here was for a PR stunt. Kallie was making more out of it than it was.

"Let's just hope the morning papers have something nice to say."

"Oh, don't count your chickens before they've hatched. You've got a long way to go before all is forgiven," she reminded me and took a step back. "I'm going to take off. I'll give you a buzz later on today, and we can discuss your PR schedule for next week."

"Wait. You're leaving?"

"You didn't expect me to stick around here all day, did you?"

"Well, no. I guess not. What are you doing after you leave here?"

"I've got some calls to make and research to do. I need to dig up info on local events that may be good for you to get involved in."

"No rest for the weary," I teased. "I guess I should be thanking you. I'll walk you to your car."

We stepped out into the bright sun, and Kallie pointed to the left. "That's me right over there. The red BMW."

"Nice ride, but I'll admit, it's not the car I expected you to drive. A car like that screams arrogance."

"I'm not sure how a car can say so much," she replied with a chuckle.

"A car says a lot about a person."

"I'll admit, it wouldn't have been my first choice. It was what the rental agency gave me. At home, I drive a Prius. It's better for the environment."

"Now *that* I expected. Saving the world one mile at a time, Kallie?"

She shrugged.

"Just trying to do my part. Taking care of Mother Earth is important to me. In fact, that's why I'm a vegetarian. I originally went to college for Environmental Studies. I changed majors my sophomore year after I learned how small the job field was. Unfortunately, the government moves at a snail's pace when it comes to climate change, and there's not much money to be made in the private sector."

"With all the talk about global warming, I think that will all change soon enough."

"I think it will eventually, but opportunities wouldn't have opened up before my student loan bills came due. Who knows? Maybe one day I'll go back to school for it. But for now, Public Relations it is. I can't complain, though. I love what I do."

When we reached the car, Kallie unlocked it and moved to get inside. However, when she stepped back to make room for the door to open, she bumped into me and stumbled. Instinctively, I caught her by the waist, entirely unprepared for the electric current that began to sizzle at the point of contact. It surged through my veins, robbing me of breath. There was a pulsing—an invisible thrum—and I couldn't be sure if it was the beating of my own heart or if what I felt between us was somehow its own living being. The soft scent of her hair wafted tantalizingly under my nose, and I felt her shiver. Despite the warm temperature, I could see goosebumps rising visibly on her arms.

She feels it, too.

"Easy now," I whispered against her ear.

"I'm sorry. I wasn't paying attention, and..." Her voice was breathy as she let the sentence go unfinished.

I knew I should step away or come up with something smart-assed to say, but I couldn't break the searing connection. Turning her to face me, I boxed her in against the car with both arms. I didn't want her to leave my side. I wanted her someplace where she couldn't run so easily from me as she had last night. Something had spooked her on the beach. What it was, I didn't know, but I wasn't going to let her run off like that again. The very thought of her leaving—of not seeing her until tomorrow, or next week, or whenever the hell she deemed appropriate—felt like a sucker punch to the gut.

"I don't want you to go home alone to make calls. Come to my place. We can make whatever calls you need to make together."

She blinked a few times as if gathering her thoughts, then shook her head.

"Sloan, that's not a good idea." Gone was the breathy voice, replaced by her professional demeanor.

"Why not?"

"Because you and I..." She paused, seeming at a loss for words, before motioning back and forth between us. "I'll be honest. I don't know how or why, but things got complicated in a hurry. All I know is that we really need to focus on what's important—and that's cleaning up your image."

"Right now, I don't care about my image. All I care about is being somewhere alone with you."

"Sloan, how can you say that? You barely know me."

"I know enough."

"Well, I don't. I have work that needs to be done. Going to your fancy lair is the last thing I should do."

"My lair? You make me sound like Tony Stark," I said with a

smirk. "I may have been able to fly around the track, but that's as far as it goes. No Ironman super suit is hiding in my closet."

Looking down at the ground, she puffed out an exasperated sigh.

"Sloan, I—" she stopped short, seeming to notice something. "Well, would you look at that? Damn it. I somehow managed to get grease on my hands again. I'm going to run back inside and wash it off before I get it on my clothes or all over the interior of the car."

Without warning, she ducked under my arm and hurried back toward the entrance to the track.

Oh, hell no.

Following close behind her, we closed the distance and entered the building. When I saw her disappear behind the door to the women's restroom, I looked around to make sure the coast was clear, then slipped in and locked the door handle behind me.

Kallie was standing at the sink washing her hands and looked up in surprise when she saw me. "Sloan, what are you doing? You shouldn't be in here."

"Why not?"

"Because it's not...it's not," she stammered. "It's not appropriate."

I grinned as I slowly advanced toward her.

"I don't care about being appropriate, Kallie. You should know that by now. I've never been one for decorum, so you'll have to do better than that."

"Well, I also don't trust you to be in here alone with me. You're..." She trailed off, appearing flustered, as she focused on scrubbing the nonexistent grease from her hands.

"I'm what?"

"You're dangerous for me," she blurted out.

"Dangerous?" I chuckled. "Oh, baby, you have no idea how dangerous I can be—especially when I want something. You've read my file. I like to win, and there's nothing I want to win more than you. If you tell me you don't want me, I'll walk out that door, and we'll keep it professional. But I don't think you will. I think you want us to happen just as much as I do. I don't know why you're fighting it."

"You're wrong. You don't know enough about me to know what I may or may not want. And I'm telling you I don't want this."

She wouldn't meet my gaze but instead moved over to the electric hand dryer and placed her palms under it. Hot air buzzed from the machine as I stepped up behind her and rested my hands on her hips. I lowered my head to her ear, speaking just loud enough to be heard over the dyer.

"I think you're lying. I saw it all over your face when we were out by the car. Even now, you're flushed, and your breathing is erratic. Am I wrong?"

The dryer finished, and she lowered her hands to her sides. She didn't attempt to move away from me, but she also didn't answer and instead seemed to be lost in contemplation. I needed to see her face—to read her eyes and know if this fantasy I had of being with her was just one-sided. For all I knew, her erratic breathing was from frightened nerves. The last thing I wanted was for her to be afraid of me. Spinning her body so that we were standing toe-to-toe, her bright green eyes stared up, and I held her gaze steady.

"It doesn't matter if you're right or wrong, Sloan," she finally said. "Yes, I know there's this weird, inexplicable energy between us, but you don't understand. I can't be with you."

"Stop letting a stupid contract get in the way of things. It doesn't change the way I feel. I haven't been able to stop thinking about you since I first saw you in Long Beach."

"You don't understand. It has nothing to do with our contract. Well, maybe it does, but that's not the main reason."

"Does the main reason have something to do with the warning you mentioned last night?"

"It has everything to do with the warning. Please, trust me on this," she pleaded.

"The only thing I trust is my gut, and my gut is telling me there's only one way this is going to end."

"And how is that?"

I pulled her closer, pressed my lips against the delicate skin of her earlobe, and whispered with heated breath, "With me buried deep inside of you."

She gasped in surprise, and I wrapped one hand around the base of her neck.

"Sloan, I don't think we know each other well enough to be having this conversation."

"Then let's stop talking about it. I'm going to kiss you now, Kallie. Please don't deny me."

To my satisfaction, she didn't pull away. Her cheeks flushed, and her eyes darkened to a deep green and brimmed with possibilities. I leaned in so close, and I could feel her breath on my lips. Yet still, I waited. I couldn't force her. She had to be the one to close the remaining distance.

I sensed the moment she surrendered when her breathing became shallow. I could feel the pulse in her neck quicken under my palm as she angled her head, pushed up on her toes, and brought her lips to mine. They felt soft and full, and I enjoyed every single trembling breath she took as she gained the courage to apply more pressure. Electric shockwaves coursed between us, and she let out a small whimper. I responded by pushing my mouth harder against hers.

Parting her lips, she allowed our tongues to begin a slowdance. I suppressed a groan of satisfaction, not wanting to gloat about being right. It hadn't been just my imagination. She wanted this as much as I did, and her need tasted so goddamned good.

As I kissed her desperately, my only focus was to make her feel everything I felt. Adrenaline coursed through me and my heart began to pound. I pulled her tightly against my chest, and she seemed to melt into me, giving me all the encouragement I needed to lower my hand and squeeze her firm, jean-clad ass.

"I shouldn't want this," she murmured against my lips.

"But you do," I said, my voice low and raspy as I stated the obvious. She released a soft moan, and it was as if my words bolstered her courage to explore further. Her fingers curled through my hair, then moved down to my shoulders and back, touching as if she couldn't get enough.

Moving our bodies in unison, I turned until the large block privacy windows were at her back. Lifting her onto the window's ledge, I positioned myself between her legs. There was no hiding how turned on I was in this position. My cock was rock hard, and when I heard her small gasp, I knew she could feel it through our clothing. That just made me burn for her all the more.

I devoured her, our tongues twisting and tasting. I wanted more. I *needed* more. Tearing my lips from hers, I took a second to read her hooded green eyes. All I saw was desire and longing behind those thick lashes.

"Oh, Mother of Stars... Sloan, what are you doing to me?" Her words sounded like the sweetest of sighs, and I groaned.

"Not nearly enough."

"Everything about this moment feels right, but..."

"Shhh," I hushed, placing a finger over her lips. I cupped her face and stroked her cheeks, unable to get enough by simply touching her. I knew how she was feeling. This was wrong on so many levels, yet it just felt so damn right.

"I don't want to regret this, Sloan."

"You're overthinking, Kallie. Just feel. Tell me what you want." When she didn't respond, I slipped a hand under her tank until I felt the creamy skin of her waist. It was warm and soft and everything I'd imagined. I pressed my lips to her shoulder, trailing soft kisses along the hollow at the side of her throat as I moved my hand up to cup one of her breasts. I began to massage over the lacy fabric. "This—is this what you want?"

"Yes," she breathed.

Covering her mouth with mine once more, I didn't give her a chance to say anything else. With one hand clamped on her hip, I used the other to greedily pull aside the cups of her bra, and her breasts spilled free. I pushed the thin tank up to her neck and lowered my head to capture a nipple between my teeth. She gripped my head with both hands and arched, encouraging me to take my fill. When I began to circle my tongue over her supple areola, she moaned, and I nearly came on the spot. There was no doubt Kallie would be like volcanic molten lava in bed. Even though I knew I wouldn't take things that far today, I wanted to take this moment to discover a few of the places that would make her erupt.

"Tell me what you want, Kallie," I repeated, speaking the words into her cleavage as I moved my mouth between each tit, refusing to let one get more attention than the other. "I can't assume. Not now. I need to hear you say it."

"I just want you to touch me."

"Where, Kallie? Tell me where."

"Everywhere!" She gasped out the word as if it hurt her to say it.

Sliding my hand from her hip, I positioned my thumb at the apex of her thighs and began to rub. Even through her jeans, I could feel her heat. She was driving me fucking wild.

Moving from nipple to nipple, I enjoyed the way she lifted her hips against my hand to get better friction. Her hands snaked around the base of my neck as she arched her back, searching for more, and I was determined to give her exactly that.

Banding my arms tightly around her, I slid her off the

window ledge and carried her petite body back by the sink, where I pressed her back against the wall. I swiftly unbuttoned her jeans and dipped my hand under the waistband of her panties. When my fingers connected with her wet slit, we both gasped.

"God, you're so fucking wet," I murmured against her lips. I circled her hard clit for a moment, then drove a finger inside her heated well. Her breath hitched and her hips pushed upward, taking what I offered with fevered urgency. I increased my tempo, building momentum until she was whimpering with need.

"Come for me, baby. I want you to come on my hand."

She kissed me frantically, and my fingers thrusted deeper to massage and stroke her walls, only pulling out to trace wet circles around her throbbing nub. I felt her body tense, and her shallow breathing began to come faster. She was close. I quickened the pace, flexing my fingers with more urgency until I could feel the slight tremors of her building orgasm. I wanted to give her this—to make her see that if she gave us a chance, we'd be explosive.

When I knew she was almost there, I tore my mouth from hers so I could see her face. I wanted to watch her as she fell apart. Her eyes grew wide, then snapped closed, and I was rewarded with her cry of pleasure as she shattered under my palm. Her ecstasy faded to enfolding aftershocks, and her eyes slowly fluttered open. Burying my nose in her neck, I allowed her a moment to catch her breath as I inhaled her scent—that vanilla mixed with patchouli that was already becoming so familiar.

Once her breathing began to regulate, she clasped my face between her palms and pulled my head down to hers for a slow, languid kiss. When she pulled away, there was no mistaking the glowing embers in her gaze.

"Sloan, I've never felt this way before. I'm not the kind of woman who *does* things like this. I don't know what came over me, but—"

A rattling sound at the door cut off her words. We both stilled.

"That's strange. It's locked," I heard Rochele say from the other side.

"I'll get a janitor to unlock it," I heard Cooper tell her. Their voices were muffled, but there was no doubt it was them.

"Shit!" Kallie hissed, scrambling away from me to adjust her shirt and button her pants. When I began to laugh, she shushed me and frantically whispered, "Be quiet! They'll hear you!"

"Relax. If you think Cooper and Rochele haven't had more than their fair share of clandestine hookups, you're sadly mistaken."

"That's not the point," she snapped. "As I said, I don't do things like this. Plus, I'm your—"

"Yeah, yeah. I know. You're my PR rep. You have a serious hang-up over that. It's all good. Trust me," I said and moved toward her. She backed away, rapidly shaking her head.

"Jesus H. Christ, Sloan. They're going to be back at any moment now, and I can only imagine what they'll think if they find us here together. Quick. Hide in one of the stalls."

"I am not—" I didn't get a chance to finish before Kallie pushed me into the tiny bathroom cubicle. She may have been only a couple of inches over five feet, but she was mighty strong for such a little thing. Or perhaps I was just too busy laughing to put up much of a fight.

"Lock the door," she whispered. "And for the love of all the spirits, stay quiet!"

Feeling amused, I complied just as I heard keys rattling in the door lock. A moment later, I listened to the water from one of the sinks running, followed by Rochele's voice.

"Kallie, I didn't realize you were in here. The door was locked, so…"

"Oh, yeah. Sorry about that. The bathroom I'd used earlier near the pit was just a single stall. When I came in here, I had assumed it was that same way. I didn't think to unlock it when I realized there were private stalls in here."

Single stall?

I smirked, entertained by Kallie's inability to concoct a lie that didn't sound ridiculous.

"Oh, gotcha. Got to love those single-stall bathrooms," Rochele replied, but the skepticism in her voice was clear as day. Not to mention, all Rochele would have to do is glance at the floor to spot my red-and-white men's Reeboks flashing like bullseyes under the stall door, and she'd know I was here.

"Are the boys gone?" Kallie asked, continuing the small talk. Her voice had a slightly elevated pitch, giving away how nervous she was.

"Yes. The director of Safe Track just came by to pick them up. There's a movie night planned at The Residence."

"That sounds like fun."

I heard the flushing of a toilet, then water running. It was somewhat awkward hiding out in the women's restroom waiting for them to finish their business, but it was what it was. It's what Kallie had wanted, so all I could do was stare at the gray metal walls of the stall and wait it out.

Within a few minutes, the two women exited the restroom. I waited until it was safe to assume all was clear, then opened the cubicle's door. I wanted to catch Kallie before she left the premises, but when I hurried out to catch up with her. I came face to face with Cooper. He had been leaning against the wall opposite the restroom waiting for me to come out. His knowing smile was wide as he shook his head.

"Looks like Ro owes me twenty bucks," he said with a laugh.

"But seriously, man. There's a hotel just up the way. Probably cleaner than the restrooms here at the track. Just saying…"

Without another word, he turned and walked away, but his low chuckle could be heard echoing off the concrete walls of the corridor as he left the building.

11

Kallie

I sat at the kitchen table with my laptop, staring at the slew of emails I needed to respond to. Three were from Milo Birx, barking at me to get something or another lined up for Sloan. I didn't like the man at all. To say he was rude, arrogant, and downright nasty didn't even begin to cover the bad vibes I got from him—and it went well beyond his lack of compassion for the orphan boys who lived at The Residence. There was just something evil about him. He gave me the creeps.

My inbox also contained bills that needed payment, their flashing due dates reminding me why this job was so important. I couldn't wait until the day I would gain extra pocket money after paying off my student loan debt with the bonus following my contract.

Follow-up emails from the D.C. office needed tending to as well. The bulk of them were from former clients who needed assistance in some form or another. However, I couldn't seem to focus on any of it. Only one client was first and foremost in my mind—and that was Sloan Atwood.

It had been four weeks since our hookup in the women's restroom—four long weeks of strategically making sure I was never left alone with Sloan again. When I agreed to take him on as a client, my father had instructed me to be Sloan's shadow. For the most part, I was. I'd gone through the motions of scheduling more one-on-one events with the boys at Safe Track and orchestrating in-person media interviews. I'd made sure Sloan's calendar was full, and I had been present for every single engagement.

The only problem had been coming up with ways to avoid any sort of physical contact. He was everywhere I turned, and if I so much as brushed up against him, it was complete agony. My insides would begin twisting with desire, reminding me of what his hands had felt like on my body. He knew no boundaries. I couldn't believe how a man I knew so little about had the power to possess me the way he did.

Recognizing my weaknesses, I was careful only to see him in public settings, not allowing him the opportunity to whisk me off into some kind of hidden broom closet where he could have his way with me again. It wasn't that he didn't try. I just made sure to be one step ahead of him since I clearly couldn't keep my head around the man. I needed to regain my balance after being kissed senseless twice—and then some—within just thirty-six hours of meeting him. The easiest way for me to maintain focus was to bury myself in work. Sloan and my father's firm were counting on me to concentrate on the job. Nobody would win if I lost sight of my priorities so early in the game.

Clicking out of my inbox, I pulled up the information for Drift, a professional racing school that I was hoping to get

Sloan involved with. While I'd managed to keep him busy, his schedule was on the lighter side for the upcoming weeks. I didn't want him to have too much free time on his hands, and I could only do so much with local charities to fill his calendar. Perhaps working as an instructor at the school would help fill the void racing left and help his reputation in the public eye.

Picking up my cellphone, I dialed the phone number for the operations manager listed on the website.

"Drift Racing School. This is Sheila. How can I help you?"

"Hi, Sheila. My name is Kalliope Benton Riley. I represent Sloan Atwood. I was wondering if I could speak with Joel Freidman, the operations manager."

"Just one moment, please."

After being placed on hold, I tapped a pink-painted nail on the edge of my laptop while I waited. A few minutes later, a gruff voice came on the other end of the line.

"This is Friedman."

"Hello, Mr. Friedman. My name is Kalliope Benton Riley. I represent—"

"You can save your breath, darlin'. My secretary told me. Atwood, right?" he asked in a thick Southern accent.

"That's right. I saw on your website that you're looking for instructors. Is there a time when Mr. Atwood could come in to speak with you about that? Possibly an interview?"

Joel Friedman burst out laughing as if I'd just said the funniest thing he'd ever heard. After a moment, he coughed, then calmed himself enough to speak.

"Look, I don't mean to laugh, but Atwood is the last person I want around these parts. You're wasting your time."

"But Mr. Friedman, if you'll just—"

"Atwood is a drunk, and I won't have my students put at risk. Not to mention, you've called the wrong school. Atwood isn't a drift racer. He's an open-wheel racer. I suggest you figure out the difference before you call around looking for jobs for him."

While I knew there were different types of racing, my knowledge was limited and didn't extend beyond what I'd seen in *The Fast and the Furious*. I mentally kicked myself for not doing more research. I'd just assumed racing was racing. However, I should have known better than to assume anything in the PR business. Even still, I couldn't stop the feelings of indignation—and not because I was upset over him pointing out my lack of knowledge. I was mad over what he'd said about Sloan.

"I can assure you, Mr. Friedman—Sloan is not a drunk. I've spent the past month with him, and he hasn't had one ounce of alcohol. You can't judge or assume things based on one mistake he made."

"Oh, it's more than that. I've seen those pictures of Atwood with the kids at the track in the newspaper. If you think a few photo ops with orphans are going to change what happened, you're sadly mistaken. Blood is thicker than water, darlin'. There's no changing that. His old man was deep into the bottle for years until it finally caught up to him. He was an arrogant SOB, too—thought the sun came up just to hear him crow. I imagine his son isn't much different."

I bristled, feeling thoroughly annoyed on Sloan's behalf. While he still hadn't opened up to me about his father or his feelings surrounding his own accident, I knew enough to know that Friedman's harsh judgment wasn't warranted.

"What Atwood senior did should have no bearing on Sloan's character. While I can understand how he might not be a good fit as an instructor because his racing experience isn't right for your school, it's wrong to make a son suffer for the sins of his father."

"Maybe, maybe not. But it's a chance I can't afford to take. I appreciate the call, but I'm a busy man. Good luck to you. Bye now."

"Mr. Friedman, wait—" The line went dead. "Ugh!"

Frustrated, I sat back in my chair and pinched the bridge of my nose. As Sloan's PR agent, I knew I needed to push him to tell me about his father so I could have a prepared response in situations like this. However, the more I got to know Sloan personally, the more I hesitated to confront him about it. It just seemed too personal—like an invasion of privacy—and I felt it would be better for him to tell me when he was ready.

My stomach rumbled, and I glanced at the time. It was nearing two o'clock, and I'd skipped lunch. Pushing the laptop to the side, I decided it was time to take a break and get something to eat. I walked into the kitchen, opened the refrigerator door, and scanned the contents. Deciding on a spinach salad, I pulled out all of the fixings. After I finished layering the greens with walnuts, mandarin oranges, and feta cheese, I went back to the table with the bowl, intent on making it a working lunch.

As I ate, I returned to focusing on the job at hand. Next to me on the table was a copy of a newspaper from a small local press. On the front page, Sloan's face was all smiles in a picture captured outside The Residence with Eli and Marcus. He really was handsome, with his dark hair and blues eyes—eyes that made me feel like he could see right through me. He was sporting day-old stubble on his face when the picture was taken, adding to his sexy, rugged appearance.

We had been there for a barbeque—a last-minute invitation from Rochele at Eli's request. The press hadn't been notified, but there was always someone around with a cell phone camera waiting to catch an image of a famous race car driver. In this case, it was a neighbor. I was just as shocked as Sloan was at seeing his picture in the paper the following morning.

Alongside the picture was a glowing article titled, "When Kindness is Winning."

Positive PR was always good—and when it was organic, it was even better.

Sloan was a natural with the boys, and I found myself thinking about the conversation I'd had with Joel Friedman. Friedman had been too punitive with his judgment. Sloan may have screwed up when he relied on alcohol and pills to cope, but it didn't have to define him. Perhaps if he used his experience for good, people might view him differently. That thought brought an entirely new idea to mind—one that had me pushing away my salad and tackling the keyboard once more.

AN HOUR LATER, I was feeling incredibly accomplished. A targeted internet search had opened up a ton of possibilities, and I'd been fortunate to score right out of the gate. Jeremiah Lanford, the owner and head counselor at Wings Halfway House, had been all too willing to let Sloan come in and work with the teens who struggled with alcohol and drug addiction. He readily offered to have Sloan be a guest speaker at a public event they had planned for next week.

The problem was, I wasn't sure if Sloan would be on board with it. He didn't seem like the type who would jump at giving a keynote address, but I could work with him on it. This could be an excellent opportunity for him. After spending the past month with him, I didn't believe he had an addiction problem, but he had been on a dead-end road that could have ended in catastrophe if it wasn't for the wake-up call he'd gotten in Long Beach. He could use his experience, as well as his notoriety, to possibly influence a struggling teen.

I closed my laptop, ready to call it quits for the day, but a knock at the door made me pause and look down at my attire. Even though it was after three in the afternoon, I was still wearing booty shorts and the tank top from my yoga workout that morning. My hair was an absolute wreck, piled in a messy bun on top of my head. While the exercise was part of my morning routine, I typically showered right afterward. This morning I'd been so focused on getting straight to work, I had completely lost track of the day. As a result, I was a hot mess.

"Crap," I cursed under my breath, not happy about an unexpected visitor. Moving to the front door, I peered through the security peep hole to see who it was. A man in a tan uniform shirt was on the other side, holding a bouquet.

That's odd. Who would be sending me flowers?

Feeling curious, I unlocked the deadbolt and opened the door.

"Delivery for Kallie?"

"That's me," I replied and took the arrangement from him. "Thank you."

After signing for the delivery, I closed the door and brought the beautiful arrangement of sunflowers mixed with vibrant roses, lilies, and snapdragons to the kitchen. Placing the bouquet on the counter, I removed the envelope from the vase.

Hey, Rainbow Brite! I know you've avoided being alone with me. I won't apologize for anything, but I think we should start over—for real this time. I've been patient, and the planets have aligned. Dinner at my place tonight. – Sloan

I smiled after reading what he'd written on the card. I wasn't sure what he meant by the planets aligning, but I had no intention of going to his house. It was a sweet gesture, yet a precarious one, and I couldn't help but feel a little sad about it. It would be so much easier if I could simply trust destiny to guide the way and give in to Sloan's advances.

But I couldn't.

A round with my tarot deck last night confirmed as much. The upright Strength card had presented itself, reminding me to stay disciplined—especially during times of great adversity. Putting the job ahead of my desires for Sloan had been proving to be more than just a little bit difficult. It had been nearly impossible.

As I was about to put his note back into the envelope, I noticed a cream-colored satin pouch tied around the neck of the vase. Loosening the drawstring tie from the bag, I dumped the contents into my palm. It was a beaded chakra bracelet with a notecard explaining its meaning. I didn't have to read the card to recognize that the different colored beads represented the planets.

"Is that what he meant by the planets aligning?" I said aloud to myself.

Before I could contemplate it further, my cell phone buzzed. Walking back to the kitchen table, I saw Sloan's name on an incoming text.

Today

3:32 PM, Sloan: *Hey. What are you up to?*

3:33 PM, Me: *Researching things to make you look like a choir boy.*

3:33 PM, Sloan: *Anything good?*

3:34 PM, Me: *Maybe.*

3:35 PM, Sloan: *Did you get the flowers?*

3:35 PM, Me: *I did. Thank you.*

3:38 PM, Sloan: *I picked the sunflower bouquet mixed with all the different colors because it reminded me of when you wear your rainbow hair.*

I smiled, flattered by his attention to detail. I'd suspected Sloan had a sweet side to him on the first day we met after he'd pulled me into a dance on the beach. I'd slowly learned over the past month that there was so much more to him than the assuming arrogance that was often on display. He kept things close to the vest—that much was certain. But when he let his guard down, especially around the boys at The Residence, I was able to catch a tiny glimpse of his huge heart.

Almost instinctively, I went back to the counter to retrieve the chakra bracelet. I pressed it between my palms, closed my eyes, and focused on the beads' energy. After a few moments of meditation, a sense of calmness washed over me, and my cloudy destiny seemed to clear a bit. From behind closed lids, all I could see was Sloan. My stomach began to flip. Opening my eyes, I stared down at the beads and chewed on my bottom lip, wondering if I'd been paying attention to all the wrong signs.

My hookup with Sloan at the track was so much bigger than he realized. For me, it was like I could feel him in every molecule of my body, his unbridled passion taking me to heights I'd never been before. It had been foolish of me to let things go so far—a moment of extreme weakness. I simply fell into the moment with little thought about the consequences. Afterward, all I could do was recall the gypsy's warning. I thought back to what she had said to me all those years ago.

"I see travel in your future. And the sun—the sun setting in the west."

At the time, I thought she was referencing my move to California for college. Now I wondered if she had been looking beyond my college years toward something more meaningful, as the words she'd said afterward were too much of a coincidence to be ignored.

"Destructive and doomed love surrounds you. Remember the weaknesses of a Gemini, my dear, or you'll be destined for a life of heartbreak. Your eagerness to express your emotions will be your downfall."

My breakup with Dean, followed by a hasty makeout

session with Sloan in a public restroom, made her words ring true. I'd allowed my emotions to rule me in typical Gemini fashion, which was exactly what the gypsy had warned me about. As silly as it may have sounded, I couldn't shake off all she had said. Her words were like a pulsing neon sign in my head telling me to run away.

"You will fall in love under the bright sun in the west, giving someone the power to destroy you. And make no mistake—destroy you he will. The man who tastes your lips under a California sunset will be the one to break you."

Goosebumps pebbled on my arms as I thought back to the sunset on the beach with Sloan. While I had stopped him before he could kiss me, I couldn't ignore the magnetic pull I'd felt toward him that night and every moment after that. Whether I denied him a sunset kiss or not, I knew then that he had power over me. And after our encounter in the bathroom at the track, I was sure that, if given the opportunity, the man could destroy me.

However, regardless of the fortuneteller's warning or what my tarot cards said, I knew deep down that I could not continue to run from this. Sloan possessed a fierce determination that I would have to face one way or another. And if I were honest with myself, I knew I couldn't fight him off for much longer. My heart and body wouldn't let me. I wasn't even sure why I was fighting it anymore. After all, I was a grown woman with a strong mind and a desire to go after what I wanted. Was it so bad that I wanted Sloan? It didn't have to be anything serious. I wasn't looking for that. As long as I set the pace, a psychic warning could only come to fruition if I allowed it to.

Placing the bracelet back inside the bag, I felt extraordinarily conflicted despite the clarity about the inevitable. I sighed and picked up my phone to reply to Sloan's last text.

3:39 PM, Me: *The flowers are beautiful. And the bracelet too. That was very nice of you.*
3:40 PM, Sloan: *And what about dinner?*

I didn't have to have psychic abilities to know that question was coming next. I glanced at the vase of flowers. The radiant yellow petals of the sunflowers were reminiscent of bright sun rays on a clear day. Mixed with the perfect combination of bold colors and gorgeous florals, they were an instant mood lifter. That was why I always associated the rainbow with optimism—something that Sloan knew because I'd told him as much. I could only guess that he aimed for an optimistic vibe when he added the note to have dinner tonight.

3:43 PM, Me: *I don't think dinner at your place is a good idea. But I do have something to discuss with you. How about we go out?*
3:45 PM, Sloan: *Doesn't work for me. I want to enjoy a meal and a nice California wine with you without having to worry about reporters stalking every beverage I taste. My place.*

I bit my lower lip as I considered his proposal. He had a point. It would be nice talking freely without worrying about prying eyes and eavesdroppers. However, the idea of going back to his oversized bachelor pad was intimidating. I wasn't sure why—it just was. I looked around at my surrounding space, then glanced outside to the inground pool. The thought of inviting Sloan into my space felt safer for some reason.

I looked down at my phone and reread the entire text thread. Instead of responding to his invite, I walked down the hallway to the master suite. Once there, I went over to the dresser and pulled my tarot deck from the box. Anxious butterflies danced in my stomach as I tapped the deck twice, then gave the cards a careful shuffle. After cutting the pile three times, I broke with tradition and committed to turning over one card only. I had no intention of going through an entire formation trying to interpret the meaning of each card. I already knew what my gut was telling me. I just needed one more sign to let me know if I should follow it.

When I flipped the top card, the upright Star presented itself. I audibly sighed with relief to see a symbol of hope and love in romance. The optimistic energy I'd been feeling so powerfully was reinforced by the Star card. It was telling me that I shouldn't ignore it but use it to rebuild my confidence so that I could move on to the next chapter—and my inner goddess was telling me if I allowed myself to turn the page, the next chapter included Sloan.

"I can control the pace," I reminded myself.

Impulsively, I typed my reply to Sloan before I could change my mind.

3:57 PM, Me: *How about you come here? I have wine.*
3:59 PM, Sloan: *That works. I'll bring the food and text you later for your address. Does 7:00 sound okay?*
4:00 PM, Me: *I'll see you then.*

Feeling remarkably satisfied that I'd come to a decision about which path to take, I turned away from the cards and moved to the closet. Along the way, I spotted the homeowner's smart home system and decided to take advantage of it.

"Alexa, play upbeat music," I called to the little Echo Dot sitting on the dresser.

"The station, Dance Party Favorites, free on Amazon Music," the computerized voice replied.

Instantly, "Don't Stop Believin'" by Journey began to play.

Perfect.

I smiled to myself and opened my closet to pick out something to wear. As the music played, I eyed up a light pink halter sundress. The airy, breezy ruffle design was flattering on me and appropriate for an evening sitting by the pool. Paired with a long necklace, stacked bracelets, and pink hair extensions, the outfit completely suited my current mood. Satisfied with my choice, I pulled the dress out of the closet and laid it flat on my bed. After telling Alexa to turn up the volume, I sang along with Steve Perry and headed to the bathroom to take a shower.

12

Sloan

With a takeout order from The Lucky Koi in hand, I climbed into the black leather driver's seat of the Camaro with a satisfied grin on my face. I felt like I was finally making headway with Kallie. Even though she hadn't given me the opportunity to touch her since our encounter in the track's restroom, I'd used the time to pay attention to every little detail about her and knew my efforts were starting to pay off. From remembering the food she preferred and the jewelry she wore to her beliefs in the stars and the moon, it was like the meticulous prep work that went into a race—and no detail was too small. Except now, I was preparing for an entirely new kind of race—the race to Kallie's heart.

Her unpredictability over the past month had been a challenge for me. She went from red hot to ice cold in the blink of an eye, trying her hardest to keep me at arm's length. Two weeks ago, she would have flat-out rejected a private dinner invitation from me. Her willingness to accept it today, even if it was at her place, signaled I might finally have her attention for something other than business.

Still, I knew I had to be careful. She was a wild card. One wrong bump and our tandem could be wrecked. She was the antithesis to every woman I'd ever been with, yet the attraction I felt for her was no less irresistible—it was downright consuming. Her uniqueness just made me want her all the more, and I'd committed to doing whatever I had to do to have her.

I pulled out of the restaurant's parking lot, shifted lanes, and followed the GPS map to the address Kallie had texted me. With the top down, I hit the accelerator and drove up Ocean Avenue toward North of Montana. Within fifteen minutes, I was turning onto Kallie's driveaway. Killing the engine, I grabbed the bags of food and walked up the walkway leading to the single-story home. Kallie opened the front door before I reached it.

Instantly, my breath caught, and I slowed my steps, wanting to take in every inch of her. Her emerald eyes were shadowed darker than usual, and her lips were coated in a thin layer of gloss. Her feet were bare, with pink painted toenails that matched the pink in her hair and color of her dress—and what a dress it was. It was casual and shouldn't have been nearly so devastating, but in that, she looked like a goddamned sex goddess. The halter V-neck accentuated her breasts, and all I could think of was how they had felt in my hands, how her nipples tightened with just one flick of my tongue. It would only take one tug at the tie at her neck to set those gorgeous globes free.

"Hey, there," she greeted with a smile. Her green eyes twinkled, reminding me of fuchsite sparkling under a setting sun.

"Hey, yourself." Stepping toward her, I reached with my free hand to twirl a pink lock of her hair around my finger. This was the first time I'd seen anything other than purple and rainbow colors. "No rainbows today. What does the pink mean?"

"Happy."

I cocked up one eyebrow. "What are you so happy about?"

She shrugged as if to say, 'why wouldn't I be,' and smiled. "I guess I'm just happy about the progress I made today, and I'm happy you're here. Come on inside. I've already uncorked the wine."

Enjoying the subtle sway of her hips as she walked, I followed her inside to an open concept kitchen, dining, and great room. She breezed past the interior rooms and led me to a connected outdoor living space with an inground pool. Next to the pool, I saw she'd set a patio table for two. A bottle of wine sat chilling in an ice bucket next to a plate of cheese, olives, and crackers. I set the takeout bags down on the table and glanced around.

"Nice setup you have here," I mused.

"Thanks. Make yourself comfortable. I just realized I forgot the utensils. I'll be right back."

As I waited for her to return, I rolled up the sleeves of my black button-down and went to work on emptying the contents of the takeout containers. The food selection included more rabbit food for Kallie and beef hibachi for me.

"I can't take credit for the menu," I said after she returned. "But I knew you liked the restaurant we ate at with Cooper and Rochele. I hope this is okay."

"Looks great to me. You'll have to let me know if the wine is any good. I'm not up on the best California vintages," she admitted as she began to pour the chilled white into two glasses.

"I'm no wine snob—I prefer a good whiskey or an IPA over anything else—but I can recognize a quality *vino*." I paused to accept the glass she held out and took a sip. The flavor was crisper than some of the other white wines I'd had, but I liked it. "It's smooth—not as sweet as I would have expected, but good."

We took our seats at the table, and it was hard not to notice the way the slit in Kallie's long flowy dress opened to reveal her shapely thigh. I wanted nothing more than to reach over and slide my hand all the way up, but I knew any attempt to do that just yet would be a mistake. Getting her to open up to me—both literally and figuratively—would take finesse.

Tearing my eyes away from her sexy legs, I focused on the food in front of us. Kallie began to pile forkfuls of green onto her plate, and I tried not to wonder how any of it could possibly sustain her as I added a hefty portion of beef to my plate.

We ate quietly for a time. She seemed content to enjoy the peaceful evening while I, on the other hand, used the absence of conversation to get a better read on her mindset. I wanted her—badly. Things were going well, but I knew one wrong move would shoot our delicate balance straight to hell.

"This avocado salad is so amazing," she said after we were halfway through our meal. "I can't believe you remembered what I ordered the last time. I wouldn't have."

I glanced down at her plate. Though she'd said her food was good, I found her to be moving it around her dish more than she ate.

"You've barely eaten anything," I pointed out.

"I had a late lunch. Plus, I'm distracted at the moment, so that isn't helping my appetite."

"Oh? What about?"

"Well, I think we should establish some ground rules for tonight," she announced.

I paused midchew and eyed her quizzically. "Rules?"

"Yes, rules. I came to a conclusion earlier today."

I grinned at her businesslike tone. When she talked all

professional, I found it sexy as hell. "Should I be nervous?" I teased.

"No, but I do think it's important to get this off my chest. I invited you here on the pretense of business—which we do need to discuss—but after dancing around it for a month, we both know tonight won't be all work and no play. You were right when you said there was something strong between us. There have been signs, and while I'm not entirely sure if I'm reading them correctly, I'm tired of denying the attraction I feel for you. Plus, I know how you operate, and I can predict where this night will go. If I didn't, I wouldn't have invited you here."

I nearly dropped my fork, totally taken aback by her unexpectedly relaxed stance. I was used to aggressive women coming on to me, but Kallie had always been different. Up until two seconds ago, I'd fully expected to have to work to win her over. Now she was saying there were... signs?

"What are you trying to say, Kallie?"

"I'm saying that I'm open to the possibility of there being an us, but there are important business things to go over first before you try to get in my pants."

I sat back in my chair and crossed my arms, unable to hide my amusement. She looked thoroughly satisfied—as if her declaration somehow made the inevitable easier for her to accept.

"You're not wearing pants," I pointed out.

She flushed, and I felt my amused grin widen.

"You know what I mean. It's just an expression. Would it have been better if I said, 'under my skirt?'"

"Much better. Does that mean you're going to *let* me try to get under your skirt later?" She didn't answer but merely smiled in return before taking another forkful of salad. "Alright, since you're going to play coy, why don't you tell me about these signs you speak of?"

"Nope. I already told you—business first. You need to have patience."

"Patience is the most overrated virtue."

"Maybe it is," she replied with a shrug. "But you don't have much choice in the matter now, do you?"

I eyed her curiously for a moment before going back to my food. "Fine. Have it your way. You want to talk shop, then I've got some news for you."

"Oh?" she asked, looking up from her plate with interest.

"Do you want the good news or the bad news first?"

"Yikes. That sounds scary. I didn't realize there were both. Let's get the bad news out of the way first."

"Milo called. He—" I stopped short when I saw her cringe. "What's wrong?"

"Nothing. I just don't like Milo. I mean, I've only been around him a handful of times, so it's not like I know him all that well. It's just a feeling I have. I'm not surprised his name is attached to whatever bad news you have to tell me. I've deliberately not looped him in on some of the events we had scheduled with Safe Track because I don't trust him. Whenever he's around, he gives off negative vibes."

I pressed my lips together in a tight line, understanding her astute observation perfectly.

"You're not alone there. Not many people like him, but he's good at his job." I paused, unsure if I wanted to fully commit to the words I was about to say. "I don't really need him anymore. I can cut him loose if it makes you feel better."

"No, it's okay. We all have to work with people we don't like. What did he want when he called?"

"Tanya Griffin's parents filed a lawsuit."

Kallie froze, her fork hovering over her plate.

"That's not good, Sloan. After all the work we've put into—"

"Hang on. Let me finish. We both knew a lawsuit was coming. That's the bad part, but not a surprise. The good news is, because of all the positive press you've been getting me, my lawyer thinks we'll be able to settle reasonably out of court."

Kallie's shoulders sagged with relief. "That's good to hear. That last thing I wanted was to face a public trial while we're trying to rebuild your image. People don't need a reminder of what happened. Any news on the little girl?"

"She's fine, from what I've heard. Full recovery. That fact helps my case a lot too."

"That's also good, which brings me to tell you about the opportunity I lined up for you earlier today that could heighten your positive PR even more."

Having finished my food, I pushed the plate away, topped off our wine glasses, and sat back in my chair. "More positive press is good. Let's hear it."

"Well," she began, seeming somewhat apprehensive. "Have you ever heard of Wings Halfway House?"

"The name rings a bell. Why?"

"It's a place for teens struggling with drug and alcohol addiction. I spoke with a man named Jeremiah Lanford, the owner and head counselor over there. Considering your accident and what happened afterward, I thought speaking to the teens about your experience would be an opportunity for you to do some good. Jeremiah thought it was a great idea too."

I pressed my lips together in a frown. I understood what she was trying to do, but public speaking wasn't exactly in my wheelhouse. Talking to a reporter after a race was one thing, but reciting carefully-orchestrated words to a crowd of teenagers struggling with addiction was different altogether. I may have been on a collision course, driving the wrong way on a one-way street, but I didn't know enough about addiction to give advice. The most I could say was, "Hey, kids. Don't fuck up like I did."

"I'm not sure if that's the right gig for me, Kallie. Isn't there something else you can set up with Safe Track?"

"I already have stuff lined up with them. Wings would be different. Given your past, you understand the destruction that can come with excessive drinking and drugs." She paused and reached over to place a hand on my knee. "Not to mention, your notoriety could really make a difference for one of these kids. Jeremiah offered to let you come in and speak with them sometime within the next couple of weeks. If all goes well, he said he'd be interested in exploring mentorship opportunities too."

I hesitated, not sure what to say. Yes, I could probably tell my story easily enough, but that wasn't what worried me. Kallie didn't know about my father. If she did, she would know that something like this had the potential to open up a can of worms. I didn't want to do it, yet there was something in her expression that made me feel like I had to. She was pushing at the walls I'd constructed around myself since the accident— and I was letting her.

Standing up from my chair, I turned away from her intense gaze. Looking out past the pool, I stared at nothing in particular as I contemplated what she wanted me to do. After a moment, I shook my head, then turned back to her.

"Fuck, Kallie. I can't mentor a teenager. My own life is barely on track. Up until you showed up, I was off the rails, on a road to nowhere. I just don't think I'm a good fit for that kind of thing right now—possibly ever."

"Can you at least think about it? I told Jeremiah that I'd need to talk to you about it first, but he agreed to keep the guest speaker spot open until he hears back from me. Perhaps if you meet with him and tour the facility, you can make up your mind then."

"Alright. I'll think about it."

Her ability to twist me to her will was astonishing. This girl was going to be the death of me at this rate.

"If you find yourself struggling with a speech, I can help you and—"

"Kallie, don't get ahead of yourself. I said I'd think about it. No promises."

She beamed, and I felt myself soften. Standing up, she came over to where I was standing and placed her hands on my forearms.

"Thank you."

I looked down at her wide smile. Her green eyes twinkled in the low sun, and I couldn't stop myself from reaching up to touch her face.

"I've traveled all over this country for more races than I can count. I've seen thousands of faces and just as many smiles. But yours, Rainbow Brite... your smile is my favorite."

Her grin widened, and she began to laugh—and I mean, really laugh. The sound was full and deep, the freedom of who she was coming to the forefront. Even when she quieted, there was still a slight twitch to her lip as if she were still mulling over the humor in her head.

"You've got some smooth lines, Sloan. I'm sure you've used that one on all the ladies."

"No. Just you," I admitted sincerely. The humor faded, and she flushed a subtle shade of pink. Tilting her head to the side, she eyed me with curiosity.

"I can't help but think about what Cooper said about you not keeping women around for very long. I don't know where things will go with us, and I'm not looking for anything serious, especially considering I'll only be here for another four and a half months. I have a life in D.C., and when our contract is over, I'm going back. But you should know in advance that I don't know how to do casual flings. When I give, I give one hundred percent of myself and won't be able to separate sex from emotions. Even if I try for casual, it may not end up that way for me, and when I think about where things may lead tonight..."

She wavered, and her apprehension was evident by the worry lines on her forehead.

"Look, I know what Cooper said. He's not wrong—I don't do serious, but it's not for the reasons you might think. I'm not anti-commitment. It's just that racing life is—" I pinched my brows together, trying to think of the best way to describe what it meant to spend countless hours on the road, living in trailers, and working my ass off to win one qualifying race after another. "Racing life is hard, Kallie. There's nothing glamorous about it —especially when you're first coming up. I traveled a lot, and I saw the relationship strains other drivers had with their significant others. I just wanted to focus on racing. It was all that mattered to me."

"I was never up on who was who in the racing world," she admitted. "But with minimal research, I learned what a big deal you were. When I read something that compared you to the Tiger Woods of racing, I was shocked to realize I hadn't heard of you before."

"I don't know about that particular comparison, but I do know I was at the top of my game at the time of the crash. I still hold the record of being the youngest driver ever to win three consecutive championships, but the money and fame that came with it didn't happen without sacrifice. I would never have achieved any of it if I'd had the distraction of a serious relationship."

"And now?

"Well, I'm not racing at the moment now, am I?"

"At the moment?"

"I'll always want to be behind the wheel again, Kallie. That will never change."

"I know the doctor said you couldn't race anymore, but considering how medical technologies advance, I have to ask. This is going to sound so contradictory—especially since I just said I don't want anything serious—but I'm more than just a one-night-stand kind of girl. If given the opportunity to get back into racing, where would that leave me?"

"If you're wondering that, it seems like you are, in fact, looking for something serious."

"Not necessarily. I just want to know where I'll stand if you start racing again."

"If I answer that, you might not like it, Kallie."

"Try me."

Fuck.

Unable to meet her stare, I stepped away and turned to look out over the pool once more. I didn't know how we got to this point, but I knew I had to give her an honest answer. I didn't like mind games, and I hated liars. I prided myself on speaking my mind, and people always knew where I stood. Giving her brutal honesty might ruin any chance I had with her, but I gave it to her, nonetheless.

"Racing was, and still is, my first love."

"I'm okay with that," she responded.

I spun to face her again, shocked to hell by her acceptance. "You are?"

I didn't know any woman who would be okay with being told she was second fiddle to a motorsport. I expected to have to explain more.

"Sounds crazy, right?" She sighed and began to pile up our dinner dishes. "The thing is, I appreciate the honesty. I just got out of a serious relationship, and as I said, I'm not looking for another. However, I needed to make sure I wasn't going to be a one-shot deal for you. Being another notch in someone's bedpost has never worked for me. Your response may not be acceptable for some women, but it's enough for me. I know my limitations, and now I know yours. If I think I'm getting in too deep, your honesty tonight will help me keep my emotions in check. I only want something real and authentic—someone who wants to be with me for who I am and not an idea of what they want me to be. Does that make sense?"

Taking a few steps toward her, I stopped her from clearing the table and turned her to face me. Using one finger, I tilted her chin up until her eyes met mine. "I told you once before that you deserved someone who would love you and leave you wild. I meant what I said."

She didn't respond but looked away, seeming somewhat nervous. I followed the direction of her gaze to see the sun had lowered further in the sky, creating a rainbow mirror on the pool for the surrounding landscape. When I looked back, I saw worry lines creasing her forehead again. She took a step back and returned to clearing the dishes, but I stopped her by wrapping my arms around her waist.

"Sloan, the dishes. Let me just—"

"What is it? Tell me what's bothering you."

"I...it's..." she faltered. "It's the sunset."

"What about it?"

She released a small laugh and shook her head. "You'll think I'm nuts."

She pulled away once more, but this time I didn't stop her. Following her lead, I helped bring the dirty dishes into the house. We cleaned up in silence as I waited for her to explain. When the last plate was stacked into the dishwasher, I took her hand and led her back out to the patio. Taking a seat on one of the lounge chairs near the pool, I pulled her onto my lap.

"Kallie, what's with you and the sunsets?" I asked, pointing to the sun that had almost completely disappeared. "You had the same look on your face that night on the beach."

Apprehension momentarily clouded her features before being replaced by a look of resignation.

"It goes back to something a gypsy fortuneteller told me at a carnival when I was eighteen. Her name was Madame Lavinia. I didn't want to see her, but my brother, Austin, literally pushed me into her tent, and I didn't have much of a choice. Austin knew how much I believed in destiny and fate, and he used to get a kick out of it. Still, if I'd had any sense, I would have run right out of there."

"What did she say?" I asked with genuine curiosity. I had a feeling that whatever she was about to say would give me a bit more insight into the free-spirited woman who could drive me wild with just one look.

"She said destructive love would surround me, and the man who kissed me under a California sunset would be the one to break me. That's why I ran before you could kiss me on the beach. As for tonight, I was hoping it would be dark before... Well, before anything happened."

I raised my eyebrows and grinned, amused by the solemn set to her jaw as she told her outlandish tale.

"A gypsy fortuneteller. You're serious right now?"

"I knew you would think I was nuts," she mumbled, then let out an exasperated sigh and stood up to pace. "Forget I said anything."

"No, I'm glad you told me. All this time, I thought I'd done something to spook you," I said, trying my damn hardest to stifle the laugh threatening to burst forth. "I'm happy to hear it was just a... a carny influencing you."

She stopped pacing and narrowed her eyes at me.

"You can think it's funny all you want, but it's more than what she said about being kissed at sunset. It's also about what happened with us right out of the gate. I'm a Gemini and tend to let my emotions rule me. Madame Lavinia predicted that would be my downfall. I broke up with Dean, then the very next day, I got hot and heavy with you—a virtual stranger at the time—in a public restroom."

As ludicrous as it all sounded to me, I could tell her concern was wholly genuine, and I tried to adopt a more somber tone.

"Kallie, I don't believe in psychics. I decide my fate—

nobody else. But you've obviously had considerable worry over this. What can I do to help you get past it?"

"You don't have to do anything. I decided earlier today that I was going to let it go and just live in the moment—as long as there's no sunset involved."

I glanced in the direction of the setting sun. It had completely disappeared behind the landscape, having left behind a rainbow watercolor painted across the sky. Reaching up, I clasped her hand.

"Kallie, I don't care about the sunset. I want you. Here and now."

Her long lashes dropped before lifting to boldly meet my stare. Her demeanor shifted, and her eyes glimmered with a barrage of conflicting emotions—desire, longing, apprehension.

But when I tugged her hand to pull her back onto my lap, she didn't resist.

13

Kallie

"I want you. Here and now."

His words ricocheted through my body. Small shadows chased across his face in the dim lighting, making him look dangerously sexy. Our eyes met for a brief second, and I took in the darkness dancing in his gaze.

Holy Mother of Stars...

It was all I could think before he covered my mouth with his. I knew this moment was coming, but I'd hoped to put him off until it was completely dark—when the sun had safely hidden away behind the earth. But now none of that seemed to matter. I wanted this man in a way I'd never wanted anything else in my life.

His kiss was light at first—just a graze that drove me completely wild. I whimpered against his lips, and he responded by gripping the back of my head and pressing his mouth more firmly to mine. Within mere seconds, the kiss went from tentative to feverish, passionately demanding to take what he needed.

Our tongues danced as the rainbow sky faded into a deep purple on the horizon. His hands moved possessively up and down my back, progressing over my ribs and to my waist, skimming the sides of my breasts on the way down. I felt myself shiver at the contact, my desire building and causing a fervent ache between my legs.

Shifting my position, I arranged my skirt so I could straddle his hips. His breath was hot on my neck as he nipped his way across the line of my jaw, moving down my neck to my cleavage. He tugged the strings securing my halter with one hand while his other ran up my leg, then slid under my dress. He massaged my thigh, shoving my skirt further up as he went, brushing past the strap of the lace thong at my hip and around to cup my nearly bare behind. He held me firm and pulled the top of my dress down to expose my breasts.

"No bra," he murmured. My nipples pebbled from the appreciative way he stared at them. A moan escaped me as his magical lips leaned in to kiss the area around one tightened peak. He kneaded my breasts, pinching the erect nipples between his thumb and forefinger before capturing one with his teeth. At the same time, he slid his other hand from my backside to slip a finger under my panties. The throbbing between my spread thighs intensified, and I ached to be satisfied.

"Touch me, Sloan."

"I will, baby, but there's something in my way. I want no barriers this time. I've been fantasizing about seeing you bare for far too long." He grabbed hold of my hips with little effort and lifted us both from the chair until we were in a standing position. Looping one finger through the side of my thong, he said, "I want these off."

He tugged the thong all the way down to my feet and I

willingly stepped out of them. He kissed his way back up my legs, starting near my ankles, then over my knees until he reached the apex of my thighs. A fire burned fierce in my belly, and I couldn't think straight. I was nearly naked with him holding my dress up around my hips, the fabric barely clinging to my body by the elastic band under my bustline. When he began to pull that down, too, I grabbed hold of his hand.

"Sloan, maybe we should go inside," I breathed. "Somebody could see. The trees only hide so much."

"No. I want you here. Naked. If someone's out there, let them watch." To prove he was serious, he quickly yanked my dress down and it pooled around my ankles, leaving me completely exposed. It was an extraordinary sensation to feel the soft coastal breeze dance lambently across every inch of my skin as I stood there, stark naked, with Sloan. It was incredibly liberating. Stepping back, he admired his handiwork for a moment before breathily whispering, "You're so fucking gorgeous."

Then he lunged for me and began the merciless attack on my mouth once again. Pulling my naked form tight against him, he coaxed me back onto the lounge chair. Pressing me back, he hovered over me and positioned his body between my legs. Using one hand, he raised my arms above my head and leaned in to nip his way around my collarbone. His free hand softly brushed along the curve of my breast, pausing only to flick at a rigid peak, then slid down over my stomach to the juncture of my thighs. When he ran a finger through my wet slit, my breath caught, eliciting a gasp of unadulterated pleasure.

Never before had I felt so uninhibited and free. I didn't care about the gypsy's words, my tarot cards, or the fact that there were still dark purple streaks across the sky from the setting sun. I didn't even care about the possibility of being seen. It was as if nothing in the world mattered except for his touch.

"Oh, God... Sloan. I feel like I've waited a lifetime for this."

Releasing my arms, he sat up and used both hands to spread my thighs further apart. Continuing a slow exploration of my most intimate parts, he lazily circled my clit with his thumb, spreading the moisture around before sliding two fingers inside. I wanted to cry out from sheer ecstasy, but I worried about the neighbors possibly hearing, so I held back. My back arched, and my stomach tightened. I was coming apart at the seams.

"You like this?"

"Yes, don't stop!" I shamelessly begged.

Lowering his head, he pressed his mouth against my folds. Instantly, an electric shock surged through my body, eliciting a moan from my lips. His tongue moved against the pulsing nub, flicking up and down and filling me with the most intense pleasure I'd ever felt.

"I want you to come, Kallie," he murmured between licks. "Then we're going to take this party to the pool. I want to feel your naked, wet body sliding against mine."

Fire coursed through me at his words, the ache turning into something vicious, and I could only moan again in response. I wanted him—desperately. I needed to know what he'd feel like inside me. I'd never before had a lover linger in all the right places in order to find my most sensitive areas. If his hands and tongue could work so much magic, I could only imagine what it would be like when we officially joined for the first time. Images of Sloan and I moving together in unison in the pool filled my mind. It was enough to send me reeling over the edge.

"I'm going to come!" I gasped. The words had barely passed my lips when wave after wave of the sweetest, most intense ecstasy rocketed through me. It started low and deep, bursting forth in a kaleidoscope of colors that took my breath away. My body shuddered and convulsed, but Sloan wouldn't let up on the merciless flicks of his tongue against my throbbing bundle of nerves. I squirmed, but he held me to the spot with his firm grip on my hips.

"Be still, baby. Just feel," he ordered.

I was so sensitive to his touch that my natural reaction was to pull away. Still, even if it was nearly impossible, I did as he told me. I loved the way he made me feel but hated it at the same time. It was as if my mind, heart, and body were not my own, but something only he commanded.

Holding as still s as possible, I focused only on the tightening sensation that was quickly building deep in my belly once again. His fingers circled my walls as his tongue applied pressure to my clit. I could feel a second orgasm on the horizon, but he kept me on edge, never quite allowing me to get there. I bucked involuntarily, craving the relief I was so close to getting. I was beyond the point of wanting. He was driving me insane, and I was desperate, completely lost in an ocean of sensations.

He must have sensed my urgency because he plunged his fingers deeper into my core and increased the intensity of his tongue. My insides constricted, and my mind went hazy. In one blinding moment, white-hot pleasure shot through my veins. I cried out, unable to suppress my screams.

Time passed. I didn't know if it was seconds, minutes, or hours. I was only aware of the tingling sensation all over my body as I slowly opened my eyes to meet his. His lips parted slightly, and his deep blue eyes were a violent inferno of desire. Moving up my body, he took the lobe of my ear between his teeth before tracing the outline with the tip of his tongue. A shiver ran through me.

"Let's go to the pool," he whispered.

Climbing off the chair, Sloan began to unbutton his shirt.

"No, let me," I told him. My legs felt weak as I stood from the lounge chair, but I kept myself steady as I closed the gap between us and reached for the buttoned seam of Sloan's shirt. Starting at the top, I unfastened each button to expose his chest at a painstakingly slow pace. As much as I wanted to rip the clothes from his body, I wanted to enjoy this moment of seduction even more.

Once his shirt was removed, I lightly trailed my fingertips over his rock-hard abdomen to the line of muscle leading to his groin. I heard his sharp intake of breath as I reached to undo the buckle of his belt, allowing me easy access to unzip the fly of his jeans and release his straining cock. After pushing his pants down his legs, I took a step back to admire the hard lines of his body. He would make any sculptor weep. I could see the faint lines of his scars on his left hip and arm, and I wondered how many came from the crash and how many were from the resulting surgeries that followed. The imperfections somehow made him look more rugged and sexy. He was magnificent in every sense of the word—from his muscular thighs to the rippled power of his rock-hard abs and broad, bronzed shoulders—the perfect specimen of the alpha male.

I took in the dangerous glint in his eyes before allowing my attention to travel down past his tapered V to settle on his long, thick erection that looked impossibly hard. Moving forward, I gave him a slow and lazy kiss. He wrapped his arms around my waist to pull me closer, but I shook my head.

"It's my turn, Sloan. I want to taste you."

Lowering to my knees, I took his virile cock into my hand. His breath hissed between his teeth as I closed my lips around the lush head, flicking my tongue leisurely before taking him further into my mouth. He was hot, silky, and soft. His taste ignited my senses, and I greedily sucked, worshiping his manhood. Sloan fisted his hands through my hair, encouraging me to take more, so I pushed forward until I felt him hit the back of my throat. Tightening my lips, I pulled back to swirl my tongue, then pressed deep to suck him in long, drawing pulls.

"Holy fuck, Kallie. I'll never last at this rate," he groaned and pushed forward into my mouth. My sex tightened in pleasure from his words as his thick veins throbbed against my tongue. His thighs tensed and I could feel his shaft swell deep in my throat. His breathing became ragged, and I knew he was close.

I pulled back, not wanting him to come just yet. I wanted to feel him inside me when he did. I looked up at him and our gazes locked. The raw hunger in his eyes mirrored my own as he hauled me to my feet. I saw him reach down and snatch a condom from the pocket of his jeans before moving to lift me effortlessly. He positioned my legs, scissoring them around his hips. As he walked us to the pool, I swiped my tongue up the side of his throat, relishing in the intoxicating smell of his cologne and the subtle saltiness of his skin.

Lowering us to the top step, he sheathed the condom over his length, then captured one of my nipples between his teeth to tease the hardened point. With me straddling his hips, he trailed kisses up my neck, fisting his hand in my hair and yanking my head back to ravage my mouth like he was starving. Water lapped around my knees, and a fire began to build low and deep in my belly. It flowed through me, hot like lava.

With my knees firmly planted on the top step of the pool, I tightened my legs against his hips. I could feel his erection pressing hard against my heat as his teeth bit into my lower lip, the sharp sensation cutting through me and intensifying the ache in my belly. I needed him inside me—now. Slick with anticipation, I reached between us to position his tip to my entrance, then lowered onto his scorching heat with painstaking restraint. He pierced me, stretching me inch by divine inch until he was rooted deep in my essence. Our unification was more fulfilling than I could have possibly imagined, and I could almost see actual sparks flying in the air.

"Magic," I breathed.

"You can say that again," he agreed as he pushed up and gripped my hips.

I tightened around him. My already rapid-heartbeat increased in tempo, fueling my veins with even more desire for him. With my hands braced on the concrete behind his head, I began to move. As if the gods had created us for each other, we easily found our rhythm. His motions were determined, matching me thrust after thrust. We rocked together and the water sloshed, adding an erotic melody to our union. I kissed him again, our breaths mingling as we rose to new heights.

I gripped his shoulders, needing something more than concrete to hang onto, and felt his rippled muscles bunch beneath my palms. Before long, I was overflowing with arousal.

"Oh, God!" I gasped. I was so close.

"Fuck, Kallie," he growled with a satisfied groan. "You're driving me wild. Give me your orgasm. I need to feel your sweet pussy tighten around me."

Reaching between us, he began to circle my clit with his thumb as he pushed up harder inside of me. My muscles clenched involuntarily as he brought me closer to that glorious peak. I was amazed at how he knew exactly what to do to please me—how to torment me with delicious pleasure, teasing me just long enough to ensure my climax would be cataclysmic.

With every inch of his length buried inside me, I dug my nails into his shoulders. I was right on the cusp and could barely think.

"I'm almost there," I panted. Tightening my legs around him, I braced myself for that delicious moment when I would be sent over the edge. I trembled, losing more of myself with every passing moment. I became desperate, the promise of release all-consuming.

"Now, Kallie. Give it to me now!"

Strong hands gripped my hips, pulling me down as he pushed up in a hard thrust. Over and over again, he plunged impossibly deeper. As he continued to power upward, that slow build in my belly burst. I was mindless, wildly grinding against him as I split apart at the seams. I tossed my head from side to side and let out a harsh cry of fantastical release. My sensitive tissues rippled until I began to spasm uncontrollably in a long, shattering, heart-pounding orgasm.

"Sloan!" I cried out and unraveled around him, overcome with a sensation of blinding heat. Colors flashed before my eyes as the rush surged through me.

My fingernails clawed at his back, pulling him closer when I felt him tense beneath me. I clung to him, waiting for the moment he would follow me into the abyss of mindless release. With one last plunge, his body convulsed before momentarily falling still. When his breath hitched, and I felt the delicious pulsating of his cock, we spiraled together and his climax burst forth.

A rush of air escaped my lungs as my hammering heart worked its way back to a normal rhythm. With his arms banded tight around me, the raw strength of him enveloped me. I slumped down and wrapped my arms around his broad back. A calm stillness held fast to the air as he pressed his forehead against mine, then softly ran his hand up and down the curve of my spine.

"Goddamn," he murmured into my ear. "I knew the moment I met you that you'd be a firecracker, but I had no idea... That was pyrotechnics on steroids."

I smiled and let his words linger in the air for a moment.

"I think you were right when you said the planets have aligned. Venus and Mars definitely played their part tonight." I felt the rumble of laughter in his chest more than I heard it and pulled back to look at him. "Why are you laughing?"

"I'm laughing because I have no idea what you're talking about."

"Mars is the planet of sex. Venus is the planet of love. When they align, they promote sexual attraction and compatibility."

His grin widened, and he placed a light kiss on the top of my nose.

"Whatever you say, Rainbow Brite."

"It's true!" I protested.

"Maybe it is. Why don't we go inside and see if your theory is correct?"

"We could, but the outcome depends on certain things."

"Such as?"

"Your birthday. When is it?"

His brows pinched together in confusion.

"May 2nd. Why?"

I eyed him knowingly as a slow smile spread across my face.

"You're a Taurus. That's a good match for me—a Gemini—especially if you want to test my theory," I told him before leaning in so I could whisper in his ear. "Because make no mistake, you'll need great endurance in the bedroom to keep up with me."

14

Kallie

My eyes fluttered open at the sound of floorboards creaking. I yawned and rubbed the sleep from my eyes. Rolling over onto my back, I saw Sloan standing at the foot of the bed in the morning light, completely in the buff and entirely shameless. He had just come from the shower and was towel drying his wet hair, the action causing droplets of water to rain down from his head and glisten on his shoulders and chest. I sighed inwardly. He was truly magnificent.

"Good morning, gorgeous. Did you sleep okay?" he asked.

Perfectly content admiring his physique, I let my gaze roam over his body one more time before answering.

"Really good, actually. What time is it?"

"It's almost nine."

"Nine! I never sleep that late. If I were home in D.C., I would have already finished my morning yoga routine and be in my office by this point."

"Don't beat yourself up over it. I kept you up late—you know, that whole endurance thing," he added with a wink, then flashed me one of his cocky and swoon-worthy smiles. "Besides, skipping yoga once isn't going to hurt. You proved last night how flexible you could be."

I nearly melted as I recalled the heights he'd taken me to during the night—over and over again—once more in the pool, then twice in my bed. But now, my body was craving something else. Holding the sheet up to cover my naked chest, I sat up.

"I can't handle your tricks pre-caffeinated and on an empty stomach. I need sustenance."

"My tricks?" he asked as he slipped into the jeans he'd worn last night. They were tight in all the right places, yet slightly faded in spots, as if he'd spent countless hours working on cars while wearing them.

"Yeah. And you're doing that smilking thing again. Cut it out."

"Oh, so you like that, do you?" he countered with a suggestive smile, emphasizing his smilk even more until my toes wanted to curl.

I frowned and tossed a pillow at him.

"Food first."

Catching the pillow in the air, he laughed and tossed it back.

"You're cranky in the morning before you eat. Good to know. I'll go whip up some grub while you get dressed."

"You don't have to do that," I told him, but it was too late. He was already out the door.

I rolled out of bed and did quick work in the bathroom. Within twenty-five minutes, I was showered and dressed in frayed jean shorts and a gray off-the-shoulder T-shirt. I'd skipped putting on makeup but clipped my pink hair extensions into my ponytail before heading out to the kitchen. Once there, I saw Sloan had managed to find all the tools he needed and was working on our breakfast. Wearing those oh-so-snug jeans and nothing else, he looked glorious standing over a pan of eggs sizzling in a frying pan—like my very own sexy chef.

"Do you want help?" I offered as I watched him pull bread from the toaster.

"Not unless you can procure bacon out of thin air."

I scrunched up my nose in disapproval.

"Pigs will never be on the menu in this house as long as I live here. Sorry, not sorry."

"I'm just teasing you. I'm good with this. Have a seat. There's coffee in the pot," he said, pointing to the coffee maker on the counter. "I would have made you a cup, but I wasn't sure how you take it."

"I'm not a big coffee drinker. I prefer black tea."

He cocked his head to the side, looking perplexed.

"Oh. I'll drink it then. When you said you needed caffeine, I just assumed you meant coffee. I didn't realize..."

He didn't have to finish his sentence to remind me about how few personal details we knew about each other—right down to the basic things like coffee or tea. Yet here I was, consumed with unyielding seismic feelings after a night of unbridled passion. While we might not have been total strangers anymore, there was still so much we had yet to learn. Pushing the nagging worry aside, I filled the tea kettle with water and placed it on the stovetop to boil.

"Don't sweat it, Sloan. How could you know?"

"Next time—and there will be a next time—I'll remember," he promised as he placed two plates of piping hot eggs on the table for each of us.

Next time.

Anticipation coursed through me after hearing just those two words, only to be replaced with disgust as I watched him douse his eggs in ketchup.

"You put ketchup on your eggs?" I asked incredulously.

"Along with fifty-four percent of Americans."

"That's gross," I said with a laugh.

"I honestly prefer hot sauce, but you didn't have any in the fridge. Ketchup isn't bad, though. It's pretty tasty. You should try it."

I grimaced.

"No thanks. A little bit of salt and pepper is good enough for me."

Suddenly feeling ravenous, I focused my attention on my own plate and speared a piece of the scrambled egg with my fork. We ate in the quiet for a while, content to enjoy our start-of-the-day meal. When we finished, I stood to clear the dishes. As I was stacking them into the dishwasher, the doorbell rang.

"That's strange," I mused. "Who would that be?"

Sloan cocked up a curious brow, then shrugged and continued to sip the remains of his coffee. Drying my hands quickly on a dishtowel, I made my way to the front door. When I opened it, my mouth dropped open. Gabby was standing there beside a suitcase on the other side.

"Surprise!" she said with a wide grin. Without giving me a second to absorb my shock, she rushed in and wrapped me in a tight hug.

"Gabby! I'm so glad to see you! I wasn't expecting—" I stopped short when I felt her stiffen. Taking a step back, I followed her gaze and saw that she'd spotted Sloan. He was still sitting at the kitchen table, in all of his shirtless glory, looking just as stunned as I was.

"I wanted to surprise you, but it looks like I should have called," Gabby said somewhat indignantly as she pushed a lock of chestnut hair from her forehead. To say there was tension in the air was an understatement. I could only imagine what the scene looked like to her—and it was exactly as it appeared.

"No! I'm glad you're here. Austin mentioned that you were

going to visit, but I wasn't expecting that to be for another few weeks. Come in. There's someone I'd like you to meet." Pulling her inside, I closed the door, took her suitcase, and wheeled it off to the side. I stood there between Sloan and Gabby like a pickle caught in the middle, then nervously motioned to Sloan. "Gabby, meet Sloan. Sloan, this is my best friend, Gabby."

Standing up, Sloan approached us and extended his hand to her.

"It's a pleasure to meet you, Gabby."

"Likewise. Kallie has told me all about you."

Sloan cocked up an eyebrow in surprise.

"Has she?"

"Yeah," she replied with a slow nod of her head. "She apparently skipped a few details."

I cleared my throat uncomfortably, knowing I owed Gabby a huge explanation. While I had talked to my friend several times over the past month, I'd never once mentioned my physical involvement with Sloan. All she knew up until three minutes ago was that he was my client.

"Gabs, I'll fill you in later. Right now, Sloan and I were just finishing up breakfast. Are you hungry? I can make you something."

"No, I'm good. I snacked on the plane. But thanks," she said, never taking her eyes off of Sloan. She seemed to be sizing him up. Her watchful gaze was suspicious, but Sloan seemed unruffled. If Gabby thought she could intimidate him, she would be sadly disappointed—Sloan was the master at intimidation.

"How about coffee then?" Sloan offered. "There's still some left in the pot."

"Coffee would be great. My flight left at five this morning, east coast time. I could use the boost."

Without another word, Sloan nodded and went back to the

kitchen. After pouring Gabby a mug, he looked over his shoulder and said, "Cream? Sugar?"

"Just a little bit of cream, please," Gabby told him.

He handed her the mug of steaming java.

Thanks," Gabby said, and her scrutinizing stare seemed to soften. The fact that Sloan was shirtless, showing off his impeccable abs, was definitely helping the situation. Gabby was never one to shy away from a fine specimen of male beauty.

"No problem," he replied easily. "Well, ladies. I hate to cut this introduction short, but I should be heading out. I'm just going to grab my things, and I'll be off."

While Sloan was in the bedroom getting what I could only assume was his shirt, an awkward silence fell over the table. I offered Gabby a slight shrug and a smile, almost apologetic, as I waited for us to be alone so I could explain. She smiled at me in return, but her grin didn't quite meet her eyes.

When Sloan emerged from the bedroom, he was fully clothed with his keys in hand. Leaning over, he kissed the top of my head.

"I'll call you later," he said. I moved to stand and walk him to the door, but he stopped me. "It's all good. I can see myself out. You two have catching up to do. Gabby, it was nice to meet you. I hope to see you again soon."

I silently watched him walk to the front door. Once the door was closed, I turned back to Gabby. She had gotten up from the table to snatch a leftover piece of toast off the counter. When she looked back at me, she placed one hand on her hip and stared at me with accusation.

"You have some explaining to do," she said, pointing the piece of toast at me like it was a jousting lance. She sounded mad—and rightfully so.

"I know, I know. I should have told you. The problem was, I didn't even know how to explain it to myself, let alone somebody else. It just sort of happened."

"Happened? Last I knew, you broke it off with Dean and wanted to take time to reflect on things. I bumped up my vacation time and booked a flight here, assuming you would appreciate some girl time after just breaking up with your *fiancé*," she said, emphasizing the last word.

"He wasn't my fiancé," I reminded her.

"Whatever. Who cares about the technicalities—he proposed," she waved off, then tossed the uneaten toast back onto the plate on the counter. "Bottom line is that you and Dean were *serious*. Yet, when I get here, I see you're shacking up with the hottest guy I've seen since Bradley Cooper. Now spill it. And I want *all* the tea. How long has this been going on for?"

I chewed on my bottom lip, hesitant to tell her the truth. I was a terrible liar, and if I wasn't forthcoming from the beginning, she'd find out eventually. So when she narrowed her eyes with suspicion, I knew honesty would be best. Getting up from the table, I went into the family room and plopped down on the couch. Gabby took a seat in the armchair adjacent to me, crossed her arms, and waited not-so-patiently for me to continue.

"It began the first day I met him. I went to his house to introduce myself, lay out the PR strategy, and all that jazz. We talked for a while, then... Well, to make a long story short, when I was leaving, he kissed me. Don't ask me to explain how it happened—it just did."

"He kissed you! Wait—you were still with Dean at that point, right?"

"Yes."

"Did you kiss him back?"

I groaned.

"Yes, I kissed him back. And you don't need to remind me— I know I'm a terrible person."

"No. I don't think that. I just think you and Dean weren't

meant to be. Everybody around you knew it. You just had to figure it out for yourself. Go on," she prompted with an impatient twirl of her finger.

"After I left his place, I knew I never would've let that happen if I was truly in love with Dean. Later that same day, I called Dean to break it off. You know all about that part."

"Yeah—and he was a complete dick about it, in my opinion. Not buying the ring because he was worried about losing interest in his bank account? I mean, really," she scoffed. "I still can't believe he admitted that to you."

"It doesn't matter," I brushed off, refusing to disclose how much it stung. I'd made my choice and felt confident it was the right one, but it was hard knowing the person I'd been with for over two years appreciated his money more than me.

"So, on day one, Sloan kissed you. Where did it go from there?" Gabby prompted.

I tossed her a meaningful look, unable to contain my smile.

"Well, we may or may not have had a super-steamy hookup in a public restroom..." I trailed off as her big brown eyes went wide. Her jaw dropped open, and she began mouthing words that wouldn't come out. For once, I'd made her speechless, and her disbelieving stare made me laugh.

"You did not!" she exclaimed after finding her voice.

"We did—but I immediately regretted it," I hurriedly added. "He's my client, after all, and getting romantically involved is so unprofessional. My father will kill me when or if he ever finds out. Not to mention, if things go south with Sloan, I risk forfeiting a bonus payout that I could really use. With all of that in mind, I avoided being anywhere alone with him for weeks afterward. It wasn't until last night when we finally made it... official, I guess you could say."

"Had sex?"

I rolled my eyes.

"Yes, Captain Obvious."

"So, how was it?"

I gave her a pointed stare, then made a zipper motion across my lips.

"Nope. I never kiss and tell."

"Aww, come on, Kallie! I haven't had sex in months. Just one little detail?"

I laughed.

"He was still here this morning. If it was bad, do you think I would have let him spend the night? But I will tell you this." I paused, looking for the right words. "With Sloan, there's this inexplicable connection. It's like I can physically and mentally feel my destiny shifting by cosmic force. The pull is so strong, I can't deny him—can't deny us. It's like we were meant to happen. I never felt that way with Dean."

"Oh, shit. This is serious, Kals."

"I know."

"So, now what?"

"Well, now that I gave in to it, there's nothing I can do but let the Fates take the reins and enjoy the ride."

Gabby smiled and cocked her head to the side thoughtfully. After a moment, she set her coffee mug on the table and came over to wrap me in a hug that warmed my soul.

"I've missed you so much. And I'm happy for you—really, I am. You seem content—relaxed even. I can see it in your face and your posture. And, more importantly, this is the first time I've heard you *sound* like you in a long time. You've always had this energy about you that people could feel before you even uttered a single word. It was like Dean was suppressing that and all of the little quirks I love about you. I'm so happy you're back."

I squeezed her tight and blinked back tears of joy. I was grateful for her friendship, knowing I could count on her to always see me for who I was. Her presence brought balance to my world, and it felt so good to have her there.

***

FOUR HOURS LATER, Gabby and I were lounging outside on the patio, drinking piña coladas, and poring over the twenty-seven tabs we had opened between both of our laptops. She was only here for a long weekend, and I'd decided to dip into my limited savings and plan a short trip north to Napa Valley to make the most of my time with her. As she hemmed and hawed over which bed and breakfast we should stay at, I sipped on the coconut rum cocktail and mapped out wineries.

"I know this is super last minute. Are you sure you can get away?" she asked.

"It's not a problem. I don't have anything booked for Sloan until Monday afternoon. It's just over a six-hour drive to Napa Valley, not accounting for any traffic we're likely to encounter. If we leave tomorrow morning, that will give us Friday evening, all day Saturday, and the first half of Sunday. It's too bad there aren't any last-minute flights into Sacramento."

"A drive is fine with me. I hate flying—and even more so after the flight out here. The turbulence was brutal. Besides, I have to get back on a plane on Monday. The fewer flights I have to take, the better." She paused, clicked a few keys on the keyboard, then put her feet up on the empty chair next to her, showing off her perfectly manicured red toenails. "Okay. The B&B is all booked. We check in tomorrow at three. Checkout is Sunday at one in the afternoon."

"Perfect!"

"Did you decide on the wineries we should hit?"

"I don't think we should drive around ourselves—especially

since we'll be drinking. I was thinking about booking this wine train tour—scenic views, antique rail car, wine tastings. It sounds fun."

"Yes—book it! Ooh, I'm so excited!"

Raising my frosted glass to clink it with hers, I grinned ear to ear.

"Road trip!"

15

Sloan

I woke up Friday morning feeling like something was missing. I rolled to the side, reached out, and came up with a fistful of cold sheets. It put me in a foul mood. After spending only one night in Kallie's bed, it already felt strange to wake up without her in my arms. I wanted her with me—always—and as I remembered her call last night to tell me about her weekend trip with Gabby, it made my mood sink even lower. I wouldn't get to see her again until Monday.

Flipping so I was flat on my back once more, I stared at the ceiling. Practice races were happening at Motor Club Speedway later on today. A day at the track would be better than sitting around my place sulking. The sooner I showered and headed out, the sooner I'd be able to push Kallie's absence from my mind. Shoving a frustrated hand through my hair, I swung my legs over the side of the bed. When I stood, a stabbing pain shot through my hip.

"Shit!" I yelled to the empty room, grabbing the nightstand to steady myself. Chronic pain after any joint replacement was common. For me, mornings were always the worst because that's when the muscles surrounding the joint were the stiffest. I knew better than to put too much weight on my left leg right away. Instinctively, I opened my nightstand drawer to reveal the little orange bottle of painkillers. There were still two remaining pills. I hadn't taken one since before meeting Kallie.

Guilt clawed at my chest, knowing she would disapprove if I took one—especially since I didn't really need them for pain management anymore. It usually took a good thirty minutes or so for the muscles to naturally loosen, but once they did, I was generally fine as long as I made sure not to put too much weight on that side of my body throughout the day.

Slamming the drawer closed, I decided to wait out the pain. After a few minutes, the sharp stinging began to subside into a dull ache. Carefully moving toward the master bathroom, I looked forward to the long, hot shower that was sure to help loosen me up.

"SOMETHING FEELS OFF," Cooper said, elevating his voice to be heard over the music blaring from the grandstand of Motor Club Speedway. "The Distance" by Cake was always a staple as pit crews scrambled to prepare for the next practice race, but the music seemed extra loud today.

I'd just arrived at the track twenty minutes earlier. I hadn't expected Cooper to be there, as his team wasn't on the schedule today. However, he'd been invited to observe and give pointers to a racing team as they practiced. The driver was a friend of ours, Tyler McDermott. His recent success in the European circuit made him a favorite to win the Motorsports

International Legacy League, more commonly known as the MILL.

"Feels off in what way?" I asked.

"Shit has been going wrong all day," he explained. "The crew just replaced the rear bearings for the second time today, and the car has only been around the track a few times. That shouldn't be happening. I'm trying to think of what the team might be overlooking."

"Has anyone on the team looked at the clutch plate? When I first arrived, I noticed the car sliding around a bit."

"Yeah, everything checked out."

"I'm sure it's fine, Cooper. Tyler has a good team. They'll figure it out."

"I hope so. Tyler needs everything to be perfect for the MILL. Bets are on him to win, but he needs the money more than the title."

I frowned and turned my gaze away from the track to look at Cooper. There was an urgency to his voice that made me think there was more to the story.

"The money? Tyler makes a good buck from endorsements. I heard Kapton Motor Oil paid him a mint to promote their product. Don't tell me he blew through it all."

"You didn't hear?"

"Hear what?"

"Man, you really have been out of the loop, haven't you? I'm talking about his wife, Amy."

"What about her?"

"She was diagnosed with an aggressive form of cancer about six months ago. I don't remember what kind, but the prognosis is bad. My heart breaks for both of them. They've spent almost every penny they have on her chemo. Tyler said he wanted to take her to Switzerland for some experimental treatment, but the price tag is insane. So, as I said, he could really use the prize money from a win—not to mention all the extra endorsement money that will follow."

I shook my head over the devastating news.

"Wow... I didn't know. Tyler and I used to talk all the time, but I haven't spoken to many people since my accident. I feel bad that I didn't know. I should call him."

"You had a lot going on. I'm sure he didn't want to worry you."

"Still, Tyler is a good guy. I met Amy a few times—a real sweetheart. For both of their sakes, I hope he wins this." I stared absently at the track and rubbed my chin thoughtfully. "What about doing a fundraiser? If we pulled in enough drivers, I'm sure we could raise the money he needs."

"Ro is looking into it, but I'm not sure if she made any headway. Maybe you could ask Kallie to get with her on it."

"That's not a bad idea. I—"

The rumbling sound of a car engine cut me off. Whatever was wrong with the rear bearings must have been fixed because Tyler's car pulled out onto the track once more. Cooper and I moved up to the bottom row of the spectator stand to watch the open-wheel single-seater take position.

Within minutes, the car was moving around the track at a blistering speed. I thought Tyler took the cornering speed a little too slow, not utilizing the aerodynamic downforce the car naturally generated to push the car down onto the track. I was about to comment on it but paused when I saw he hadn't gotten back up to speed on the straightaway. Then I spotted the smoke.

Instinctively, I gripped the railing in front of me until my knuckles turned white. Everything happened so fast. The only thing I could do was watch helplessly as Tyler's car—its back end on fire—spun out of control and crashed into the center barrier.

Everything around me glitched into slow motion. Cooper

hopped the rail and took off running. The fire marshals scrambled. I heard screams from the observers and yelling from the pit crew, but it was all a distant echo. I couldn't move or look away from the wreckage. Completely frozen to the spot, it was as if Tyler's crash were my own, and in that moment, I was unable to prevent myself from being thrown back in time to that day.

I SLIP my arms into the sleeves of my flame-resistant racing suit and zip up the front. Walking over to the waiting open-wheeled race car, I use all the energy I have to push down my anger over the information I found out about my father. My sole focus must be on the practice race I'm about to run.

I climb into the car and allow a crew member to adjust the Hans device until I am safely secure in the head and neck restraint. Gripping the steering wheel, I wait for Benjamin to signal me out onto the track to join the pack of ten cars. Once he does, I move into position at the back of the group. The purpose of today's practice is to teach the rookies how to take the lead from behind. Nothing else matters except the cars on the track.

When the flag drops, so does my foot on the accelerator. Moving the steering wheel from left to right, I weave between cars and make my way to the front. I keep my eye on who I'd pass, knowing I've yet to reach Tripp Lucas, an arrogant S.O.B. who is still a few cars ahead. Little does he know, he's about to get schooled.

The engine revs as the wind whips around the car. I feel the tires roaring beneath me as I nose just ahead of Tripp. I shift, and the car lurches. A rush of adrenaline surges, making me feel alive in ways only racing could. The only thing that could make it better is if this wasn't just for practice but the real deal.

As I creep past Tripp, he taps the gas and pushes slightly ahead of me. I do the same, the noses of our cars playing a virtual tug of war. When he gets the advantage, I don't bother to chance a glance in his direction. I know the cocky bastard is probably smirking. He doesn't know I'm just toying with him. Making him think he is winning is all part of the psychological game. I haven't even begun to push my car to its limits yet. The rookie has a lot to learn.

As we whip through the first lap, I catch a glimpse of my mother standing next to Cooper and Benjamin in the pit lane. The image of them is fleeting, their forms nothing but a blur as I speed past—and it's a good thing, too. The last thing I want is to see her. My teeth clench as I tamp down my anger once more and focus on the turn ahead.

I bank left around the bend and prepare for the straightaway. Easing my foot off the clutch, I shift into final gear and press the gas pedal to the floor. I can see Tripp's car losing speed in my peripheral, and I grin. I have him now. When I think it's safe to look, I cast my gaze in his direction. Sheer panic is written all over his face, knowing he is about to be lost in my dust. Instinctively, my grin widens.

However, my smile is short-lived. It takes me less than half a second to realize Tripp's panic had nothing to do with losing the race and everything to do with the smoke billowing from the engine of a slowing car up ahead.

"Son of a bitch! Where's the goddamn caution flag?"

I have a split second to decide. If I swerve left, I will hit Tripp's car. If I brake too hard, I will risk being hit by the two cars right on my tail. My only hope is to ease off the gas, slowing just enough for Tripp to pass me so I can get around the smoking car. I remove my foot from the gas, hoping Tripp will take the cue. Thankfully, he does —but he isn't fast enough.

The slowing car comes closer and closer. A shiver of fear races down my spine. Officially out of time, I have no choice but to bank left. I hear a crunch and immediately know the front bumper of my car connected with Tripp's rear. My car spins out, skidding along the track backward. I am all but blind as I brace for impact.

. . .

WHETHER A FEW MINUTES or a few hours had passed, I couldn't be sure. All at once, everything seemed to fast forward into real time. I saw Tyler's body being carried away on a stretcher. Cooper appeared at my side, his breathing heavy.

"He's alive. I'm not sure of the extent of his injuries. They're taking him by helicopter to Bayfront Hospital. It'll take me a while to get there by car. I'm going to leave now. Do you want to —" Cooper stopped short and grabbed my arm. "Sloan. Hey, man. Are you alright? You're as white as a sheet."

Slowly, I turned my head to look at him.

"Yeah, it's just that... the crash. It reminded me..."

Cooper released my arm, stepped back, and shook his head.

"Shit. I can't imagine what seeing that must have been like for you. Don't worry. Tyler was conscious and talking. I don't think his injuries are life-threatening. It was nothing like your accident. Do you want to ride with me to the hospital?"

"It's all good. You go on. I'm going to hang back. Maybe look into what went wrong with the car."

Cooper seemed wary as he studied my face, but I ignored him and turned my focus back to the track where the fire crew was still dousing the flames.

"I don't like the idea of leaving you here alone. Are you sure?"

He sounded torn.

"I'm sure. Tyler needs you more than I do," I replied without looking at him.

At some point, Cooper must have left. I didn't remember him walking away, nor did I remember the long drive back to my house. One minute I was at the track, and the next minute I found myself at my kitchen table with an unopened bottle of Jack and my last two remaining oxycodone pills sitting in front of me.

16

Kallie

Three hours into the drive to Napa Valley, Gabby and I sang along with The Ataris—completely off-key and not caring one little bit. "Boys of Summer" was one of our favorites, and it brought back so many memories from our younger years.

Having just driven through the flat and dusty terrain of Bakersfield, we'd finally gotten past the obstruction of oil pumping units and agricultural fields to a more scenic route—if one could call it such. The narrow asphalt road on which we traveled was full of twists and turns, with steep drop-offs. I nervously looked ahead, seeing nothing but tumbleweeds and potholes to avoid.

"You seem antsy," Gabby said.

I eyed her questioningly.

"Antsy?"

"Yeah. I wonder why they call it that anyway—antsy. It's kind of a dumb word when you think about it. Ants don't seem anxious. They seem pretty calm and hardworking when building their little anthills."

I laughed.

"I guess I never thought about it. But then again, why do we call someone 'nutty' when they're acting crazy? Or what about harebrained? I don't think the peanuts and rabbits of the world would take kindly to the reference," I pointed out.

"True."

Glancing at my cell phone mounted on the dash, I flicked my finger against it as if somehow the action would spark cell service. My phone had been fading from one bar to no bars ever since we got off I-5 and headed toward Bakersfield.

"Gabby, I have no clue where we are."

"Just keep driving toward the mountains, then we'll double back the way we came."

"Mountains? All I see are big brown hills. What looked like mountains from a distance turned out to be a whole lot of nothing."

"Because we haven't gotten there yet. Besides, it's an adventure! For someone who's usually so free-spirited, you're worrying too much. Just go with it."

"I don't think we should go any further. I'm going to turn around. I'm getting really nervous about being in the middle of nowhere without a cell phone signal. I mean, what if—" I was interrupted by a loud thud from underneath the car. "Oh my god! Did I just hit something?"

"I don't think so. I didn't see an animal or anything."

My heart sank, thinking I may have run over a furry critter when I distractedly looked at the GPS map.

"Gabs, I'm pretty sure I just killed Thumper."

However, the drumming sound continued, making me all but certain I hadn't hit anything. I began to wonder if there might be something wrong with the car itself. My concern grew as the incessant thump-thump noise continued over and over again in a steady rhythm.

Gabby turned down the radio to hear where the sound was coming from. Then she laughed and pointed to the side view mirror.

"No, you didn't kill Thumper, but you may have run over a nail or something sharp. Or maybe it was the pothole you hit a mile back. I'm pretty sure you have a flat tire."

"A flat! Why are you laughing? That's not funny!" I scowled, annoyed that she somehow found this humorous, and cautiously maneuvered the car to the side of the road until it came to a stop. Looking at my phone once again, I saw the words 'no service' where the little bars should have been. "Do you have cell signal?"

Gabby pulled her phone from her purse and glanced at the screen.

"Nope."

"What are we going to do now? Without cell service, neither one of us can call AAA."

"I can change a tire. No sweat. I've got this, *chica*. Pop the trunk."

I looked under the dash in search of the trunk release as Gabby climbed out. After finding it, I killed the engine and joined her at the back of the car. She stood with her hands on her hips, staring down into the trunk, seeming perplexed.

"What's wrong?" I asked.

"Tools. There's a tire and a jack here, but no lug wrench."

"So what does that mean?"

"It means I can't change the tire."

"You have got to be kidding me." She just shrugged, and I threw up my arms in exasperation. Pinching the bridge of my nose, I began to pace. I knew I shouldn't have listened to her and stayed straight on the route to our intended destination. Turning back to the car, I opened the door to the backseat, pulled our luggage out, and set the bags down on the side of the road.

"What are you doing, Kals?"

"I'm looking for tools. Maybe the rental agency put them in the backseat for some reason."

"I doubt it," she said skeptically.

Glancing back at her, I let out a breath in frustration.

"Maybe, maybe not. Are you just going to stand there watching me, or are you going to help me look?"

Gabby went to the opposite side of the car and began to search around. We lifted the floormats and flipped down the back seat but came up empty-handed.

"Damnit!" I cursed, slamming my hand on the top of the car.

"I'm sorry."

"Not for nothing, but when you spotted the mountains and wanted to take pictures, my gut told me it was a bad idea. But no—instead, I listened to you when you said, 'We have time, Kallie. Just detour through Bakersfield.' Now, here we are, somewhere on route 178, with a flat and no way to call for a tow. Even if we could fix it, I have no idea how to get us back."

"I'm really am sorry, Kallie," she repeated. "But, in my defense, the rental company is to blame for the missing tools. I would have been able to change the tire if it weren't for that."

"We should have just stuck to GPS. At least then we wouldn't have ended up in the middle of nowhere," I grumbled. "The last thing we passed was a gas station about ten miles back."

"Someone is bound to come down this road eventually. Until then, I packed wine."

I tossed her a skeptical look.

"Wine? How is that supposed to help?"

"Wine always helps," she said, her voice full of optimism as she began rummaging through her suitcase on the side of the road. "When I went out this morning to grab snacks for the trip, I picked up a couple of bottles for us to drink at the hotel."

As I watched her struggle with the corkscrew, I couldn't help but laugh and hoped she was right. Someone would have to drive by eventually. Until then, all we could do was wait it out.

Closing the trunk, I climbed onto the back of the car and took a seat. The sun was blisteringly hot, and my hair was sticky on my neck. Using the hair tie I had wrapped around my wrist, I bound the pink and blonde into a loose bun on top of my head. Feeling the heat just as I was, Gabby mimicked my actions and then handed me a bottle of white.

"I didn't think to pack cups," she told me after she took a swig straight from a bottle that she'd kept for herself.

"I don't think we need to worry about being civilized when there is literally no sign of civilization anywhere," I joked. Holding up my bottle, I clinked it to hers, then took a sip. "If it weren't so damn hot, I'd suggest we walk back to the gas station."

"I second that. I'm not walking anywhere in this heat," she agreed.

"What did you buy for snacks?"

"Lots of stuff." Reaching into the backseat, she procured two large Ziplock bags of goodies, then took a seat next to me on the back of the car.

"If Sloan were here, I'd bet he would be able to change the tire without tools," I said through a mouthful of kettle chips.

"There's no way to MacGyver your way through changing a tire. I don't care how sexy he is—he's not a miracle worker. What we need is a fairy godmother to come bibbiti-bobbiti-boo us out of this."

"Maybe. Chip?' I offered, holding out the bag.

"Sure." As she crunched away, her expression was thoughtful.

"What are you thinking about, Gabby?"

"Honestly? I'm thinking about you and Sloan. I'm still a little surprised by it. I mean, I'm not judging you in the least bit —that man is fine as hell. But I am curious about what's going through your mind. Is this just a fling to get over Dean, or is it something more? Rebounds can be fun but also destructive if you aren't careful."

I considered her question for a moment, not entirely sure of the answer.

"It can only be a rebound if I had a broken heart. The crazy thing is, I never felt like I did. Sure, I was sad for a few days after Dean and I split, but I wasn't sad because I missed him. I was sad because I felt like I wasted two years of my life with someone who didn't make me happy. As for how I feel about Sloan... It's tough to say. It's not just a fling, but it's too early to tell if there's more to it. I just know I felt something strong the minute I met him. I've been thinking about the gypsy's warning a lot too. You remember Madame Lavinia, right?"

"Yeah. How could I forget? She predicted I'd have a tragic accident, and then I broke my arm the next day. I know it was just a coincidence, but it was super spooky at the time."

"What if it wasn't a coincidence?"

"You can't be serious." She paused and looked at me incredulously. "Kals, please don't tell me you've been carrying around what she said to you about sunsets and doomed love for all of these years."

"I can't help it. There are just too many coincidences to ignore. She's one of the reasons I spent a month avoiding being anywhere alone with Sloan. I was nervous. But I have to wonder—"

"Kallie, listen to me. It's not—"

"No, hang on. Just hear me out. I recently began to think I misinterpreted the warnings. Getting lost in my emotions and worries may be the reason she predicted destructive love.

Perhaps I've been the one who's been getting in my own way by overthinking everything. Maybe it has nothing to do with Sloan —or any other guy who may have kissed me at sunset—and everything to do with the way I let my emotions rule me."

Gabby's eyes grew wide, and she looked genuinely worried. When she spoke, her tone was apprehensive.

"Oh, no... You've been stressing way too much about this, Kals. I need to tell you something, but you have to promise you won't get mad."

I chuckled.

"How can I promise that if I don't know what you're going to say?"

"Good point," she responded with an ironic smirk. "What I have to tell you has to do with Austin."

I rolled my eyes.

"Oh, God. What did my brother do now?"

"I swear, Kallie. I thought you knew, or I would have told you. I didn't know you were carrying this around all of this time and—" She stopped short, and I narrowed my eyes.

"And what? What did he do, Gabby?"

She sighed and shook her head.

"When we were in high school, the two of us used to play Charlie-Charlie all the time. One of the times we were playing, Austin wanted to join in. Do you remember that?"

"Yeah, why?"

"Austin sort of... well, he moved the pencil to make you believe that the guy who kissed you during a sunset would be your soulmate."

"Sort of?" I said with a laugh. After taking another sip from my wine bottle, I smiled. "When we were playing, I suspected Austin of deliberately pushing the pencil. Why would I be mad about that? It was just a silly game. I haven't really thought about it since."

"Well...that's not all, which brings me to the psychic gypsy.

Austin knew how freaked out you were about my so-called tragic accident, so he may or may not have paid off the psychic to tell you all of those things."

I froze, unable to find words as I processed what she was saying. When I finally found my voice, the words came out slow and laced with disbelief.

"May or may not have paid her off?"

"Kallie, as I said—I swear I thought you knew. I would have told you before now had I known. Austin thought it would be funny to get the gypsy to say the opposite of what the Charlie-Charlie game said. He knew it would mess with you. His logic was to make sure you didn't get too serious with a guy when you went away to college. I suppose it was his twisted way of being an overprotective brother, but I thought he would have told you the truth by now. Are you mad?"

I stayed quiet, looking down at the busted-up asphalt road for a moment before bringing the wine bottle to my lips. I took a long pull. I always knew there was a possibility that the psychic was a fraud, just as I knew there was potential to change any negative reading from happening in the future by my own free will. I just never thought I would be betrayed by Austin that way.

"No, I'm not mad. Just feeling stupid, I guess."

"If it makes you feel any better, I don't think Austin thought you were still hanging on to this either. It was only a joke—we were practically kids at the time. You know he wouldn't deliberately hurt you."

I gave her a small smile.

"I know he wouldn't."

I stared at the endless road covered in dust and tumbleweeds feeling disempowered. I felt foolish and even found myself second-guessing my tarot cards. Something that once gave me peace, comfort, and guidance during difficult times suddenly seemed childish and trivial. It was as if everything I believed was just an illusion.

DARKNESS HAD FALLEN HOURS AGO, yet not a single car had passed. We'd consumed most of the snacks, and there wasn't a drop of wine left. Resigned to spending the night in the car, Gabby and I decided to sleep in shifts. It was my turn to keep watch. We agreed that at daybreak, before it got too hot, we'd walk back to the gas station we hadn't wanted to walk to when the sun was high in the sky. Our only saving grace was knowing we had a few bottles of water in the car to get us through the hike.

I looked out the front windshield at the star-filled sky. Being so far away from the city lights, thousands of twinkling dots could be seen as far as the eye could see. For me, stargazing was like dreaming with your eyes open. I was convinced that our destiny was written on the very stars which I looked upon, and no matter what anyone did to change it, the outcome was always fated. I'd always been someone with immense energy and an ambitious drive, and I believed anything was possible if I just followed my path. But after hearing about Austin's ruse, I now felt disenchanted, and it upset me on a profound level.

As I sat there in the dark, I began to wonder about every single aspect of my life. I had obsessed for years over the tiniest details, always trying to find the deeper meaning to reassure me of my path to happiness and success and also help to prepare me for anything terrible looming on the horizon.

What if it's all a bunch of hocus pocus and misguided intention?

It was too much to process in my exhausted state, and I fought back a yawn. The combination of the hot sun during the day and consuming too much wine was a terrible mix for someone who needed to stay awake half the night. I glanced at my phone to check the time. It was after one in the morning, and I wasn't due to wake Gabby until two.

My eyelids felt heavy, and I blinked rapidly in an attempt to keep them open. I thought about getting out of the car to stretch but was nervous about doing so after hearing the high, quavering cries of coyotes from somewhere nearby. Inside of the car was safer, especially since luck was clearly not on my side today.

Perhaps if I closed my eyes for just a minute...

17

Kallie

I woke to the sun blazing through the windshield. I blinked, becoming aware of a relentless knocking on the driver's side window. Turning my head, I nearly jumped out of my skin to see a gray-bearded man with a wide-brimmed hat peering through the window. Glancing at Gabby, I noticed she was still fast asleep.

"Gabby!" I hissed as I shook her. "Wake up!"

Groggily, she opened her eyes and jumped the same way I had when she saw the man.

"Shit! What time is it?" she asked.

"I don't know," I told her as I turned the key in the ignition so I could power down the window. Glancing up at the man, I smiled and said, "Hey, there! Sorry. You startled me."

"It's alright. Everything okay?" he asked.

I pointed over my shoulder in the direction of the deflated tire.

"We caught a flat tire last night, and we couldn't get cell service to call for a tow."

"You ladies slept here all night? Holy smokes—that wasn't too fun now, was it? You never know who could come around the bend in these parts. You're lucky nothing happened to you," he added with a shake of his head. "You got a spare? I can change it for you so you can be on your way."

"I have a spare, and it's so nice of you to offer, but unfortunately, the tools are missing from the trunk."

"That's no problem. I keep a toolbox on the tractor," he told me and thumbed toward a large-wheeled yellow farming tractor parked on the opposite side of the road. "Just give me a minute to get what I need."

"That would be great! Thank you so much!" I said, not hiding my immediate relief. After he walked away, I turned to Gabby. "It looks like our fairy godmother sent help."

"Thank goodness, too. I'm stiff as hell," she complained as she opened the passenger door to stretch her legs. I followed her lead and watched as the man walked back toward my car, lugging a large red toolbox. When he reached us, he set the box down and extended his hand to me.

"I should have introduced myself. My name is George Calhoun."

"I'm Kallie, and this is Gabby. Believe me when I say it's more than just a pleasure to meet you," I joked. "If you hadn't shown up, we'd be walking ten miles to the nearest gas station to find a payphone."

"I can believe that. Cell phone service around Bakersfield is known to be the worst in the country. There's not much around these parts. Where were you ladies headed to, anyway?"

"Napa Valley from Santa Monica, but we took a minor detour and ended up a little lost," Gabby said.

"A minor detour? You're halfway to Death Valley. I'll say you were lost!"

He shook his head and chuckled, then sat on the ground next to the flat tire and began to work. Fifteen minutes later, the full-sized spare was secure. George stood up and wiped the dirt off his hands on his tan coveralls.

"You should be all set now. The air in the tire is a little low. You'll want to fill it at the next gas station. Just try to avoid any potholes in the meantime."

"I can't thank you enough," I told him. "Is there anything I can do to repay you? I have a bit of cash on me and—"

"Don't you worry your pretty little head about it. You don't need to give me anything. I'm happy to help," he assured, then smiled to reveal the deep age lines on his tanned face. After he collected his tools, we bid our farewells and watched as he puttered down the road on his tractor.

"Man, did we ever catch a break!" Gabby said.

"For sure. At the rate we were going, I thought we'd never make it to Napa Valley. You ready to go?"

"Yes, but...about Napa Valley." She hesitated, and I was pretty sure I knew what she was thinking. By the time we got to Napa and checked into our room, the wineries would most likely be closed for the day—and forget making it there in time for the wine tour by train. While we could still go on as planned tomorrow, it seemed pointless to drive all that way for just one day.

"Do you want to scrap the trip and just head back to my place? I'm sure we can call the B&B and get a refund if we explain what happened."

"Kals, I'm so glad you said that! After yesterday and last night, I just can't get excited about it anymore. I was afraid to say so because it was my idea to detour in the first place. I just think I've had enough adventure for a while," she said with a small laugh. I couldn't agree more.

As I drove back in the direction we came, Gabby repeatedly checked our cell phones for service. We stopped at the next gas station to add air to the tire just as George suggested we do, asked for directions, then continued on our way. The clerk's explanation of how to get back to where we needed to be was meandering and hard to follow, so I just tried to follow the landmarks I remembered passing, even if they were scarce.

When we reached Bakersfield, I sighed with relief to know we were heading in the right direction. And when our cell phones started chiming with notifications, I nearly wept.

"Finally, we have service!" Gabby announced. "It's weak, but it's something. I'll pull up the directions back to your place, then screenshot them in case we lose service again."

"Good idea."

"You've got a bunch of voicemails on your phone. Want me to play them on speaker?"

"Sure."

My mother's voice was the first to sound through the speaker.

"Hey, Kallie! It's mom. I was just calling to see if you and Gabby got to Napa okay. Call me when you get this."

My mom was a forever worrier, so her message was no surprise. However, the following message was unexpected.

"Kallie, it's Cooper Davis. When you can, give me a call back."

As he rattled off his phone number, I wondered how he'd gotten my number but then realized he must have gotten it from Rochele. When my inbox advanced to the next message, I was shocked to hear Cooper's voice again.

"Kallie, it's Cooper again. Hey, I'm sorry to bother you, but I can't reach Sloan. I was wondering if you've heard from him. Give me a buzz back."

I frowned as a computerized voice told me it was the end of my messages. I glanced at Gabby in confusion.

"That's strange. I wonder why he's trying to get a hold of Sloan."

"Kals, I just looked at your call log. That guy Cooper called three more times after the last message. Sloan called once, too, but didn't leave a message. You don't think something bad happened, do you?"

My stomach did a nervous flip, and I bit my lower lip.

"I don't know. Can you dial Sloan for me? His number is in my contacts."

"Sure."

I waited as the phone rang. After the fourth ring, a loud beeping sound came through the line signaling the call had failed.

"Lost service again," Gabby said.

"Damn it. Did you manage to pull up the driving directions at least?"

"Yeah. I grabbed them on my phone while your voicemails were playing."

"Good. That's all that matters. I can try calling Sloan again when we get home."

Still, despite my words, Sloan *did* matter, and I was concerned over why he wasn't answering his phone when Cooper called him. Whatever it was, it must have been serious enough for Cooper to reach out to me. What it could be was anyone's guess, but I couldn't shake the angst-ridden feelings for the remainder of the drive back to Santa Monica.

"THE IDEA of a shower never sounded so good," Gabby said as we dumped our bags in the front hall of my house. "I'm going to take one if that's okay."

"Go for it. I'm going to try to reach Sloan again. I'll shower after. Just don't use up all the hot water," I added, knowing Gabby's penchant for long, hot showers.

"I won't," she promised, but I knew better. If I she wasn't

quick, there was no doubt I'd be washing under lukewarm water.

After Gabby disappeared down the hall, I pulled my cell from the back pocket of my jeans and dialed Sloan's number. It was my third time calling him since we gained steady signal strength, but there was no answer once again. I began to pace. Feeling frustrated, I pulled up my missed call log to locate Cooper's number. He answered after the second ring.

"Kallie, hey. I'm glad you called back."

"Yeah, sorry. I just got your messages this morning. I was on a road trip, got lost, and had no cell service. It's a long story. Anyway, I've tried calling Sloan, but he hasn't picked up for me either. Is everything okay?"

I heard Cooper sigh on the other end of the line.

"There was an accident at the track. A friend of ours, Tyler McDermott, was banged up pretty good and was sent by helicopter to the hospital."

"Oh, no! Is he okay?"

"He'll recover. But he's not the reason I called you. I'm worried about Sloan. He was at the track when it happened. I left him there to go to the hospital, but I didn't like how he looked. I think the crash really shook him up. When I called him later, and he didn't answer multiple times, I started to get even more worried. I have a meeting that I can't miss this afternoon, but I planned to head over to his place to check on him as soon as I finish. I should be able to get over there by three."

Glancing up at the clock hanging on the kitchen wall, I saw it was nearing noon. If I hurried in the shower, I could be to Sloan's place by one.

"No, it's okay. Thanks. I'll head over there myself in a bit."

"Are you sure? I don't mind. I just want to make sure he didn't do anything stupid."

"It's all good. When I see him, I'll make sure he gives you a call."

After thanking Cooper for reaching out, I ended the call and went to the front hall to grab my suitcase, then began rummaging quickly through it to find my shower toiletries. A few minutes later, Gabby came down the hall with a towel wrapped around her head.

"Fifteen minutes. That might be a record for me!" she joked. "There should be plenty of hot water left."

"Thanks, Gabs. Listen, I hate to leave you alone since you'll only be here for a short time, but I need to go out for a bit. I just spoke with Cooper, and I'm worried about Sloan. I'm going to check on him. Will you be okay here for a few hours?"

"I'm a big girl. Do what you need to do. While you're gone, I'll take advantage of that glorious pool you have in the yard."

"Are you sure?"

"Positive."

I smiled, grateful for her easy understanding, then hurried to the bathroom to shower.

18

Kallie

Shortly after one, I pulled into Sloan's driveway. His black Chevy Camaro was parked haphazardly in the middle of the drive. It was at an angle, and I couldn't pull up all the way. That wasn't a good sign. After ensuring my back end wasn't sticking out in the street, I parked near the end of the drive, then got out and walked up to the front door.

After ringing the bell four times, it was clear he wasn't going to answer, so I walked around to the back. Thankfully, the gate to the backyard wasn't locked. As I rounded the back corner of the house, my steps faltered when I saw a patio chair tipped on end and the glass patio doors partially open. My stomach dropped, and panic began to set in.

I hurried toward the open doors. Once inside, I looked around but didn't see Sloan. The place was a mess—but in a different way than it had been when I was there the first time. Takeout containers and clothes no longer littered the floor, but almost every piece of furniture had either been shifted to awkward angles or knocked over. One of the end-table lamps had toppled onto the floor, and the glass top of the coffee table had slid to balance precariously on the frame. Automatically, I bent to reposition it so it didn't fall and break.

As I stood back up, I froze when I spotted an orange prescription bottle on the floor. The lid was off, and it appeared empty. Picking it up, I read the label.

It was oxycodone.

The pit in my stomach grew.

"Sloan?" I called out in alarm. I listened for his answer as I picked up the lamp and put it back in its proper place on the table. Stepping over an empty bottle of Jack Daniels, I made my way upstairs with the hope of finding Sloan there.

I tried not to worry about what the empty pill bottle and liquor could signify, but my anxiety only grew with every step I took. Halfway to the top, I heard a loud bang, then a thud. I gasped and began to sprint up the last remaining stairs. I hurried along the hallway toward the sounds. At the end of the hall, I came to what I could only assume was Sloan's bedroom. The bed was unmade, and the room reeked of whiskey—but that wasn't what caused fear to wrap like a vice around my heart. It was seeing Sloan lying face down on the floor that made my blood turn cold.

"Sloan!" Rushing to him, I skidded to a halt and tried to flip him over. His dead weight made it a struggle, but I eventually got him to shift onto his back. He looked up at me with glazed eyes, almost as if he couldn't focus. Judging by the smell of him, he probably couldn't. His pupils looked normal and not constricted like I'd expected them to be. That was a good sign. It meant he might not have taken the prescription drugs after all.

I pressed my lips together in a tight line, glanced around the room, and tried to think of what to do. There was a balcony off of Sloan's bedroom, and he was lying just inside the open doors. The wrought-iron curtain rod hanging over the door had been pulled from the brackets, falling until it skewered one wall. My quick guess was that he tripped coming inside and tried to grab ahold of something to stop himself from falling. The rod puncturing the wall was most likely the source of the bang I'd heard, and the loud thud was probably Sloan's heavy body hitting the floor.

He groaned and attempted to sit up. I quickly shifted to help him. That's when I noticed he had another bottle of Jack —this one half-empty—clutched tightly in his hand. Despite his fall, he managed not to spill a drop. I did a mental calculation, combining the bottle he was holding with the empty one at the base of the stairs, to figure out how much he'd likely consumed since last night.

Fighting to push himself up with his free arm, the two of us managed to get him into a sitting position. Shifting his body, he leaned back against the side of the bed, almost as if it were too much of an effort to stay upright on his own. Dark circles shadowed his eyes, and his face was pale. He looked fragile and broken.

Have I been blind over the past month? How did I not know he could be triggered so easily?

Speechless, I could only stare at him. I was kicking myself for failing to ask more probing questions about his accident and what happened with his mother and father. As a trained PR agent, I knew how to ask the hard questions, yet I'd avoided them and allowed my personal feelings to get in the way.

After a moment, he seemed to regain some semblance of focus and glared at me.

"What are you doing here?" he slurred viciously. I flinched from the venom in his voice. I'd never heard him talk to me like that before.

"I talked to Cooper. He told me about the crash. I was

worried when you didn't answer the phone, so I came here to see if you were okay."

At my words, his face momentarily softened.

"I called you."

"I know, but you didn't leave a message. Sloan, what happened?"

"No rainbows," he mumbled instead of answering me. Reaching up, he fumbled the blue extensions I'd clipped in today. "Why blue?"

"Blue is when I'm sad. I was sad when Cooper told me what happened. I'm even sadder now to see you like this. Why, Sloan? Why did you do this to yourself?"

Instantly, his menacing look was back. He scowled and tried to stand up. I quickly moved to help him, but he batted my hand away.

"I've got it!" he snarled. Once on his feet, he swayed a bit but didn't topple over like I thought he might. With him standing at full height, I was able to take in his appearance. He was clad in nothing but a pair of boxer briefs, and there was a long cut extending from his right shoulder to his sternum. It wasn't deep, but it would still need tending to.

"Sloan, you've scraped yourself up pretty good. Let me get something to clean—"

"If you've come here to save me, you can forget it. I don't need you to fix me anymore. Get out!"

"You're drunk!" I snapped back. It was foolish to point out the obvious, but I couldn't think of anything else to say. I'd never seen him in such a state, and I didn't know how to handle it.

"Well, thank you for pointing out what I already knew. In my opinion, I'm not drunk enough. Now get out so I can finish this here—" He stopped slurring to point a wavering finger at his bottle. "This here bottle needs to be finished."

He took a few swerving steps toward the balcony doors. I

moved, afraid he might fall on me, but I was also scared of him going outside near the railings.

"Wait. You shouldn't go out there. It isn't safe in your condition. Please, Sloan. Stay in the house," I begged and placed a hand on his arm. He glanced down at it with disgust, as if it were an annoying fly he wanted to swat away.

"Why do you even care? You're wasting your time. You can't stop history from repeating itself. I am who I am, baby. It's in my blood!" he shouted and jabbed a finger into his chest.

History? His blood? Is he talking about his father's drinking?

"What are you talking about?"

"Jesus Christ! I told you I don't want you here! Don't you have someone else who needs fixing?" Ignoring me, he continued another few steps toward the door. I knew he was only acting like an asshole to get me to leave. It stung but little did he know, I wasn't going anywhere.

"Sloan, stop this right now. You're not your father!" The words were out before I could think. Sloan's steps faltered, and he turned his head to glare at me through narrowed eyes.

"What did you say?"

"Nothing," I responded hurriedly, not wanting to say anything else to upset him. "Just forget it. Let's go downstairs. I can make some coffee and—"

I stopped short, my breath catching in my throat as my fears came to fruition. When he reached the balcony door, his foot caught on the threshold and caused him to stumble. Before I could think to react, he grabbed hold of the doorframe to stop himself from falling. In the process, he dropped the bottle of Jack Daniels. The glass bottle hit the tiled floor of the balcony and shattered into hundreds of tiny glass pieces. The brown liquid slithered like a toxic snake to disappear over the edge.

"Fuck!" he hissed.

Throwing his arms up in a rage, his forearm hit my face, and I stumbled back a step. It smarted only a little, and I knew it was an accident, but that didn't change the fact that I wanted to cry. The shock was the only thing preventing my tears from falling. I couldn't believe I was seeing him like this. The person standing before me wasn't the man who was kind and patient with orphan boys, the man who slowed danced with me on the beach, or the man who called me Rainbow Brite and whispered sweet flirtations into my ear.

No. This was a man who had his whole life ripped away from him in one tragic moment, and he was spiraling out of control as a result—and breaking my heart in the process. I didn't want to be anywhere near him, yet I knew I couldn't leave. I couldn't abandon him at a time when he needed me the most—and not as his lover, but as his agent.

Tucking my emotions away, I donned my professional hat.

"Enough. You're a complete train wreck, and I know you to be better than this. Time to sleep this off. No more talking until you've sobered up."

He glowered at me, looking as if he wanted to argue, but couldn't muster up the energy. When I took his arm, he didn't push me away this time but allowed me to lead him to the bed. Once he seemed settled comfortably, I pulled the blankets up to cover him.

"I don't know why you want to be with someone like me. I'm sorry, Kallie," he mumbled quietly. I didn't respond, too afraid my voice would crack if I did. I wasn't mad at him—although I knew I should be. I just couldn't be angry when my heart hurt after seeing this powerful and captivating man be made small by things he had no control over.

I waited until his breathing was even, signaling he was asleep, then exhaled a sigh of relief. Moving to the chair in the corner, I sat down quietly and allowed myself a moment to relax for the first time since before getting the flat tire yesterday. It was strange to think I'd been stranded on a road to nowhere mere hours ago. It felt like it had happened weeks ago.

Remembering that I was supposed to update Cooper, I took my phone from my purse and shot off a quick text to him.

Today
1:37 PM, Me: *Hey, Cooper. I just wanted to let you know I'm with Sloan. He's okay. He indulged in too much whiskey and is currently sleeping it off.*

His response came almost immediately.

1:40 PM, Cooper: *Dumbass. Thanks for letting me know. I'll call him later. If you need anything, you know where to find me.*
1:41 PM, Me: *I appreciate it.*

After dropping my phone back inside my purse, I set it on the ground near my feet. My gaze shifted up to wander over Sloan's glorious body. His face, typically so intensely alert, was peaceful and relaxed while he slept. He no longer looked like the cocky race car driver who could make me feel exposed and naked with just one look. Instead, he appeared young and innocent.

I stifled a yawn as exhaustion from a restless night of sleeping in the car began to set in. I leaned my head back, knowing a quick nap would be needed if I wanted a clear mind after Sloan woke. Closing my eyes, I tried not to think about the conversation I would need to have with him and surrendered myself to sleep.

A RUSTLING SOUND awakened me from my slumber. The unfamiliar surroundings disoriented me at first. It took me a solid fifteen seconds to realize where I was. I glanced out the balcony doors at the setting sun. I'd slept the entire afternoon and most of the evening.

Crap!

I hadn't planned on being here that long. I cast my eyes to Sloan. He was still asleep but stirring. The sound of his movement must have been what prompted me to wake. Reaching down into my purse, I retrieved my cell phone to check the time. When I looked at the screen, I saw there were three missed text messages from Gabby.

Today

4:03 PM, Gabby: *Any thoughts about dinner? I thought maybe we could go down to the pier.*

4:33 PM, Gabby: *On second thought, I don't feel like going anywhere. I'm perfectly content to stay lying by the pool. How about we order pizza instead? Veggie toppings only, of course.*

7:14 PM, Gabby: *Hey, is everything okay? I'm getting worried.*

Guilt washed over me, feeling terrible about leaving her after she'd flown all the way here to see me. Typing as fast as my fingers would allow, I sent back an apology.

8:06 PM, Me: *Gabs, I'm really sorry. When I got here, Sloan was a bit of a mess, and I didn't want to leave him. I'm not sure how much longer I'm going to be.*

I saw the three little dots on the screen, signaling she was typing. A few seconds later, my phone vibrated with her response.

8:08 PM, Gabby: *I figured as much. Don't worry about it. I was starving, so I went ahead and ordered the pizza. There are leftovers here for you.*

8:09 PM, Me: *I feel awful. Thanks for understanding. I'll text you when I leave here.*
8:11 PM, Gabby: *Don't feel bad at all! I'm fine. I already assumed you'd be spending the night with that hottie. I'm completely jealous, by the way. Take your time. I won't wait up. Have fun!*

I glanced at the bed, then at the bent curtain rod and the hole in the wall.

Fun?

If Gabby only knew half of what had gone on here, she'd be screaming at me to get out. There was nothing fun about what happened earlier, and I didn't expect things to get any better after Sloan woke.

19

Sloan

There was a stabbing pain piercing from one temple to the other. I tried to blink to rid myself of it, only to be blinded by rays from the setting sun coming through the balcony doors. Rolling away from the sunlight, I brought my hands up to my head and squeezed. My stomach pitched. It felt as if I'd been run over by a Mack Truck.

I lay there for a moment, waiting for the churning in my stomach to subside. As I did so, a feeling of awareness came over me, almost as if I were being watched. Slowly opening my eyes, I allowed them to adjust to the light. When my vision finally came into focus, I saw Kallie sitting in a chair in the corner of the room—and that's when it all came flooding back.

The whiskey.

The argument with Kallie.

Shit! What the fuck was I thinking?

Almost as soon as the question popped in my head, I knew the answer. Memories of my crash had blended with Tyler's, bringing back the terrible moment when my life had ended for all intents and purposes. I squeezed my eyes shut tight, trying to block out the images.

"How are you feeling?" Kallie asked.

I peered at her through squinted eyes.

"Like hell," I mumbled.

"I would imagine. How much did you drink?"

"I'm not sure."

"I saw the empty prescription bottle downstairs." Although she said it as a statement, I could tell she was fishing for an answer about whether I'd been under the influence of oxy too.

I closed my eyes again and tried to recall the order of events after I got home last night. I remembered sitting at the kitchen table, pouring shot after shot. I'd tried going to bed, but memories of the crash plagued me, and I couldn't sleep, so I came downstairs and drank some more. I recalled getting the bottle of oxy and struggling with the childproof cap. I was completely wasted by that point and had fumbled the pills, causing them to roll across the hardwood floor and disappear under the couch. I looked for them for a bit but gave up and opened another bottle of Jack instead. Everything was somewhat of a blur after that, but I was almost certain I hadn't taken them.

"Kallie, if you are wondering if I took the pills, I didn't. I thought about taking them, but I dropped them somewhere in the living room. I think they rolled under the couch."

"That might explain why the living room looked as if someone had tossed it. Do you feel like getting up? A shower and some food will work wonders."

"Maybe."

"I'll go downstairs and see about throwing together

something to eat," she told me and stood up from the chair. "While I do that, you can clean up, then come downstairs to put something other than whiskey into your system."

There was no missing the level of disdain in her voice, but her expression told a different story altogether. She was looking at me with a mix of sadness and pity. I turned away from her, embarrassed by my behavior. I didn't deserve her sympathy. I only had myself to blame.

After she went downstairs, I slowly made my way to the bathroom. Turning on the faucet, I stripped down, then stepped under the showerhead. Bracing myself against the tiled wall with two hands, I let the water stream over me and tried to think of a way to rationalize what happened with Kallie. I knew I'd been awful to her during my drunken rage. If being an asshole was an art form, I'd mastered it. After the way I'd treated her, I owed her an explanation.

Once I was showered and dressed, I felt significantly better but not great. Making my way downstairs, I found a steaming cup of coffee and a bottle of water sitting on the kitchen table. Kallie walked toward me, carrying two plates with sandwiches and potato chips. After she set the plates down on the table, I inspected the food more carefully. One sandwich was piled high with salami, and the other appeared stacked with lettuce and tomatoes only.

"A lettuce and tomato sandwich?" I asked in confusion.

"I had to make do with what was in the fridge. No worries. I didn't expect to find Tofurky in your house," she said with a laugh. "Just think of it as a BLT without the B."

"That can't possibly taste good."

"Not my favorite, but it's fine for now. You also have some blocks of cheese in there. I can cut that up if either of us is still hungry after we have this. Now, sit. Eat," she ordered and pointed to the food on the table.

After we both took a seat, I watched her from the opposite

side of the table as she sprinkled salt and pepper on the tomatoes, then dug into the blandest sandwich imaginable like it was the best thing she'd ever tasted. I shook my head and picked up my salami on rye.

"What are you doing here? I mean, I thought you were going to Napa Valley with your friend, Gabby."

"I caught a flat tire, so plans changed. It's quite the tale, to be honest," she added with a laugh. "But I think it was fated. After Cooper called, I—"

"Cooper?" I interrupted. "Why did he call you?"

"I mentioned it to you earlier, but you must have forgotten. Cooper is the reason I came here today. He was worried about you after the crash you witnessed yesterday."

I pressed my lips together in a tight line, annoyed to know Cooper had needlessly bothered her.

"He shouldn't have worried. I'm fine."

She arched up one eyebrow, her expression skeptical.

"Are you really?"

I wasn't, but I didn't want to get into it with her. Instead of answering, I focused on eating. Following my lead, she did the same. Neither of us said a word until the food had been cleared from our plates. Decidedly done, Kallie pushed her plate away and sat back in her chair. Her bright green eyes looked thoughtful, and I could sense her hesitancy before she finally spoke.

"Sloan, I want you to tell me about your accident—and I don't mean the technical stuff I can read about online. I want to know more details about the pain you experienced from your injuries, the rehab, your feelings during that time, and all the rest. I should have pushed you to tell me before now, but I allowed my personal feelings to get in the way. As your agent, I need to know every tiny detail—including the details about the argument you had with your mother over your father."

My head snapped up in surprise, suddenly remembering

what she'd said about me not being like my father. In my drunken stupor, I couldn't focus enough to press her on it. But now I was more than ready to.

"How the hell do you know about that?" I demanded.

She blinked, and it was easy to see she was shocked by the coolness in my voice. For me, it was an automatic response. Talking about the accident and my parents stirred up an ache I'd spent a year trying to bury. When she eventually spoke, it was apparent she was choosing her words carefully.

"How I know doesn't matter. Your feelings about it are all I care about. I only know a little of the story—and certainly not enough to protect you from any negative press. People talk, but I want to hear the whole thing from you. If I understand, maybe I can help you rewrite the stars."

I nearly scoffed.

Rewrite the stars. Right.

I closed my eyes, knowing I should never have expected a mundane response from someone like her. She wasn't built that way. There was always a deeper meaning.

"Kallie, I really don't want to talk about it. I've spent the better part of a year trying to forget it."

"Maybe that's why you can't get past it and why you got so drunk last night. Maybe you *need* to talk about it."

"Kallie... I can't."

She moved over to sit in the chair next to me and placed her hand on my knee. She peered up at me, and I found myself mesmerized by the intensity in her eyes. Her touch could calm the monster inside of me trying to break free. She made me a different person—a better person.

"Talk to me, Sloan," she murmured.

My throat clogged with emotion, and I tore my gaze from hers. A war raged in my head, wanting to tell her everything yet wanting to keep it all buried at the same time. She didn't understand. She couldn't hear the sounds of screeching tires and crunching metal that haunted me by day and slithered into my dreams at night. She didn't know I could still taste blood in my mouth, the metallic hints as fresh as it was on the day of the crash. Then there was the agonizing pain—both physical and emotional—that followed for months afterward.

Her warm hand shifted from my knee to cover my hand, ripping me away from a dark time and back to the present. I looked down at her slender fingers, then up her arm until my sight landed on her angelic face. Kallie stared back with eyes full of concern.

"Alright. I'll tell you," I conceded.

She smiled tentatively, seeming pleased but also cautious.

"It's a nice evening. If you're through eating, why don't we take this conversation outside?"

I nodded my agreement and stood up from the chair. Leaving the remains of our dinner on the kitchen table, I allowed Kallie to take my hand and lead me outside. Once there, I took a deep breath. The fresh air felt good and helped to clear my head. It made me realize how stifling it had become when we were in the kitchen.

I looked around and noticed one of the patio chairs toppled over. I had a vague recollection of shoving it aside in a fit of anger, but I couldn't remember beyond that. Bending over, I grabbed the arm of the chair to flip it upright. I motioned for Kallie to sit down, then took a seat next to her.

"Where do you want me to begin?" I asked.

"I don't know. It's your story." Sympathy and understanding were prevalent in every line of her expression, but the pity was also back in her eyes once more. It was the last thing I wanted. Tearing my gaze from her, I stared out across the yard. The sun had set entirely, leaving faint hints of purple to blend with the dark night sky.

"I suppose I should start with the morning of the crash. That's when everything went bad. I was heading up a practice session at Motor Club Speedway. Before we got into the cars, I'd instructed one of the crew members to play America's "Ventura Highway" on one of the portable speakers we kept in the pit. Like you believe in the stars and the moon, I have my own superstitions. I never race—for practice or competitively—before letting the song play through." I paused, not wanting to admit that hearing the song now just made me want to vomit. "Anyways, this punk-ass reporter showed up and started asking me a bunch of questions about my father. I didn't want to talk to him, and I was pissed that he was interrupting my pre-race routine."

"What was he asking you?"

"It was the usual bullshit questions at first, but then he wanted to know why I never apologized for what my father did. I didn't know what he was talking about, and I tried to ignore him, but he was a persistent fucker who wouldn't let up. Back in the day, my father was a big deal in the racing world. He was a Formula One racer—a really good one. Still, he wasn't unlike every other racer. He worried about fatal crashes on the track but tended to think he was invincible on the open road. Before hitting the height of his career, he died in a ten-car pileup on Ventura Freeway. Hence the reason "Ventura Highway" was my jam—it was kind of like a salute to him. Naturally, reporters speculated about my chosen career path because of that, but this reporter started saying stuff no other reporter had."

I eyed Kallie for a moment, noticing that she didn't look surprised by anything I was saying.

"Go on," she prompted.

"Do I need to? It looks like you already know everything I'm saying."

"Not everything."

"Have it your way." I shook my head and sighed. "Anyways,

the reporter accused my father of being responsible for the accident on the freeway. He said my dad was drunk at the time of the crash. I was taken aback since that was the first time I'd ever heard anything like that. My mother happened to be at the track that day, which wasn't uncommon whenever I was practicing or competing. I immediately confronted her about it. She was hesitant to tell me at first but couldn't deny the reporter's accusations in the end. They were all true."

"I can't imagine that was easy to hear."

"No, it wasn't. It was a blow like I can't describe. You have to remember that there wasn't internet back then, so any reporting on his accident was all in newspaper archives. Why would I think to dig up the information when I thought my mother had already told me all I needed to know? I was just a little kid when my dad died, but I'd idolized him all my life. It pissed me off to find out my mother had lied, and I wanted more details, but it was time to get behind the wheel. I stormed away. And then..." I trailed off and raked my hands through my hair as I tried to tell the story without hearing the sounds that lived in my memory. "Then the crash happened fifteen minutes later. If you've ever been in an accident, you know the sound of metal crunching. I can still hear it to this day. Everything just happened so fast—one minute, I felt cocky about schooling a rookie, and the next, I was spinning out. I have a vague recollection of the spectator crowd cheering like crazy after they pulled me out of the car, but that's all I remember."

"I'm so sorry, Sloan."

"For what? I knew better than to get behind the wheel when distracted. I preached to my crew, and other drivers about the importance of staying focused all the damn time, yet I didn't follow my own advice. That was one the first thoughts I'd had when my crew arrived to cut me from the wreckage—that I'd fucked up and lost focus."

"What about what happened after? With..." She hesitated. "With your mother."

"My mother," I spat out bitterly. I paused and took a deep breath, steeling myself before I had to tell her the rest. The mere mention of my mother grated on my nerves, but it also caused the most severe kind of ache—a contradiction of emotion I had never been able to sort out. Closing my eyes, I pictured her blurred face as I raced by her on the track right before the crash. It was the last time I saw her, and my words preceding that had been laden with anger. "Why do you want to know about my mother?"

"Well, I know she committed suicide," she answered softly.

"Fuck. Is there anything you don't know? What else did Cooper tell you when he called?" I demanded, feeling incredibly betrayed.

"Cooper didn't tell me anything. I've never discussed any of this with him. Rochele is the one who told me the night we all went out for dinner. She was trying to explain why you got so snippy with me when I'd asked about your parents."

Pushing up from the chair, I shoved a frustrated hand through my hair and began to pace the patio.

"That was over a month ago, Kallie. You've known this whole time?"

"As I told you, I only know a bit. I didn't press you because I thought you would talk about it in your own time. Rochele wasn't able to explain how you feel—only you can do that."

"Yeah, well—she's got some fucking nerve. Rochele knows what it feels like to be plagued by memories of a car accident. She's been through it. She had no business telling you anything about what happened."

"Sloan, please. Don't be mad at her. She was only trying to help."

I wanted to be angry, but I couldn't be. Kallie was right. Rochele didn't do anything wrong. I was glad Kallie had heard it first from someone I trusted, rather than reading tabloid articles full of half-truths. I was just upset because I didn't want to be talking about this. It made me feel unsettled and vulnerable, knowing that every protective barrier I'd built to protect myself was violently crashing down with every word I spoke.

I turned my back to her and looked out across the yard. The sky was now dark and bleak, the only light coming from the moonbeams peeking out occasionally from a passing cloud. It matched my current state of mind—as if Kallie was the only ray of light cutting through my darkness.

"My mother killed herself three days after the accident. She slit her wrists in the bathtub," I said quietly, not entirely sure if I was talking to Kallie or myself. "I'd been put in a medically-induced coma and didn't find out about what she did until a month later. When the doctors said they didn't think I would survive my injuries, it was assumed that she couldn't handle losing me on top of losing my dad. I don't know that for sure, though—as I said, it's just an assumption. She didn't leave a note or any other form of explanation. Some claim that people take their own lives due to mental illness, but all I can see is her selfishness. There's no excuse for what she did. What kind of mother abandons her son when he's fighting for his life?"

I felt a hand press softly on my arm and glanced over to see Kallie looking at me with sad eyes.

"I'm sorry, Sloan. She should have been there for you."

"You're damn right she should've been! I was alone, stuck in a hospital bed, with the left side of my body completely immobile. I had a concussion, several broken ribs, and needed a ventilator just to fucking breathe. When the doctors woke me from the coma and removed the vent, I was scared out of my mind. I was terrified I'd never walk again. I couldn't even hold a goddamned spoon with my left hand. It took eight months of rehab, five days a week, to get me back to almost normal—almost being the keyword," I added bitterly.

"Tell me what 'almost' means. Why did the doctor say you can't race anymore?" she asked tentatively, almost as if she were afraid to voice the question. I understood her hesitancy—I felt it too. I was scared to say the prognosis out loud for fear it would somehow make it truer than it already was.

I turned to face her and found nothing but patience in her wide emerald eyes as she waited for me to continue.

"About a month before you showed up, the rehab facility arranged for me to go into a car simulator. I was pushing the docs hard to clear me for racing. Dr. Haskell, my surgeon, conferred with the physical therapists, and they decided to test my reflexes to see how I'd fare before giving me clearance. I didn't pass their test."

"Why not?"

"I suffered too much loss of stamina. I couldn't press the gas or brake pedals for long periods without experiencing extreme pain in my left hip. Even now, I have to be careful with the way I stand. Mornings are the worst, though, because that's when the joint is the stiffest."

"How do you manage to drive a regular car?"

"Custom paddles on the steering wheel. I only switch over to them when my hip is acting up. The technology is great and has helped me a lot, but it isn't up to snuff for race cars."

"I never would have known. You've never given any inclination that your hip bothered you."

"Most days, it's fine. I was relentless with my PT to make sure of it."

"It had to be a tough road, and going through all of that without family..." She trailed off, looking thoughtful. "My mother has always been so supportive of me—and my father too, even though I didn't meet him until I was seventeen."

I cocked a curious brow at her. "Seventeen?"

"Yeah. My parents are kind of a not-so-perfect second-chance romance. If you ever meet my father, I'm sure he'll tell you—right down to his *Fade Into You* tattoo that ended up being my parents wedding song."

"Mazzy Star. Good tune," I mused.

Kallie smiled wistfully for moment, almost as if she were lost in a memory.

"He loves to tell everyone about the summer he met my mother by the lake at Camp Riley. They fell in love under the stars but were tragically separated until he became—as he likes to joke—her very own Colonel Brandon seventeen years later. He gets all sentimental about it, but that's a fairytale for a different day. My point is, I've always had parental support. I can't imagine having to go through what you did all by myself."

"It wasn't easy. Before my mother killed herself, she had always supported me. She never missed a single race. I may have been mad at her for not telling me the truth about my dad, but I would have gotten over it with time. However, I don't think I can ever forgive her for leaving me alone when I needed her the most. I'd always been independent, even as a kid. But this time, I couldn't do it by myself. There were moments of both debilitation and exhilaration as I fought to take a step or hold a utensil just to feed myself. It was humbling in ways I can't explain. I'm just grateful I had good friends to help me through the worst of it. Cooper was there a lot when the rehab got really tough. He understood racing was all I had left and knew why my recovery was so important. I fought so damn hard and did everything I was told to do in order to get behind the wheel again, but now..."

I let the sentence go unfinished, unable to articulate what 'now' meant for me anymore.

"I get it, Sloan. Really, I do."

I shook my head, needing her to understand how I'd gotten to this point.

"Before my accident, I rarely drank because I thought it clouded the mind. I hated not feeling in control. It seemed like drinking was the only thing I *could* control after my accident, and it gave me an escape. When I saw Tyler crash, everything just came flooding back. All I could think of was making those memories go away. I didn't want to feel anything, so I came home, grabbed a bottle, and—"

"You don't have to explain anymore," she interrupted and wrapped her arms around my waist.

Grateful she was giving me a reprieve, I pulled her tight to my chest and buried my face in her hair. I was emotionally spent, yet I also felt like I could finally breathe. Perhaps she was right—after holding it all in for so long, maybe I did need to get this off my chest. I suddenly realized how much of a struggle things had been and how exhausting it was to go through the motions day in and day out, knowing racing was forever out of my reach. Since meeting Kallie, those endless moments felt easier to endure, as if she alone had the power to keep me grounded.

She pulled back to look at me and afforded me a small smile. At that moment, I was completely lost in her. I returned her smile and silently wondered what it was I did to deserve this eccentric rainbow goddess. Reaching up, I touched a blue lock that was intertwined with her natural blonde, recalling what she'd said about the blue.

"I hate knowing that I made you sad. I don't want to see you wearing blue ever again, Rainbow Brite. If it means I can never have another drink again, so be it—no more drinking, no more worry about pills. You deserve better."

"Sloan, when I came here today and saw you the way I did..." She trailed off, seeming to collect her thoughts. "I can't explain what it felt like. I just know I can't do anything like that with you again. If there's a repeat of what happened earlier, I'll be on the first plane back to D.C. I need you to promise me—no more getting completely wasted and no more pills."

"I promise."

Placing a finger under her chin, I tilted her head up so I could lean in and press my lips to hers. She tentatively opened for me, her tongue sliding over mine. After the turmoil of the past twenty-four hours, she tasted so damn good. All I wanted was her.

20

Sloan

Our slow kiss quickly evolved into frantic heat. It was as if all the strained emotion from the past hour had suddenly combusted into a flame. I pulled back, wanting Kallie to understand how desperate I was for her at this moment. I cradled her face in my hands and stared into her eyes. Her cheeks were flushed, and her gaze was like molten fire. The passion burning in those expressive pools of green was almost too much to bear. I'd never felt this way about anyone before—never felt so desperate. I didn't know how or when it happened, but I was falling hard for this woman. I needed her more than she realized. My throat thickened with overwhelming emotion.

"I want you, Kallie."

Tracing her fingertip along the neckline of my t-shirt, she gave me a coy smile.

"So, what are you waiting for?"

Within a matter of minutes, we were stumbling up the stairs

to my bedroom, tearing at each other's clothes with an animal-like frenzy. She kicked off her shoes as I yanked her shirt over her head. By the time we made it to my room, she was wearing nothing but her bra and thong panties.

Snaking my arm around her back, I lifted her effortlessly and set her onto the bed. After shedding what remained of my own clothes, I climbed naked on top of her and brought my face down to her breast, biting at a taut nipple through the thin lacy material of her bra. She gasped and threw her head back. Her need was just as hot as mine. Her bodily responses to my touch were the strongest of aphrodisiacs, driving me to the point of madness.

I flicked my tongue up the side of her neck and stopped to nip at her ear. The rapid succession of her breath matched mine, both of us fueled with nothing but pure carnal need. Moving back to her mouth, we kissed frantically, tongues colliding as her back arched. She moaned into my mouth, causing my body to buzz with endorphins.

Reaching beneath her, I wound my hands behind her back and unclasped her bra. Her glorious tits spilled free, allowing me to roll each peak between my thumbs and forefingers. The air already smelled of sex, creating an all-encompassing vapor designed to intoxicate—and I was drunk on her as her hands unabashedly roamed to explore my body.

I prowled down her torso, my mouth moving over her firm stomach, all the way down to kiss the inside of her knee. When I pushed aside the crotch of her panties, I found her already wet for me. I smiled, loving the way we could go from zero to ten on the Richter scale in just a matter of moments. I slipped a finger inside her heated well and began to stroke her walls. She all but rocketed off the bed, hands fisting in the sheets as her ecstasy slowly built. I slid another finger in and began to flick my tongue over that hard bundle of nerves. Her hips pushed up against me, trembling and fraught with desire, searching in desperation for quick release.

"Oh, Mother of Stars..." she breathed, writhing and panting beneath me. "Please, Sloan. I don't want to wait. I need to feel you inside of me."

Her begging for it may have been the biggest turn-on yet. I grunted, not wanting to waste another minute. A fire burned through my bloodstream. My need to be inside her was fierce.

Pulling my fingers from the clutches of her body, I brought them to my mouth. She watched me with intense arousal as I made a slow act of licking them clean. She whimpered and reached for me. Leaning in, I kissed her, allowing her to taste the sweet tanginess of her essence on my tongue before moving to sit up. Sliding my hands down her waist, I looped my thumbs through the sides of her panties and pulled them down her legs.

Now that she was completely naked, I took a moment to appreciate every line and every curve. She had a body that would make any man lose rational judgment, and I wasn't exempt. As she stared up at me with eyes filled with unadulterated lust, my brain all but short-circuited.

"Tell me again, Kallie," I growled. "Tell me what you need."

Her eyes flashed with desire, causing my cock to throb and ache, knowing I was so close to feeling her snug heat. She didn't hesitate with her response.

"I need you inside me—now!" she gasped.

After making quick work with a condom, I positioned my body to hover over hers. Bracing one hand on the headboard for balance, I used the other to notch my throbbing tip to the outside of her waiting entrance.

"Are you ready for me, baby? This won't be gentle."

"Sloan, please," she begged again.

In one quick thrust, I plunged my shaft through her tight clasp until it was completely sheathed. She cried out and brought her legs up to wrap them around my hips. Pulling me in closer, she gave me all the leverage I needed to drive all the way home. A low groan rumbled from somewhere deep in my chest.

"Fuck, Kallie. It's like you were made for me." I drove into her again, and she let out another gasp as her body worked to accommodate my girth. "That's it. Take me. All of me."

The rippling of her heat drove me wild, but I held steady as I waited for her to get there. I hissed through clenched teeth and pushed harder. By the time I felt her building orgasm clench around me, I was ready to explode. Invigorated by the feel of her slick walls, I increased the speed of my thrusts.

"Sloan!"

"That's it. Scream my name as loud as you want. No neighbors can hear you this time."

Over and over again, I impaled her as she came, each plunge deeper than the last and filling her completely. She met me thrust after thrust, her eyes rolling back as her moans surrendered to screams. Her fingers laced through my hair and tugged in the most erotic way.

The woman in my arms was all fire, and I was entirely lost in her flame. It was an overload of sensations, consuming me with inexplicable, mind-altering need. She made me forget about everything—the past, my injuries, racing. It was as if all her talk about fate was true, and we were destined in the most fundamental ways—like nothing could have stopped us from being together.

She raked her hands down my chest, then back up to grip my shoulders. She squeezed tight, and I could feel her second orgasm begin to pulse around my cock. When she burst apart, something inside me seemed to snap, releasing whatever measure of control I'd been hanging onto. Her cry of ecstasy was all I needed to lose myself. It was my turn.

Dizzying shimmers of white began to dot my vision. I sunk

deep and hard, filling her completely, until my seed erupted. Energy spiked, and I came with such a violent force that I was left shuddering and trembling in her arms.

Our hearts beat wildly against each other. I didn't want to move and break our connection but knew I needed to remove the condom before long. Rolling onto my back, I shed the rubber and tossed it into the wastebasket next to the bed. Sliding my arm beneath Kallie, I pulled her tight to my side. Her heated body curved into mine as we allowed our racing hearts to return to a normal rhythm. We lay there perfectly content, her hand resting peacefully on my chest while I traced the lines of her tattooed shoulder.

I couldn't be sure of how much time passed before the tranquility was broken by the ringing sound of my cell phone coming from downstairs. I ignored it and continued tracing small circles around Kallie's tattoo. The ringing stopped, only to begin again a few minutes later.

"You should get that," Kallie murmured. "It could be Cooper calling to check in."

I groaned in irritation.

"Fine, but don't move. I'll be back in a few."

Swinging my legs over the side of the bed, I pulled on a pair of boxer briefs and made my way downstairs. It took me a minute to locate the phone because I didn't remember where I'd left it. When it began to ring again for the third time, I ended up finding it on the floor next to the couch. Still feeling annoyed over having been ripped from Kallie's arms, I snatched up the phone. My aggravation only grew when I saw Milo's name lighting up the screen.

"What's up, Milo?" I briskly answered.

"Sloan, what are you doing on Monday?"

I scratched my head and tried to remember if Kallie had anything lined up for me.

"Ah, I'm not sure. I'll have to check. Why?"

"Whatever you have going on, cancel it. It turns out Tyler McDermott is going to be out of commission for at least a month. He's banged up pretty bad—concussion and a few fractured ribs—but he's expected to make a full recovery."

"That's fantastic news," I said with relief.

"Yeah, well... not for his sponsors. McDermott won't be cleared in time to race the Motorsports International Legacy League in San Antonio. They're pushing hard for a replacement driver, opening up a huge opportunity for you."

"For me?" I asked in confusion.

"Yeah, you. NASCAR was willing to make an exception and allow a replacement driver in a similar situation a while back. The MILL is following their example. Tyler's car did well in the European circuit, and his sponsors think it could do even better in the U.S. After evaluating the damage, it turns out Tyler suffered more harm than the car did. Mechanics are working around the clock, and the car should be fixed and ready to go within the week. The only thing the sponsors need is someone to drive it. That's where you come in."

I froze, fixating on a proverbial carrot dangling just out of my reach. Substitute drivers were a gray area. Technically, the car qualifies—not the driver. Some argued that replacement drivers made sense for racing teams going for owner's championships. Others said replacement drivers shouldn't be allowed because it isn't fair to fellow competitors who fought hard to earn titles all season long. However, all of that stopped mattering for someone like me the moment my doctors labeled me a disabled driver.

"Milo, you know I can't race."

"Why? Because of a little hip pain? Come on, man. It's one race. I can get you what you need to numb the pain. Don't worry about that."

I knew Milo's offer to help me "numb the pain" ultimately meant one thing—prescription oxy. However, oxy didn't only mask pain with a temporary high. It also slowed the user's reflexes which could have catastrophic consequences for anyone operating a vehicle, even under normal conditions. Milo obviously didn't understand that. I may have stupidly popped a few pills when I shouldn't have, but I'd been aware of how easily someone could become addicted to opioids and recognized the dangers of building a tolerance. I'd been lucky up until this point, and I wasn't sure if I wanted to risk traveling that road again.

"Milo, the entire racing community knows I haven't been cleared to race."

"They don't know shit. For all they know, you took early retirement. Just let me handle the technicalities. This prize money is too big to pass up. All I need to know is if you're in. If you are, I'll need you to report to the track at eleven on Monday morning so we can begin practices and prep. You'll need to get acquainted with a new car and Tyler's crew, as well as get fitted for new gear and schmooze the sponsors. You know the drill."

I fell quiet. Milo's mention of prize money made me pause —not for myself, but Tyler. I recalled what Cooper had said about Tyler's wife, Amy. If I did this and won, I could give the prize money to him, and Amy could get the experimental treatment she needed in Switzerland. However, it was more than just that. Charity aside, I wasn't a saint. The idea of getting behind the wheel again was more than just appealing—it was like being offered the forbidden fruit I couldn't refuse. To know I could feel the rumbling of the engine again in just a matter of days was almost too much to wrap my head around.

As I considered Milo's offer, I began to think about the possibility of pushing through the pain on my own. The occasional painkiller could help if the ache in my hip became too unbearable, just as long as I was sober when I was behind the wheel. I didn't know if that was even an option because I had yet to try—but that's what practice was for.

What if I could prove the doctors wrong? Maybe I can race again.

"Let me think about it," I finally said.

"I need to know by tomorrow."

"Alright, I'll call you."

I ended the call and stared at the blank screen, unsure how to process the turn of events. Setting the phone on the coffee table, I went back upstairs to where Kallie lay naked and waiting. Perhaps if I talked to her about it, she'd help me work through the decision. But on second thought, there was a very good possibility she wouldn't approve—especially if racing meant I had to kill the pain with pills.

"Who was that?" she asked when I entered the bedroom.

"Milo."

"Oh, what did he want?"

I hesitated with my answer, buying time as I shed my boxers and climbed back into bed beside her. Pulling her to my chest, I kissed the tip of her nose. I moved my lips over her cheek, across her jawline, and down to her neck. My cock hardened again, anxious to feel her slick heat once more. I shifted my weight, pulling her on top of me until she was straddling my hips.

"Why he called isn't important," I told her. "The only thing that matters right now is you riding me for the victory lap."

21

Kallie

G abby shuffled into my family room on Monday morning with a loud yawn.

"Ouch! That looks like it hurts," she said when she spotted me standing in a triangle pose in the middle of the room. "I don't know how you do that so early in the morning."

"It's after eight-thirty. It's not early. In fact, it's late for me," I said with a laugh. "Yoga in the morning increases blood flow, stretches your mind, and sets the tone for the day. It's energizing, Gabs. You should try it."

"Mediation does a lot of that, too. Personally, I'd rather sit and meditate with a cup of coffee and let the caffeine stretch my mind—especially after staying up so late," she joked as she pulled the bag of coffee grounds from the cabinet.

"We did get to bed late, but at least we got to make up for the lost time. I still feel horrible about Saturday," I said guiltily, thinking about how I didn't get home from Sloan's house until after one in the morning. To make it up to Gabby, I'd spent all day with her on Sunday. I took her shopping in L.A., and we did the not-so-glamorous walk on Hollywood Boulevard, looking at the terrazzo and brass stars embedded in the sidewalk. We had dinner afterward at an eclectic little restaurant on the Sunset Strip, then came home and talked about everything and anything under the sun long into the night.

"Will you stop stressing about it? I've already assured you—I was perfectly content by the pool all day," she repeated for what must have been the tenth time in the past twenty-four hours.

Standing up, I wiped the sweat from my brow.

"I'm going to take a shower. Your flight leaves at three-thirty, right?"

"Yeah."

"Alright. That gives us the morning together. I thought maybe we could head over to the Santa Monica Pier and—" I stopped short when the sound of my cell phone vibrating on the end table interrupted me. I snagged it and looked at the caller ID. I didn't recognize the number.

"Hello?"

"May I speak to Kallie, please?" said a male voice on the other end of the line.

"This is she."

"Kallie, it's Jeremiah Lanford from Wings Halfway House."

"Oh, hi! I didn't recognize the number. What can I do for you?"

"Last we spoke, you said you would get back with me on when would be a good time for Sloan Atwood to come in and speak. As it turns out, I have a cancelation for this week Friday. Do you think he would be interested in filling it?"

I mentally went through Sloan's calendar for the week. A few engagements were on the schedule with Safe Track, the first one being later on today, but I was reasonably certain

Friday was open. Still, I remembered Sloan's hesitation about speaking with the teens.

"I think Friday will work, but I'll need to get with Sloan first. I'll ask him and get back to you within the hour."

"Excellent! I'll look forward to your call."

After I hung up, I immediately called Sloan. When he answered, he sounded half asleep.

"Let me guess. You need me to pose for a picture in an hour," he said groggily.

"Not exactly." I laughed. "Sorry to call you so early, but I just got a call from Jeremiah Lanford, the guy who runs Wings Halfway House. He wants you to speak on Friday."

"Kallie, I—"

"Before you say no, hear me out. You don't have anything scheduled until four this afternoon. I thought that maybe after Gabby leaves for the airport, the two of us could pop over to Wings for a quick tour. You could get a feel for the place, then decide."

"Yeah...about this afternoon." He paused, and I sensed his hesitation. "Something came up. I need you to cancel everything on my schedule for the next couple of weeks, maybe longer."

My brow furrowed in confusion.

"Cancel? But why?"

He hesitated again.

"I'm going to try racing again, Kallie."

I blinked several times, trying to figure out if I'd heard him correctly.

"But you can't, Sloan. The doctors said—"

"I know what the doctors said, but there's a chance I might be able to push through it. I won't know unless I try. Tyler McDermott's accident means his sponsors need a driver to replace him. I thought about it and told Milo yesterday that I would do it. Racing in the MILL is huge, Kallie. I can't pass up the opportunity without trying."

I had no idea what the hell racing in the MILL meant and didn't waste time trying to figure it out. Instead, I zeroed in on one thing—Milo. My jaw clenched at the mention of him. I thought back to Saturday night when he'd called Sloan. I'd have bet my last dollar that this sudden opportunity was discussed on that call—and Sloan hadn't said a word to me about it.

"It would have been nice if you'd clued me in," I said somewhat curtly. As his agent, I was annoyed that he'd kept it from me, yet knew I had no right to be mad on a personal level. He was a grown man who could make his own decisions. Still, I couldn't help but think about his past injuries and worry that he could somehow hurt himself. After everything he went through, a setback could be devastating.

"Kallie, don't be upset."

"I'm not upset," I lied.

"Yes, you are. I can hear it in your voice."

I sighed and pinched the bridge of my nose. I spotted Gabby out of the corner of my eye, looking at me with concern.

"I just don't want to see you have a setback. Against all odds, you've made almost a complete recovery, but you still have issues with your hip—you told me so yourself. There's a reason the doctors didn't clear you."

"I told you why the doc didn't give me clearance—it was only because my stamina pressing the gas and brake pedals was shot. It had nothing to do with the replacement joint and everything to do with the pain I experienced. I want to see if I can work through it."

"But Sloan—"

"Look, Kallie," he interrupted impatiently. "I'm headed to the track in a couple of hours. This week is just setup and practice.

The MILL isn't for another six weeks. Why don't you come down to the track with Gabby? You can see for yourself how it all works. I promise to know my limits. And when you come, make sure to wear your rainbows. I need your optimistic energy."

Before I could respond, the line went dead. I pulled the phone away from my ear and stared at it in exasperated disbelief. I hated being hung up on—especially when I wasn't through talking. Fighting off the urge to throw the phone across the room, I tossed it on the couch where decidedly much less damage would occur.

"Damn, he can be so infuriating," I grumbled.

"What? What did he do? What happened?" Gabby hurriedly asked.

I looked at my friend's alarmed expression and sighed in resignation.

"Want to hit the race track today? I can explain on the way there."

WHEN GABBY and I arrived at the track a couple of hours later, we stood off to the side of the pit lane and watched the flurry of activity. Fans dotted the stands, excited by the possibility of seeing celebrity race car drivers, while AC/DC blasted from the speakers strategically placed around the track. Even though there wasn't a race today, there was no denying the exhilarating energy in the air. Everywhere I looked, people buzzed about. Judging from their various tasks, I could guess who the crew members were, but the two men talking to Sloan were a mystery. They were decked out in expensive suits, making them stand out among the crew members wearing tattered jeans, stained T-shirts, and baseball caps boasting various racing emblems.

"Who are those men Sloan is talking with? That one guy in

the navy suit is F-I-N-E fine," Gabby said appreciatively, and I laughed.

Sloan must have heard me because he turned away from the two men and glanced in our direction. The confidence and ease with which he stood made his presence bigger than the entire track. When his eyes landed on me, he smiled and didn't bother to mask the heat in his stare. I watched his gaze skirt up and down my body, causing butterflies to flip in my stomach. I loved the way he looked at me sometimes, as if he were picturing me naked beneath him, touching and exploring every inch.

His intoxicating gaze lingered on me for a moment longer before turning back to the two men and pointing to where Gabby and I stood.

"I'm not sure who those guys are, but it looks like we're about to find out," I said. "They're headed this way now."

"Kallie," Sloan said as he approached. "Just the woman I was looking for."

"Oh?" I said in surprise, looking from Sloan to the other two men.

"Yeah. I want you to meet Wyatt Bates and Joe Corbin, representatives from Kapton Motor Oil, the head sponsor for Tyler's car that I'm going to race." I raised an eyebrow but didn't comment on Sloan's certainty about whether he *could* actually race or not. Instead, I extended my hand to the two men.

"It's a pleasure."

"Wyatt and Joe, this is Kallie and her friend Gabby. Kallie is my..." Sloan trailed off, not seeming to know how he should introduce me. In truth, I didn't know either. I supposed we could have assumed I was his girlfriend. However, we had yet to discuss making our relationship public. I thought it was best for Sloan's reputation to keep it quiet, and until I told my father about us, it was best for me too. The last thing I needed was for him to hear about me carrying on with a client from the press.

Smiling, I took the lead and broke the awkward silence.

"I'm Sloan's P.R. agent. Gabby is a friend of mine. She's in town visiting, and I thought I'd bring her down to the track to see what the fuss was all about."

"It's nice to meet you," Gabby said.

Wyatt held out his hand for her, which she readily took. He was the guy in the navy suit who she'd been eyeing up, and I could easily see why. The man oozed sex appeal, and if his arrogant stance was any indication, I thought he knew it too. He gave Gabby a flirtatious wink, and she all but swooned at his feet. I wasn't sure if I wanted to laugh or roll my eyes.

"Is it safe to assume I'll be working closely with your company over the next few weeks?" I asked, hoping to save my friend from embarrassing herself.

"Yes, ma'am. We're expecting good things from Sloan," Wyatt said.

"We were thrilled when he agreed to come out of retirement and fill in for Tyler," Joe added.

Retirement?

"Yes, well... I guess everything happens for a reason," was all I could say as I discretely flashed Sloan a questioning look. He didn't notice my confusion, nor did he seem surprised by what Joe had said.

"We should plan a time for you to come down to the Kapton Corporate offices and meet with our marketing team," Wyatt suggested. "We have our own PR strategy already in the works, but since you know Sloan better than we do, we'd like to pick your brain on ways we might be able to heighten that PR."

"That sounds great," I agreed and reached into my purse for a business card. "My number is on here. Give me a call, and we can set something up."

"We'll look forward to it," Wyatt said as he pocketed my card. "Sloan, we're going to head out. Ace Apparel should be here in an hour to fit you for new gear with the Kapton logo.

The car should be ready to go by Wednesday. Joe and I will be back then."

"Sounds like a plan," Sloan said. The three men shared a hearty handshake, then Joe and Wyatt walked away. Sloan turned back to Gabby and me. "Come on. I want to show you something."

"Wait. I need to go over a few things with you first. Before driving here, I made some calls to change your schedule. I've canceled your Safe Track events for this week and put off Jeremiah for the time being." I paused, suddenly remembering what Joe Corbin had said about Sloan coming out of retirement. "Also, why does Kapton think you came out of retirement? What was that all about?"

"Milo told them that, and I just went along with it. I didn't get into the details with him."

"Well, don't you think you should, especially since it's not entirely true?"

"Kallie," he interrupted, clasping my face between his palms. There was a mischievous sparkle in his eye that piqued my curiosity. "Thank you for clearing my schedule, and as much as I'd like to debate with you about what Milo said, does it matter? I'm more interested in something else right now. I'm going to try racing again, and that's all I'm focused on. Are you with me?"

"Yeah, Sloan. I'm with you."

"Good." He beamed and reached for my hand, but I pulled away and shook my head.

"I think it's best if we keep our relationship on the down-low for now," I explained. "You'll be in the spotlight again soon enough, and we don't need to give the press any reason to speculate more than they already will."

Sloan shrugged.

"Whatever you say. You're the boss. But just so you know, it's going to be hard keeping my hands off of you if you continue showing up at the track in those little shorts."

I flushed, and Gabby snorted a laugh, which only caused my blush to deepen. I looked down at my black t-shirt and cut-off jean shorts. I hadn't expected to conduct business today, or I would have dressed more appropriately. I'd deliberately worn these clothes, knowing I wouldn't care if I accidentally brushed up against grease like I had the last time I was at the track.

Seeming oblivious to my embarrassment, Sloan turned to walk away. Gabby and I followed him across the track and toward a set of tall, wide double doors.

"I think it's pretty ironic that Kallie, of all people, is going to be working side by side with a motor oil company," Gabby pointed out as we walked.

"Tell me about it. I was thinking about that when I shook their hands. I know it's part of the business, but I'm going to have a hard time overlooking the fact that they're one of the biggest culprits of air pollution. I'm going to have to make a sizable donation to Greenpeace just to ease my conscience."

"Just remind me not to tell you what the gas mileage is for these babies," Sloan said with a chuckle as he slid open the large metal doors. A parking lot opened up on the other side, revealing four large red trailers, three of them built around matching semi-trucks. They stood tall, sleek, and shiny, with the Kapton Motor Oil logo emblazoned in black and silver lettering along the sides.

"Fancy," Gabby remarked.

"This is how we'll get to San Antonio, Texas for the race. International races would have a different transportation system for obvious reasons, but U.S. races typically travel by road. That right there," he said, pointing to a windowless trailer, "that's the hauler. It's how the car will be transported. The other three are totor homes for the top-ranking crew members. Most likely, additional haulers will be added for equipment, but these are to showcase."

"Showcase?" I asked.

"The sponsors can go a little overboard with these things. It's like there's this unspoken competition to see which team can pull up looking the best. The drivers never mind because it's to our benefit." Reaching up, he unlatched the door to the totor home that had Tyler McDermott's name written on the side, and I wondered if the name would soon be changed to Sloan's. "Step inside, and I'll show you what I mean."

Climbing aboard, I looked around the surprisingly luxurious layout. There was a spacious kitchen and dining area, complete with smaller-than-average stainless steel appliances. Black leather armchairs and a couch occupied what could only be described as a living room, with a large screen T.V. hanging on the wall adjacent to them.

"Wow! You weren't kidding about these being a showcase!" Gabby gushed, sliding her hand over the black and silver veined marble countertop in the kitchen area. "It's gorgeous in here."

"The sides pop out, which makes for more room. It can sleep up to eight, but the king bed in the back is reserved for the driver. That's me," he added with a wink.

I eyed him curiously, once again biting my tongue about whether or not he could even race, as I followed him toward the back. He sounded so happy and excited. I'd never seen him quite like this before—he was like a little kid on Christmas showing off his new toys. Who was I to kill his spirit?

When we reached the back room, a small master suite with a private bathroom came into view. The composite wood walls were painted a muted gray, and the bed was covered with a plush red comforter and black throw pillows. It matched the overall sleek and extremely masculine style of the upscale RV.

"I like it," I said as I stepped past Sloan to get a better look at the room.

Moving to the left to make room for Gabby to enter, Sloan took advantage of the tight space by placing his hands on my hips. With minimal effort, he pulled me back, so the curve of my spine was against his hard chest. He leaned in, and I could feel his breath hot on my neck while he not-so-subtly slid one hand under the hem of my T-shirt to connect with the bare skin at my waist. I shivered at the contact but quickly pushed his hand down and cast a side-eye at Gabby to see if she'd noticed. She was looking around the room, seemingly unaware that Sloan was trying to feel me up right in front of her.

"I can't wait to feel you naked in that bed," Sloan whispered softly into my ear. I stifled a gasp as I felt his fingers graze under my shirt once more.

"Um," Gabby said, making a loud show of clearing her throat. "I'll just step outside and leave you two to it."

"No, it's fine!" I said hurriedly and slapped Sloan's hand away. "Sloan just needs to learn how to behave."

I angled my head to give him a pointed stare. He laughed and held up his hands in mock surrender.

"Hey, don't blame me. I told you what I think about those shorts."

"We should head back anyway," I told them and stepped back out of the bedroom, away from Sloan's wandering hands. "The apparel people will be here soon, and Gabby needs to get to the airport by—"

"Sloan!" yelled a male voice. Startled, I turned and saw Milo poking his head inside the door to the totor home.

"What's up, Milo?" Sloan asked.

Milo looked right past Gabby and me as if we weren't even standing there and motioned with his head toward the track.

"Stop fucking around in here. You can have a threesome *after* the race," he snapped. My spine instantly stiffened in indignation. "Ace Apparel just arrived. You need to go get fitted."

"I'll be right there," Sloan replied.

"When you're through with that, I need to talk to you. Meet me in the sponsor's lounge." Milo paused, his gaze quickly flashing to my face, before looking back at Sloan. "And when you come, come alone."

Then he was gone, leaving the totor home door to slam closed in his wake.

"I really don't like that man," I murmured.

"I'm pretty sure the feeling is mutual," Gabby observed.

"Milo just hates it when his drivers are distracted by women," Sloan rationalized. "I'm sorry, Kallie. I know he can be a real dick, but I can't cut him loose now. I wouldn't be here today if he didn't land this opportunity for me. I'll talk to him, though. He needs to cut that shit out. There's no reason for him to be so rude to you."

"Don't worry about it. It's not worth it," I tried to assure. However, inside I was seething. I never wanted to slap someone as much as I did Milo. He was an asshole—plain and simple. There was no other word to describe him.

The three of us exited the totor home and made our way back to the track.

"Things are moving along pretty quick, Sloan. Have you talked to your doctor or physical therapist about all of this?" I inquired as we walked.

"Not yet."

"Why do I get the feeling that you're not going to?"

"I'll think about it. How long are you two planning on sticking around the track?" he asked, clearly trying to change the subject.

"Not much longer. I thought Gabby and I could take a quick walk around the inside corridor, maybe stop at the gift shop, then leave for the airport."

"So, I'll see you later then?"

I shrugged.

"Possibly. The day sort of flipped upside down on me. I haven't thought much past bringing Gabby to the airport."

Sloan stopped walking, forcing Gabby and me to look back at him.

"Gabby, if you don't mind," Sloan said as he grabbed my hand. "She'll be right back."

Without warning, Sloan all but dragged me a few yards away toward the spectator stands until we rounded the corner into a small secluded alcove behind the seating area.

"Sloan, what are you—" I protested but was immediately silenced when he pressed my back against the concrete wall.

I gasped, but he stifled any protest I may have had by covering my mouth with his. Within a matter of seconds, heat exploded through my veins. His kiss was deep and demanding. I didn't care about who might walk by and see us or about what they might think of a returned celebrity racer caught in a liplock with his PR agent—all that mattered was the passionate power of his lips on mine.

I surrendered to him, allowing his tongue to push past my parted lips. Pulling my hips sharply against him, he forced my back and neck into a slight arch and angled his head to get better access. He groaned against my mouth, the vibration causing my nipples to stiffen in response.

"God, Kallie. I'll never get enough of you," he murmured, then continued to ravish me like a starving man who couldn't get his fill.

I reached up to tangle my fingers through his dark waves, pulling him closer and encouraging him to take more. But much to my regret, he broke the kiss and pulled slightly away. I was breathless from the electrifying sensations coursing through my body, leaving me charged with nowhere to go.

"Well, that was some goodbye kiss," I joked in between pants as I tried to catch my breath.

Pressing his forehead to mine, his blue eyes bored into mine with such intensity that goosebumps formed on my arms.

"That wasn't a goodbye kiss, Kallie. That was a promise of later."

Stepping back, he flashed me one of those lopsided, sexy grins I loved so much, then turned and walked out toward the track. I was left momentarily stunned. Shaking my head to clear it, I followed his path only to find Gabby staring at Sloan as he passed by her. She had a look of total bewilderment on her face.

"What the hell was that all about?" she demanded. I shrugged sheepishly but didn't answer. I couldn't take my eyes off Sloan as he sauntered away. I didn't want him to go, yet I couldn't stay. All I knew was that, after I dropped Gabby off at the airport, I would be counting down the seconds until I experienced Sloan's promise of later. It was crazy how much I always looked forward to our time together. He'd quickly become the reason my sun and moon rose and fell. He was why the stars seemed to twinkle a little brighter and...

Oh my God.

A heaviness began to build in my chest, welling in my throat until I thought I might choke. And at that moment, a sense of perfect clarity burst forth.

I'm falling in love with him.

I knew when I agreed to pursue this thing with us, it would be risky. My emotions had a mind of their own, and I knew I could fall for him. I just never anticipated I would fall this hard and this fast. The realization crashed over me like a tidal wave, crushing me upon impact.

At first, I was flooded with happiness—until the brutal reality washed it all away as I remembered the gypsy's words. Gabby may have told me that Austin paid the fortune teller to say those things, but what if it wasn't all a ruse? What if her words were a real premonition, and I was setting myself up to be broken? If that was the case, it was too late to turn back now. I had a full heart—full of blossoming love for a man who I wasn't sure would love me back. Our relationship was supposed to be temporary. I would be going back to D.C., and if all went well, he'd be going back to his first and only love—racing.

I didn't know how much time had passed, but I was brought to attention by a hand waving in front of my face. I blinked and focused my gaze on a wide-eyed Gabby.

"Sorry, Gabs."

"Shit. You've got it really bad for him."

I studied Gabby's face and wondered if I should share my thoughts.

"I do—I *really* do. I'm not sure what to do about it either," I admitted.

"What do you mean?"

"This is going to sound so stupid, especially after you told me the truth about what Austin did, but what if the gypsy wasn't faking her predictions after all?"

"Oh my God, Kallie. Stop right this minute."

"I told you it would sound stupid," I said with a small laugh that I didn't really feel. "I guess it's been such a foundational belief in my life for so long that it's hard to shake the foreboding feelings about what the gypsy said. Even though I now know it was all a ruse, it's almost like the damage has already been done. Plus, I just can't help considering my history of falling for the wrong guy. I have no illusions when it comes to Sloan. We aren't a fairytale. In a few months, my contract will be over, and we'll go our separate ways. And when that happens, it will be just like the gypsy said, regardless of whether she knew it then or not—my heart will be broken."

"Who says you have to leave when your contract is over?"

"Gabby, I can't stay here. I have a whole life in D.C., and I could never stay away permanently. I'd miss my parents and little sister too much. Emma is growing so fast. I wouldn't miss that for the world."

Gabby tilted her head, seeming to contemplate something for a moment, before giving me a small smile.

"Do you know what I think?" she asked.

"What?"

"I think everything you've experienced in your life has brought you to this moment—the gypsy, Austin's prank, Dean, the job transfer to California, and even the dumb Charlie-Charlie game we used to play. I think the universe was preparing you for something bigger. And maybe, just maybe, Sloan is that something. You'll never know unless you take a chance."

22

Sloan

Kallie and I entered the front door of my house after
having spent the morning at the track. I'd been behind
the wheel practicing almost every day of the past two weeks,
and my hip was feeling the result. Kallie had been by my side
for it all. I loved having her there, but I hated it at the same
time. Her constant presence made it difficult to disguise the
pain when it got really bad. I wasn't sure why I continued to try
to hide it. Perhaps it was my ego not wanting to make me look
weak. She'd been so supportive, and I didn't want her to worry
or second guess my decision to do this.

Deliberately falling behind to stay out of her line of sight, I
followed her into the living room with a slight limp as I
attempted to shift my weight away from my left hip. I managed
to make it to the couch just before she turned toward me.

"How are you feeling?" she asked.

"I'm feeling great," I lied and flashed her a bright smile. "I'm happy with the progress we made today on the track. Tyler's crew and I have really clicked. They're starting to feel like my own now. It's always a good day when we manage to shave a few seconds off the clock."

Her expression was doubtful, but I didn't let my grin falter.

"If you say so," she said with a shake of her head. She walked over to the patio doors, folded her arms, and stared out across the yard.

"Don't believe me?"

"Not really." She sighed, then turned to face me once more. "You try to hide it, but I can see you're hurting, and I don't understand why you're pushing yourself so hard. I get that you want to race again, but why push so quickly for this race in particular? There are other races you can enter, ones that would give you more time to prepare. As it stands right now, you've barely gotten through the past two weeks, and there are still four more weeks to go."

I knew she was right, and I should probably do as she suggested. The pain I felt after only one day behind the wheel had been enough to give me a reason to reconsider. However, after the conversation I had with Tyler a few days earlier, I quickly realized it was too late for me to pull out. He needed me to win this.

"The thought has definitely crossed my mind, but I can't. Not now. It's not just about me, Kallie. It's about Tyler McDermott too."

"Tyler? What about him?"

I leaned back and rubbed my forehead, remembering the anguish in my friend's voice when he talked about Amy.

"It's his wife. She has cancer. After Tyler got home from the hospital last week, I called him. Amy, his wife, is in rough shape —much worse than I realized. He's been in touch with some doctors about an experimental treatment available in Switzerland. He wants to take her there, but the price tag is insane. It's basically going to cost him two-hundred grand just to walk in the door, then seventy-two hundred dollars per treatment after that, spanning three days a week for four months. His wife qualifies for the trial, but he needs the prize money from the MILL to do it."

"I'm not following you. If you race, how does it help him?"

"If I win, it's three million dollars, minus the crew and Milo's cut. That doesn't include any contingency dollars put in by sponsors. Even if I don't win but finish in the top ten, there's still a sizable amount of bonus money to be paid out. Obviously, I'm going to race to win, but I don't plan to keep any prize money. I don't know how I could after hearing about Amy. Tyler is desperate. I'm going to give any winnings I get to the McDermotts so they can get Amy the treatment she needs."

She just stared at me for a few seconds, seeming to take a moment to absorb what I'd said, then walked over to where I was sitting.

"That's a lot of money to give up, Sloan."

"It is," I agreed.

Taking a seat next to me, she placed a soft kiss on my cheek.

"You're a good man," she said softly. "I can't believe you're going to give it all away. I don't know anyone who would do that."

"Don't kid yourself," I brushed off. "I might be doing a good thing, but I have selfish reasons for doing it too. Competing in the MILL will give me the exposure I need to reinstate myself into the racing world. There will be other purses to win."

She eyed me thoughtfully, then clasped my hand between hers and stood up.

"Maybe, maybe not. I just hope you don't kill yourself in the process. You need to be careful with that hip. That said, come on. Let's do some of the yoga techniques I taught you. You need to stretch after racing this morning."

Fuck.

Stretching was the last thing I wanted to do right now. I could barely move from the red-hot pain blistering across my left hip. If I stood up and attempted to twist myself into a pretzel as she did, she would immediately know how bad I was hurting today.

"I will later," I told her. "Right now, I just want to chill for a bit."

"Alright. Take your time. Just make sure to do it. If you don't mind, I'm going to use your shower. I need to get the stink of exhaust out of my hair. I have to meet with the marketing team at Kapton Motor Oil at three, and I don't want to walk in reeking like their product."

"The shower is all yours. I'll take one afterward."

She narrowed her gaze suspiciously, and I knew what she was thinking. Kallie had spent more time at my place than hers as of late. She'd taken numerous showers here—many of which I'd climbed in to join her. However, just the thought of doing that today made the stabbing pain in my hip seem all that much worse.

If she was questioning my sudden lack of libido, she didn't voice it. Instead, she quietly made her way upstairs to the master bath. It wasn't until I heard the faucet turn on that I let out a quiet groan. Shifting my weight, I stood up. Pain shot down my leg, and I winced as I slowly made my way to the kitchen for an ice pack. Alternating cold and heat seemed to work the best when it got this bad.

After securing the ice pack inside the waistband of my tactical racing pants, I went back to the couch. Twenty minutes later, I heard Kallie turn off the shower. Thankfully, my hip was feeling remarkably better—not great, but at least I could stand up without wincing. All I needed to do now was quickly get heat on it, and the shower usually worked best to loosen it up. After I did that, I would attempt the stretches Kallie had suggested.

Placing the ice pack back inside the freezer, I made the seemingly impossible hike up the stairs. When I entered the bedroom, I stopped dead in my tracks. Kallie was standing by the bed digging through her overnight bag, her hair wrapped in a towel, the ends of her hair dripping water down her shoulders onto the carpet. The afternoon sun was shining in through the balcony door, casting a glowing halo around her. She looked like a beautiful, blonde angel.

Not bothering to fight the gravitational pull I always felt from her, I walked over to the bed and sat down on the edge.

"Come here, gorgeous," I said.

When she turned to face me, I reached up and began to pull the towel from her body, but she caught my hand to stop me.

"Sloan, we don't have time. I have to—"

"Shhh. I know you have to leave soon. Trust me and just sit down," I told her and patted the bed next to me. Doing as I asked, she released my hand, allowing the towel to fall from her body. I caught it as she moved to sit naked beside me. "Turn so your back is to me."

Again, she did as I'd instructed. I loved that she was so trusting, even when in the most vulnerable state. It only made me want to be buried balls deep inside of her. If it weren't for the pain in my hip, I'd tell her to blow off the meeting with Kapton so I could do precisely that. I'd spread her wide and savor every inch of her until the sun came up the next day. However, that wasn't my current reality, so I settled for second best instead—and touching Kallie in any way was always at the top of my list of things to do.

Using the towel that had been wrapped around her, I

brought it up to dry her hair, then moved down to wipe away the droplets of water from her arms. I took my time drying her, slowly brushing the soft cotton over her upper body, suddenly overcome with the need to take care of her just as she had been taking care of me for the past couple of weeks.

Leaning in, I kissed along her shoulder, over the delicate outlines of her star and moon tattoo, until I reached her neck. Her breathing became short, coming out in little gasps when I moved the towel around to dry her breasts. My cock grew hard in my pants, and I had to shift to make room for my girth. My movement caused her to turn her head and look at me. Passion had ignited in her emerald greens, a fire burning so hot, my dick instantly stiffened to a near painful level.

"Fuck, Kallie. You can't look at me like that."

"Like what?"

"You know what. You'll never make it to your meeting if you keep it up. You're too damn tempting."

Pulling her naked body against my fully clothed one, I brought my lips to hers. She moaned against my mouth, moving her body against mine to deepen the kiss. I gripped the back of her neck as her hand ran over the span of my chest, digging into the muscles. Sliding her hands under my shirt, her fingertips skimmed the tips of my nipples.

"Shit," I hissed, knowing I wasn't going to be able to put off the inevitable for much longer at this rate. And when she moved her hand to cup the bulge in my pants, I was reminded of how this beautiful, rainbow mermaid goddess could destroy me with just one touch.

Almost reluctantly, Kallie pulled back. Her cheeks were flushed, and her lips were swollen from our kiss that had been cut short.

"Promise me we'll finish this later?" she asked.

"I don't need to promise anything, baby. I can guarantee it."

"I need to get dressed. I have to be out the door in twenty minutes."

Reaching around to squeeze her backside, I gave it a light slap before giving her a quick peck on the nose.

"You better hurry then. Kapton is waiting."

Climbing from the bed, she grabbed her overnight bag and rushed into the bathroom to get ready. I lay back on the bed, suddenly realizing how much I enjoyed having her here. In fact, I didn't like the idea of her *not* being here. While we'd barely been together long enough to say we should move in together, I couldn't help but fantasize about making that a reality one day. When we weren't lighting the sheets on fire, we'd developed into an easy relationship. Sometimes we would talk long into the night. Other times we didn't need to speak at all, and I never found those moments of silence to be awkward —it was golden. She knew who she was, what she was, and she owned it. And more importantly—she knew who I was and accepted it.

When Kallie emerged from the bathroom fifteen minutes later, she'd been completely transformed. I sat up, only to feel pain spread through my hip. I winced but pushed down the ache to take a moment to appreciate her. Dressed in a long skirt and an airy peach blouse, she'd pulled her hair back into a rainbow braid. I looked forward to unraveling all of those multicolored locks later.

"Okay, I'm off," she said as she slipped into a pair of sling-backed heels. "I'm hoping we can wrap this meeting up in a couple of hours. Fingers crossed."

Coming over to where I sat, she planted a quick kiss on my lips, then hurried out the door. I stayed seated on the bed and watched her leave, needing to be sure she was out of sight before I attempted to move. The shooting pain I'd experienced a moment earlier made me terrified to stand up. I should have gotten into the shower sooner. I mentally kicked myself for getting distracted and giving the joint time to stiffen.

I waited a few minutes until I heard the opening and closing of the front door, then gingerly moved to stand. Instantly, pain like molten fire radiated from my hip.

"Fuck!" I hissed as I took a few steps toward the master bath. My body shook, and I had to grab the doorframe for support. I gripped it so hard, my knuckles turned white as I allowed a few minutes for the pain to subside. Once the tremors settled, I slowly continued until I reached the vanity. Yanking open the drawer, I pulled out the bag Milo had given me that first day at the track. The reason he wanted to see me alone in the sponsor's box—without Kallie—was because of the contents in the clear plastic Ziplock. Inside, there were fifteen pills of oxycodone.

I recalled Milo's words as he shoved the bag into my hand.

"I can get more if you need it. All you have to do is ask."

I shouldn't have accepted them. I should have thrown the pills in his face instead.

But I didn't.

Although I wanted to push through this on my own, there was a small part of me that knew I might need them one day—and that day had arrived. With a shaking hand, I unsealed the bag and pulled out a single pill.

I stared at it for what seemed like forever before looking up at my reflection in the mirror. Pain was clearly written across my face, my eyes seeming hollow from the days spent trying to endure it. With the race still four weeks away, I had to do what I had to do. After that, I could take a break and give my body time to heal again. There was no point in suffering this way if I had something readily available to numb the agony. As long as I wasn't under the influence of the pills when behind the wheel or downing them with a shot of Jack, what difference did it make if I took them? It wasn't like before when I searched for the pleasant emptiness only the opioid pills and booze could bring. This time, I wasn't trying to chase a high—I just wanted to douse the excruciating fire in my hip so I could race. It was the only thing that mattered.

Looking back down at the pill nestled in the center of my palm, I brought it to my mouth and placed it on my tongue.

23

Kallie

Over the past three weeks, Sloan and I had settled into an easy routine. Since I was needed at the track for various reasons, I'd chosen to do as much as I could remotely from my laptop rather than work from home. Each morning, we would drive to and from the track together. It had been my idea, suggesting it would be better for the planet if we drove my car since it got better gas mileage, and he had readily agreed. While I always cared about the environmental impact of my choices, this time, it had merely been an excuse. Doing all the driving also meant Sloan didn't have to drive home after a hard day of practice.

While he practiced with his crew, I would head up to the sponsor's box and strategize. Never before had I been so devoted to a client. I'd been his shadow, essentially working fifteen to eighteen hours a day ever since he returned to the track. I spent my time working diligently on setting up events to increase public awareness of Sloan's accomplishments. Carefully-orchestrated press releases and public appearances with Safe Track brought positive attention from community leaders, resulting in additional photo ops with prominent members of local society. I worked hand-in-hand with Kapton Motor Oil's marketing executives to spotlight the Atwood Racing and Kapton brands through various media platforms. And thanks to Cooper's connections, I even managed to get Sloan a guest spot on Jimmy Kimmel the week after the MILL.

Through it all, I somehow managed to avoid Milo. I let him handle the endorsement opportunities flooding in from numerous motorsport products, all vying for Sloan's face to appear in their commercials. The endorsements were dollar signs, and I'd quickly learned that was all Milo cared about anyway.

The only problem I ran into while working remotely was the interruptions. From the people coming in and out of the sponsor's box for various reasons to the loud rumbling of the cars on the track, it was hard to concentrate at times. Popping in a set of earbuds tended to drown out most of the noise, but that didn't always work. The constant distractions often meant I had to write press releases and respond to emails late into the night —much to Sloan's complaint.

While I hadn't actually moved into his place, I found myself spending more nights at his house than mine. It seemed to work better with the routine we'd established. It also allowed me to keep a closer eye on Sloan's physical condition after a day of hard practice—and by the look of his current state when he entered the sponsor's box where I was working, today had been a tough one.

He smiled as he approached, and I pulled my earbuds from my ears. I studied him, seeing the way he was trying to cover up his limp. He couldn't fool me. He was hurting again but trying to hide it.

"Hey, Rainbow Brite. Listening to anything good?" He asked, and leaned over to plant a kiss on my forehead.

"Ruelle. How are you feeling?" I asked—just like I had every day since he decided to get back behind the wheel. Before he spoke, I knew what his reply would be.

"I'm feeling great," he predictably answered.

Liar.

I didn't voice the thought out loud because it wasn't worth the argument.

"You don't look too great."

"Thanks for the compliment," he sardonically replied. "Are you ready to go?"

"Yeah, just give me a minute to get my stuff together." Glancing back down at my computer screen, I saved the press release document I'd been working on, then closed the laptop. After gathering my things, Sloan and I headed out.

Out the corner of my eye, I monitored him as we walked across the parking lot at Motor Club Speedway toward my car. When we reached it, he opened the driver's side door of the BMW for me, then made his way around to the passenger side. As I buckled my seatbelt, I watched his movements while he climbed in. He was cautious, and I caught his wince when he thought I wasn't looking.

We were supposed to leave for San Antonio, Texas in two days. The big race wasn't for another week, but my concern for Sloan had grown steadily with each passing day. I wasn't convinced he'd be able to pull it off. He practiced hard, but the actual race would be even more challenging, and it would come with more risks. It was one thing to practice in a controlled environment with a couple of other cars on the track, and something completely different to be going up against forty or more other racers on race day. I suspected Sloan might have been thinking the same, as his mood had become increasingly sullen over the past week.

"Have you thought any more about calling your doctor?" I asked. "PT might help considerably right now."

"Kallie, don't. I told you. I'm fine," he replied irritably. He ran a hand through his dark waves, and his eyes flashed. It was impossible to miss the fiercely determined set to his jaw.

I pursed my lips and shook my head in frustration. He was as stubborn as a mule and resolved to see this through. The only thing I could do was continue to support him.

"I packed a hemp extract in my overnight bag. It's a pain relief cream. When we get back to your place, you should rub some of it on that hip. Afterward, I can help you stretch," I offered rather than push the issue further. "I'll need to stop by my place at some point too. We leave for San Antonio in two days, and I still need to pack."

He turned his head to look out the window but didn't respond. Suppressing a sigh, I turned the key in the ignition and began the drive back to Sloan's house in Beverly Grove. An awkward silence fell between us, and I flipped on the radio for some background noise. After fiddling with the controls, I settled on an alternative music station. Green Day's "21 Guns" began playing through the speakers.

I tried to focus on the lyrics, but my effort was in vain. All I could think about was how much it hurt to see the man I fell in love with suffering so much. While I hadn't told him I loved him yet, I was sure about the depths of my feelings. I just hadn't found the right time to tell him amidst the insane schedule we'd been keeping. By the time I finished work for the night, it was almost always close to midnight. We'd fall into bed, make love into the early hours of the morning, only to have the alarm go off all too soon, and we'd start the routine all over again.

However, deep down, I knew I could have found the time to tell him. My excuse was really only for myself because I was terrified of Sloan's reaction once I told him. It could significantly complicate things if my feelings weren't reciprocated. Neither of us needed that kind of strain a week before his race. It would be better for all if I kept my feelings to myself for a bit longer.

When I pulled into Sloan's driveway almost an hour later, we still hadn't spoken. After I killed the engine, Sloan began to climb out of the car. I turned to look at him. Pain was prevalent in every line of his face, distorting his perfect features with dark shadows. I hurried out and walked around to his side of the car to help him. I reached for his arm, but he pushed it away.

"I've got it," he snapped, letting his pride outweigh his need for help.

"No, you don't. Stop being a fool," I told him and wrapped an arm around his waist. "I might be small, but I'm stronger than I look. Put your weight on me."

He didn't protest this time and leaned into me. When we got to the front door, I reached into his front pocket for the keys to his house.

"Careful. If you dig deep enough, you might find something else," he teased.

"You're incorrigible," I said with a small laugh. "You can barely walk, yet you zeroed in on the least important thing at the moment. Is sex always on your brain?"

"Only when it comes to you."

We entered the house, and I led Sloan over to the couch. After he sat down, he released a small groan. I worried my bottom lip, hating to see him this way.

"Stay here. I'm going to run and grab that hemp cream I told you about."

"I can assure you—I'm not going anywhere."

Not wasting another minute, I hurried up the stairs and into his master bathroom to where I'd left my overnight bag. After locating my makeup tote, I pulled it out and sifted through the contents until I found the cream. I hoped that the combination of hemp and other organic ingredients, including menthol and arnica, would soothe the muscles supporting his joint. Since he still refused to work with his doctors and therapists, the cream combined with stretching would have to do for today.

"Here you go," I said after I returned to the living room. "Just scoop out a good dollop with your fingers and rub it directly over the painful areas. While you do that, I'm going to head back upstairs and change into clothes more suitable for stretching. Do you want me to grab you a pair of shorts or something while I'm up there?" I asked, not wanting him to do the stairs if at all possible.

"Please. There are gym shorts in the second drawer of my dresser." I turned to walk away, but he called out. "Kallie?"

"Yeah."

He hesitated, and his brow furrowed. His expression held a certain amount of sadness mixed with resolve. But there was also a longing I had never seen before.

"Thank you," he eventually said. "I'm not sure if any of this would be possible if I didn't have you with me."

I smiled, but my concern for him prevented the smile from reaching my eyes. I was worried sick. As much as I tried to understand his reasoning, I wished he would end this insanity.

"Of course," was all I could say, then hurried upstairs to change.

When I returned to the bathroom, I quickly stripped out of my jeans and slipped into a pair of yoga shorts. I left my red Atwood Racing Enterprise T-shirt on, a recent wardrobe addition I'd snagged from Sloan's latest merchandise shipment, then pulled my hair back into a ponytail.

"What is this crap, Kallie? It smells weird," I heard Sloan yell from downstairs.

I chuckled to myself as I smoothed my hair fly-aways with a brush.

"Just put it on," I called back. "I'll be down in two minutes after I put my stuff away."

I moved to toss the hairbrush back into my bag. In my haste, I banged my hand against the marble top of the vanity.

"Damn it!" I cursed when I saw I'd broken a nail. It was only partially torn, but it had broken near the nail bed. Reaching into my makeup tote, I dug around for nail clippers but came up empty-handed. Wondering if Sloan had any, I opened the bathroom vanity drawer and began rifling through the contents. I didn't see a pair at first glance, so I bent to look into the back of the drawer and pulled the contents forward.

I didn't find nail clippers, but I did find pills—and they didn't appear to be the over-the-counter kind. They weren't cold pills or aspirin, nor were they in a bottle from a pharmacy. Instead, the little white tablets were in a clear plastic Ziplock bag. Upon closer inspection, I saw letters and numbers carved into the pills. My heart began to pound in my chest.

Bending down to where my jeans lay on the bathroom floor, I pulled my cell phone from the back pocket to do a quick Google search. I forced myself to relax, hoping beyond hope the pills were not what I suspected. Maybe I was wrong —perhaps it was just flu medicine or something of the like. However, deep down, I didn't think that was the case. Copying the indented text from the pills, I typed "white tablet M 05 52" into the browser and waited for the results to populate. Once they did, I sucked in a breath and felt my eyes widen in disbelief. Although the internet pictures varied slightly, an educated guess said the bag in my hand was full of oxycodone.

The betrayal was a slap in the face—both personally and professionally. On a professional level, I worried about what would happen to the Quinn & Wilkshire name if this got out— especially after all I'd done to bolster Sloan's image. While improving his reputation was in my job description, it was what

I did during off-hours that made Sloan unique to any other client—that was personal.

I'd spent the past month watching him silently suffer, unable to do anything but show my support in every way I knew how. Hours upon hours had been spent caring for his physical condition. From learning his PT exercises and teaching him yoga to researching the best natural remedies for pain, I'd done everything in my power to make sure he could get out of bed each day and do what he loved most. But it was more than how much effort I had poured into this—he had made a promise to me. No more booze. No more pills.

And I had believed him.

Have I been nothing but a fool?

My heart felt heavy, my emotions twisting up into a knot. I loved Sloan with my whole body and soul. To know he would disregard his promise to me and risk everything for a few pills not only made me feel betrayed but angry. Fury at what he had done surged through my veins and pulsed at my temples. My brain scrambled to organize every feeling and thought I ever had about him, trying to make sense of it all. I knew he'd been in pain, but I hadn't realized it was so bad that he had to resort to taking painkillers.

Why didn't he just tell me?

I hurriedly tossed the rest of my things into my overnight bag, then stalked out of the bathroom with the bag of pills in hand. Going downstairs, I found Sloan sitting on the edge of the couch with his pants pulled partially down on one side, massaging cream into his hip.

"This stuff isn't half bad," he said. "I already feel it working."

"Sloan, what are these?"

He glanced up and frowned as he focused on what I was holding. The moment he realized what it was, his furrowed brow raised, and he momentarily froze. Shaking his head, he looked back down at his hip to return to the task at hand.

"It's nothing," he brushed off.

"I don't think these are nothing. Is this oxy?"

His head snapped up, and regretful eyes raked over me. It was as if he were processing a million thoughts. However, whatever he was thinking was quickly masked with a blank expression.

"So what if it is?" he challenged.

"Are you serious right now? I had to practically scrape you off the floor after you saw Tyler's crash. You drank yourself into a stupor, admitted to wanting to take painkillers but decided —." I stopped short as a new realization came over me. "Or maybe you did take the pills after all. Is that why you promised me no more booze *and* pills?"

"Kallie, listen to me. I—"

"No. You listen to me! I've bent over backward to make sure you've received positive coverage by the press. I'm going above and beyond what is expected of me based on our contract. I get that you want to race again, but this isn't the way. I thought I was helping you, but you've been lying to me this whole time!"

He slammed frustrated hands through his hair, then stood up to adjust his pants back into their rightful place and began to pace.

"Kallie, it's not what you think. Milo gave them to me and—"

"Milo!" I covered my mouth and choked back a sob. "Of course he gave them to you. Why the hell would he give two shits as long as you win and he gets a chunk of the prize money? What's his cut in all of this?"

"Ten percent, but that's beside the—"

"Ten percent! Wait a minute—who's paying Quinn & Wilkshire for me to be here? You or him?"

"I don't see why that matters."

"It matters because it lets me know how much stake Milo has in all of this."

"Technically, I'm paying for it. Milo just signs the checks."

I wasn't sure what I thought about that. I never thought to ask before now, but now that I knew, it somehow made me feel like an overpriced prostitute. That just infuriated me further.

"I still can't believe you would do this for him. That man is a snake!" I snapped.

Sloan stopped pacing to look at me. His face hardened, and his eyes bore into me, flashing with accusation. "At least he knows how to get me behind the wheel again. And he also doesn't throw around baseless allegations—which is more than I can say for you!" he thundered.

My head snapped back in surprise as the meaning of his words sunk in.

"Are you saying you didn't take the pills?"

"Maybe I did, maybe I didn't. Why would you care either way? All that matters is that I look good in the public eye. Isn't that right?"

Spine stiffening hard and straight, I glared right back at him and snapped.

"It's not just about the press coverage, and you know it. It's about everything I've done to help you *personally*—all because I fucking care! I've spent almost every day of the past three months with you, and a good portion of one of those months was spent doing your PT exercises and practicing yoga to make sure you were doing this the healthy way. And this," I said, pointing to the bag I held up, "this is not healthy."

"What does healthy even look like, Kallie? For fucksake, healthy isn't the way I was living a few months ago. It felt like I was walking on broken glass day after day, and the only way to numb the pain of what I'd lost was to escape into a bottle. I was miserable—resigned to the fact that my life had been ruined. But now, things are different. I have a chance to do what I love again. I told you before that racing was my first love, and I'll do anything I have to do to hang on to it. If you want to be by my side for it, fine. If not, you know where the door is."

I stilled, his immobilizing words cutting me to the core, slicing open my heart, and draining all the optimism I'd felt about our future together. Staring at him with wide eyes, I saw all of his pain and heartache for his one love—and that clearly wasn't me. My eyes stung, and I shook my head in disbelief, suddenly filled with indescribable resentment. There was no stopping the tears that began to fall freely down my cheeks. I always wondered how many broken hearts one person could handle. Whether broken hearts from unforeseen disasters or broken hearts delivered by those I loved the most. I'd experienced many—but this was, without a doubt, the absolute worst.

I'd foolishly allowed myself to love Sloan so freely and so openly. I should have known better. The universe had shown me all of his arrogance and chaos, yet I still allowed myself to fall. My instincts had been wrong. I should have listened to the gypsy. I should have listened when Sloan said racing was his first and only love. Those were my mistakes. Now all I felt was a hollow emptiness.

"So that's it then?" I asked. My eyes burned with more tears, but I refused to let them fall anymore. "Either stick by your side and watch you destroy yourself or get the hell out? Those are my choices?"

He shrugged.

"If that's how you want to look at it."

He acted as if he didn't care—as if I didn't matter to him one little bit. There was no going back now—no undoing what he'd said. The hard truth was just something I'd have to swallow.

"I can't believe you would be so callous. After everything..." I whispered, unable to say more without losing all sense of composure.

"Kallie..." he began and reached for me.

"No. Don't. Just leave me the hell alone. I have to go."

Turning on my heel, I tossed the bag of pills on the kitchen table, grabbed my keys, and rushed to the front door.

"Kallie, wait!" I heard Sloan call out as I yanked it open.

I didn't look back.

24

Sloan

I tried calling Kallie for the rest of the day but she wouldn't pick up. Instead of fighting with her, I should have told her the truth. And the fact was, I didn't take a single one of the damn pills Milo had given to me. Before I could swallow it, all I could picture was Kallie's face, and I ended up spitting it out into the toilet at the last minute. I should have flushed the whole bag—which is exactly what I did after she stormed out.

Later that night, all I wanted was Kallie. I wanted to see her, smell her, and feel her. It was as if I was going through withdrawals. Instead of alcohol and pills, Kallie was my drug of choice. I craved her as if my life depended on it.

I'd tossed and turned all night long, and when my alarm went off at seven the following day, I knew I had to go to her and make things right. I was supposed to be at the track by eleven to help load the totors for the road trip. We were scheduled to leave for Texas tomorrow morning, needing to get there early for weigh-in and heat races, but I had no intention of doing anything until I fixed this mess with Kallie.

After a quick shower, I made it to her house by eight-thirty. Her car wasn't parked in its usual spot in the driveway, and I wondered where she would be this early in the morning. It was too early for her to have left for the track. Worry for her whereabouts gnawed at me as I made my way to her front door and rang the bell, hoping she'd just decided to break with habit and park her car in the garage.

When she didn't answer, I rang it a second time and tried the door handle. It was locked. Peeking through the sidelight window next to the door, I saw suitcases lined up in the hallway. I sucked in a surprised breath when I saw how many there were. A pit in my stomach began to grow. I had a sinking suspicion the bags were not packed for Texas. She didn't need to pack that much for a week-long road trip.

Pulling my cell from my back pocket, I dialed her number. Again, there was no answer. Shoving a frustrated hand through my hair, I dialed Cooper. I knew he would be at the track soon, assuming he wasn't there already. With any luck, maybe Kallie was there too.

"Cooper," I said after my friend answered.

"Hey, man. What's up?"

"Are you at the track by any chance?"

"I just got here."

"Is Kallie there?" I asked, trying to keep the anxiousness out of my voice.

"I haven't seen her. Why?"

"Ah, I fucked up. We had a stupid argument yesterday. She basically told me to go to hell—which is exactly where I went. Last night was one long, miserable night. Now I can't find her."

"Shit, man. You definitely have a way of stepping in it," Cooper said with a slight chuckle. "Can I do anything?"

"Not really. If you see her, can you just let me know and ask her to call me?"

"Will do."

"Thanks."

I ended the call and began to walk back to my car. I racked my brain, trying to think of who else I could call. I'd spent almost every day with Kallie over the past three months, making me all but certain she didn't have any friends around here outside of my inner circle. I thought about calling Gabby to see if she'd heard from her, but quickly scratched the idea when I remembered I didn't have her number.

Just as I reached for the door of my car, Kallie's red BMW pulled into the driveway. I breathed a sigh of relief. Her gorgeous eyes were wide and steely when she saw me. She looked at me like she didn't even know me as a civil war battled across her face.

When she climbed out of the car, I stared at her. She looked hot as hell in a red halter top and those cut-off jean shorts I loved. I could tell she was braless, reminding me so much of the first night we had sex in her backyard when all I had to do was yank at the ties on her neck to free those glorious tits.

With her arms folded across her chest, she stared back at me, hurt dimming her normally bright emerald depths. Deep blue and siren red flowed through her golden blonde ponytail, and I could tell she was angry. She had every right to be. I should have been straight with her—I shouldn't have been so cruel. In her eyes, I was probably nothing more than a liar. The only defense I had was the truth. But first, I needed to feel her in my arms.

Quickly crossing the distance between us, I wrapped my arms around her. She stiffened and didn't hug me back. I didn't care. All that mattered was that she was here.

"I was worried when I didn't know where you were," I

murmured as I fingered the red and blue streaks in her hair. I pulled back to look at her. "Do I dare ask what the red means?"

"Red is the color of the devil. It's what I wear when I'm flaming mad."

I chuckled at her no-nonsense tone even though I knew I shouldn't, considering the seriousness of the moment. My only excuse was that I was giddy with relief, knowing she hadn't run off somewhere.

"I'm sorry, Kallie," I earnestly said as I stroked my hands up and down her arms.

"I don't want to hear your apology," she said stiffly. "You've already said enough."

"No, actually, I haven't. All I did was say all the wrong things. I came here today to tell you what I should have right from the get-go yesterday. I didn't take those pills."

She blinked, seeming confused.

"You didn't?"

"Not a single one. After you left, I flushed them."

"Why didn't you just say so yesterday instead of leading me to believe you did?"

"I don't know. I was sore and irritable, but that's really no excuse. I guess I went into defense mode when you accused me, and I immediately turned into an asshole. Milo gave me those things a month ago. I'll admit—I thought about taking them, but..." I trailed off, trying to find the words to explain how she was the one who ultimately stopped me. Wrapping an arm around her shoulder, I turned her toward the house. "Let's go inside, and I'll try to explain."

"No," she said, stepping back and shrugging my arm away. "Sloan, I'm happy you didn't take the pills and decided to get rid of them. But for me, it's more than that. We've been spending a lot of time together, and I think we need to pump the breaks."

"What are you talking about?" I asked, my suspicion about the suitcases coming to the forefront of my mind. "The suitcases in the hallway... those aren't packed for Texas, are they?"

She slowly shook her head, confirming what I already thought I knew.

"I decided not to go to San Antonio with you. I'm going home for a while instead. I've booked a flight home for the day after tomorrow. It's not about the pills and whether or not you took them—it's about me not being able to stand seeing you in so much pain. You love racing so much that you'll kill yourself to make it happen. I can't sit by and watch you follow this path, especially knowing what you could lose. You have everything right in front of you, but you can't see it—you can't see *me*. All you see is a checkered flag."

"Of course I see you, Kallie."

"No, you don't. If you did, you would know..." She hesitated, biting her lower lip as her eyes glossed over with unshed tears.

"I would know what?" I prompted.

"You would know I was a fool who fell in love with a man who will never love me back."

Anguish ripped through my soul at her words. She began to rub her arms as if she were warding off a chill even though the day was shaping up to be a hot one. She looked so distraught, I knew better than to reach for her again—to touch her or try to kiss her sorrows away. Her eyes bore into mine, her expression a mix of confusion, hurt, and sadness. I looked down at the ground, unable to meet her gaze.

She loves me.

When I brought my eyes back up to meet hers, I saw the unshed tears begin to fall from her emerald greens. Knowing I was the cause for those tears shattered me.

"Kallie, I—"

She shook her head again and held up a hand to stop me from speaking.

"I wish you good luck on the race. If all goes well, I'll be back in a couple of weeks to finish our contract. As for us... I don't see how there can be an us. The gypsy tried to warn me," she said with a bitter laugh. "We've both made ourselves perfectly clear from the beginning. I told you I couldn't separate my emotions from sex, and for you, racing is and always will be your first love. Despite what I said, I can't settle for second place. Racing takes the cup. I hope she treats you well in San Antonio."

"Kallie, no. I need you there with me."

I saw the storm roll through her eyes. Grief clutched me in its fiery hold, incinerating and blistering. At that moment, everything became clear. I was going to lose her. But I couldn't lose her because...

I love her, too.

I tried to push the thought away, only for it to come roaring back with a vengeance. This was a first for me, and I could barely even think, let alone process it. But one thing was absolutely certain—it wasn't racing I needed. It was her—only her. Kallie was more than a pit stop—she was my checkered flag.

However, in her eyes, I loved racing more. It was why she was leaving. It had nothing to do with whether I took oxy or not and everything to do with her trying to run away from a broken heart. I reached out to try to pull her to me again, needing to tell her how I felt, but I wasn't fast enough. In a flash, she turned and ran toward the house.

"Kallie, hang on. Don't run from me again. Let's talk about this!" I called out as I charged a few steps behind her.

It took her less than two seconds to turn the key to unlock the front door before she disappeared into the house. I didn't chase her inside, but only because I needed to process my thoughts. I couldn't run in there half-cocked, professing my love. She wouldn't believe it—at least not right now. Kallie deserved the stars, the moon, and all the rainbows under the sun—and I'd be back later to make damn sure she got them.

25

Kallie

I peered around the edge of the dining room curtains and watched Sloan pull out of the driveway. A part of me couldn't believe he was leaving without denying what I'd said— that racing was more important to him than I was. But another part of me knew it was all my fault. I'd stood too close to the fire. I'd allowed myself to get lost in him, falling hard and fast, and let the hurricane of emotions break my soul. I'd been warned of this—whether it was a misguided gypsy hoax or a hard truth—and I only had myself to blame.

Even though I was glad to hear he didn't swallow the pills, finding them opened my eyes to the day I would eventually become second to a motorsport. I'd just been in denial. It was evident that racing was his true love—his life's passion. While I'd once thought I'd be okay with that, I wasn't anymore. I couldn't settle for second place.

I let the curtains fall back into place and walked back

through the living room to the back yard. My gaze flitted between the patio lounge chair and the pool, causing memories from the first night I'd been with Sloan to flash in my mind. I closed my eyes, picturing our moments together. It was almost too much to bear. I felt empty without him, lost in a black hole of misery.

I'd told him I'd come back after the race to finish out the contract, but who was I kidding? I could barely look at the back yard without missing him. Coming back and facing a man I loved with all of my heart but who would never love me in return would be more than just torture—it would destroy me. It was better if I left now while there was still hope of fixing the pieces of my shattered heart.

Going back into the house, I retrieved my cell phone from my purse and glanced at the time. It was still early on the East Coast, but I was fairly certain my mother would be awake. Sinking into the cushions of the couch, I punched her number into the keypad.

"Hewow?" answered the cutest voice I'd ever heard.

I smiled. My little sister was always an instant mood booster, no matter how bleak I might be feeling.

"Why, hello there, Miss Emma."

"I knew it was you!"

"You did, huh? You're up early today."

"I was hungwy."

"Hungry, huh? Did you have anything good for breakfast?"

"Mommy cut up some owanges and stwawbewies, and I had some ceweal. It was vewy good!"

I had to laugh. It had been a couple of weeks since I'd last spoken to Emma, and she still clearly hadn't mastered her pronunciations during that time.

"That sounds delicious! Now you're making me hungry too. I'll have to find out what mommy's secret is. Can you put her on the phone for me?"

"Sure."

"Kallie?" my mother said.

"I'm here. God, I miss her little face. I hear she's still struggling with the Rs and Ls."

"Yeah. I've been in touch with the school about it. They've assured me it's common, but they are going to start speech therapy with her next month."

"She'll get those pesky consonants down soon enough. Don't worry."

"Oh, I'm not too worried. Your father is another story, though," she added with a laugh. "He's already lined up a speech therapist to work with her next week when we're at Camp Riley."

"Oh, I didn't realize you were heading there! I haven't visited the camp in ages!" I thought back to the few summers I'd spent helping my parents and my Aunt Joy refurbish the property in Abington, Virginia. I could almost smell the tall pines and envision the rays of light that would streak through their branches as they arched over the quaint little pathways throughout the camp like a living canopy. It had once been a performing arts camp run by my grandparents, but after they died, the camp fell to ruin because my mother didn't have the funds to keep it running. After she reunited with my father, they worked together to turn what was left of the property into a literacy youth camp for low-income families.

"Yeah, it was a last-minute thing," my mother explained. "Aunt Joy decided to convert one of the unused cabins into a guest house and asked for your father's help with some of the renovations."

"That sounds like fun. Speaking of dad, is he within earshot?"

"No. He just jumped in the shower. Why?"

"I wanted to talk to you about something, and I didn't want him to freak out."

"What's wrong?" my mother hurriedly asked, the concern evident in her voice. I took a deep breath and steeled myself to tell her the true reason for my call.

"I'm coming home. Sloan, the race car driver I've been representing... Well, I don't think I can be his PR agent anymore. The problem is that there's still just shy of three months left on the contract Quinn & Wilkshire agreed to."

"Kallie, it's unlike you to not see a contract through."

"I know what's at stake. Financially, this is going to hurt me. I was counting on the bonus and possibly making partner so much, but it's not about that anymore."

"Your father definitely won't be happy. Why do you need to break the contract early?"

"I just can't be around Sloan anymore, but you can't tell dad the reasons. At least not yet. I'll have to come up with something—say we just weren't compatible or something. I don't know."

"Kallie, I don't know what you're trying to get at. Just spit it out. What the hell happened out there? Why can't you be around Sloan?"

I hesitated, unsure if I should tell her how far across the line I went with Sloan. I took another deep breath, then exhaled slowly. My mother had always been there for me no matter what, and I knew this would be no different.

"Because I fell in love with him, Mom."

She fell deathly silent and didn't speak for a long moment.

"Is he the reason you broke it off with Dean?" she eventually asked.

"Yes and no. And honestly, it doesn't matter now. I've already booked a flight home for the day after tomorrow, but after we hang up, I'm going to see about bumping it up." I paused and looked around the room. "I just can't be here anymore. The sooner I leave, the better."

"I don't know what happened between you and this guy

Sloan, but running is never the answer. Unless, of course—"
She stopped short, then gasped. "He didn't hurt you, did he?"

"Of course not. It's nothing like that, Mom. It's just that..." I
let my words hang in the air, afraid to voice them out loud. "It's
just that he'll never love me back. What can I say? I always pick
the wrong guy."

"Don't say that. And how do you know he'll never love you
back? I mean, look at your father and me. I thought that too,
and we wasted seventeen years because of it. Does he know
how you feel?"

"Sort of."

"Kallie..." she said in a warning tone.

"Okay, fine. I did tell him, but not in so many words. I didn't
actually say I love you because I already know where he stands.
He told me as much. Please don't push me on this. Just trust
me. I need to come home."

"Alright. I'll think of something to tell your father for now.
Like you said—you weren't compatible with the client. It's not a
lie, per se. Just know that you're probably going to have to tell
him eventually."

I breathed a sigh of relief.

"Thank you. If I can move my flight, I'll let you know and
text you the flight itinerary. Can you pick me up from the
airport, or should I plan on calling an Uber?"

"I haven't seen you in three months—of course I'll pick
you up!"

"Perfect. Thanks again. I'll talk to you soon. Oh, and is
Austin back from Japan?" I asked as an afterthought.

"Yeah. He got back a couple of days ago. He's home for a
week, and then he has to go back."

"Good. That will be enough time for me to pin him down. I
have a bone to pick with Austin," I added.

"What has he done now?" she inquired with a laugh.

"Not now—it's what he did years ago with a gypsy fortuneteller."

"You mean the one he paid off?"

My eyes widened in shock, feeling like the entire universe had been conspiring against me for years.

"You knew about it too! What the hell, Mom! Why didn't you tell me?"

"I don't know. I guess I didn't think much about it. Why are you so upset about it now? It was a long time ago."

I sighed, not having the energy to get into the entire tale.

"I'll explain it to you when I get home. Right now, I need to run so I can see about moving my flight. Love you, Mom."

"Love you too, baby girl. See you soon."

After I ended the call, I looked around the room once more and felt tears begin to prick the corners of my eyes. I felt foolish, heartbroken, and everything else in between. But one thing remained unchanged—I was really doing this. I was leaving Santa Monica.

Unless I could miraculously get over my feelings for Sloan, leaving meant I would probably never see him again. I wanted to tell myself I'd be okay, but I didn't think I'd ever really be okay again. Over the past three months, Sloan had irrevocably changed me. Our time together had taught me so much about myself. I finally knew what I wanted in a relationship and knew what it meant to give my whole body, heart, and soul to someone. I only wished Sloan could have been the one to give that to me in return.

Wiping the tears from my eyes, I grabbed my laptop from the kitchen table and went to sit down on the couch in the living room. Opening my music playlist, I put a song that seemed to fit my mood, then opened my inbox. As I listened to "Last One to Know" by Leah Nobel, I pulled up my flight itinerary and compared it with other available flights leaving later today or early tomorrow. Within a few minutes, I was able to find a flight that left at five o'clock that very evening for only sixty dollars more than my original ticket price.

"Do I want to leave that soon?" I said aloud to myself. I glanced at the clock on the top corner of the computer screen. If I left my house by two, I should be able to return the rental car and make it through airport security with time to spare.

I tapped my fingernail on the edge of the computer and contemplated my options. The chakra bracelet Sloan had bought for me was around my wrist and clicked against the side of the computer as I tapped. Staring at it, images of our time together washed over me, provoking another lone tear to slide down my cheek. Then there was this ache. It was an ache I knew I'd feel but never imagined it would be this bad. I hadn't even left yet, but I already missed Sloan so much.

Moving the mouse, I clicked 'modify booking' before giving myself another moment to reconsider. After I thought more about it, I hastily brushed my tears away. No good would come from them now. I'd made my decision.

26

Sloan

I didn't know what compelled me to do it, but two hours after leaving Kallie's house, I found myself pulling through the tall black wrought-iron gates of Oakwood Hills Cemetery. I drove through the narrow winding roads toward the back, heading to the gravesite I'd visited only once before.

When I arrived at my destination, I turned off the car engine and stepped out into the bright sunlight. A sense of serenity surrounded me as I looked around. A few groundskeepers milled about, and I could see a family of mourners off in the distance as they bid a final farewell to their loved one. Everyone was quiet, respecting this place of soulful reflection with calm tranquility.

Walking over the gravel path, I passed gravestone after gravestone. Some had sunk into the soil, their engraved words weathered over time. Others boasted fresh flowers or small

American flags, symbols of the connection people had with those who had passed on.

Coming to the end of the path, I moved across the grass and stopped to read a small headstone engraved with the name of the person I'd spent a year trying not to think about.

Charlotte Marie Atwood

September 7, 1962 – March 30, 2020

"Hi, Mom," I said to the stone slab, a symbol of the end to her life's story. I kneeled and pressed my hand over her name.

I sat there for a long while, not sure what else I should say as memories of my childhood flashed before my eyes. After my father's passing, it was almost as if my mother felt she had to make up for what I'd lost—for what we'd lost. My father had left behind a sizable chunk of change, and she had invested wisely. She'd budgeted, and we'd lived modestly, allowing her to devote her time solely to me as a single stay-at-home mom.

I could still hear her laughter on Christmas morning. It had been her favorite holiday, and she always went over the top with presents. Her eyes would light up with delight as I opened my gifts, more excited to see my pleasure than to experience her own. I also remembered her disappointment when I'd acted out, and she would have to tan my hide. Looking back, I wasn't sure who suffered more from my punishments—me or her.

I recalled her encouraging words as she taught me how to ride a bike. Those words weren't all so different from when I'd decided I wanted to race just like my father had. And when I became of age and entered the racing circuit, she was there every step of the way. She never missed a race and rarely missed a practice, her unwavering support making me believe I could be anything I wanted to be.

"Take it to the moon, my boy! Don't let the sky be your limit!" she would say.

However, the thing I remembered most about growing up was hearing her tears late into the night. She had missed my father something fierce. He had been her soulmate, her world —her checkered flag. By day, she had tried to hide her sadness from me, her sole focus being a single mother doing her best to raise a man. She had never known how many nights I had lain awake listening to her cry through the thin walls of our apartment.

I buried my face in my hands, shocked to discover wetness on my cheeks. I blinked back the tears, trying to remember the last time I'd cried—like actually fucking cried. Sure, I had cried when my dad died but I hadn't cried when I learned about my mother's death. I'd been too angry. The last time I shed real tears had to have been back when I was about ten years old and fell off the swing set and skinned my knee.

My mother had been there for that too.

Keeping my face in my hands, I let the tears fall freely, realizing that I'd been too hard on her.

"I understand now, Mom. Really, I do. I know why you couldn't stay, and I forgive you. You showed me what it means to love, and I know you loved Dad with your whole heart. After he was gone, you gave all that love to me, and when you thought I wouldn't make it..." I trailed off, taking a moment to wipe my tear-stained cheeks. I glanced over to my left to where my father's headstone sat alongside my mother's. "I met someone, Mom. I think you would like her. Her name is Kallie, and she's amazing. Because of her, I now know what it means not to be able to live without somebody. It might sound crazy, but I can't imagine my life without her. This girl is the real deal. I want forever with her. The problem is, I screwed up, and now I don't know if she'll have me."

Rising to my feet, I scanned the row of headstones. Fresh

cut flowers adorned most of them, but my father's and mother's graves were bare. A pang of guilt tore at my heart, and I made a silent promise to do better. My mother didn't deserve to be among the forgotten—she deserved to be remembered for the strong woman I knew she had been. For too many years, she'd played the part of Wonder Woman, giving all of herself and never asking for anything in return. She had coped with loss and balanced the strains of being a single parent without complaint. She was stronger than she'd realized. My only regret was not telling her that before it was too late—before she thought she couldn't endure the burden of her sorrows any longer.

I began to wonder if she would approve of me trying to race again. She knew how important racing was to me, and I had to believe she had been looking down on me as I worked to overcome the injuries from my crash. Hard work and perseverance were how I got through it—all lessons I'd learned from her.

But this was different.

The pain in my hip had steadily gotten worse with each passing day, and the recovery time was becoming longer. Instead of spending an hour alternating cold and heat, the pain remedy was now continuing well after the sun had gone down. I was beginning to think that what I was doing now had nothing to do with perseverance but more with foolish determination to see it through. After all the agony I went through during my recovery, the last thing I wanted to do was cause more damage.

I thought back to what Kallie had said to me about my attempt to push through the current pain.

"I just hope you don't kill yourself in the process."

I knew her words were rhetorical, but they gave me a reason to pause. I couldn't help but think that was exactly what I was doing. Causing myself permanent damage was not the way to honor my mother's memory. She would never approve of that —just like she would never approve of me putting my love for racing ahead of my love for Kallie.

I looked over at my father's grave once more, realizing why I'd come to the cemetery in the first place. Before I could move forward, I needed my parents' approval.

"I'm sorry, Dad. I have to give it up. It's not just about my hip injury—it's about what would happen to Kallie if I got hurt again. She's too important to me. She deserves a whole man, not a broken one. If that means I have to give up racing and find a new path, so be it. I can honestly say, though, I don't think I'll ever be far from the track. I just can't be behind the wheel anymore. I don't know... What do you think about me consulting? Or maybe I could try my hand at being a crew chief?"

As if he were sending me a message from the heavens, the California sycamore trees began to sway. The slight breeze seemed to inject a sense of balance, giving me the courage I needed to embark on a new path.

Smiling to myself, I took a few steps to my father's headstone and placed my hand on the top. Giving it a gentle pat, I whispered, "Thanks, Dad. I'll take the wheel from here."

27

Sloan

Just after three o'clock, I returned to Kallie's house. I'd stopped at a local florist along the way and tried to do my best to duplicate the same arrangement of flowers I'd sent her a couple of months back—sunflowers mixed with vibrant roses, lilies, and snapdragons—rainbow colors for my Rainbow Brite.

Flowers in hand, I walked up to her front door and raised my fist to knock. However, I paused right before my knuckles connected with the door. The suitcases in the front hall were gone. Spinning around, I looked at the driveway. Her car was gone too.

Panic gripped my chest as I tried to remember when she said she would be flying home. I was sure she'd said the day after tomorrow. Instinctively, I pulled my cell from my pocket and tapped Kallie's name in my contact list, but my call was immediately sent to voicemail.

"Shit!" hissed.

I was pacing back and forth on the front walkway, trying to decide my next course of action, when a white van pulled into the driveaway. The words Tidy Maids were painted across the side in bright blue lettering. My brow furrowed in confusion when the female driver exited the vehicle and slid open the side door to allow two other women to file out.

"Can I help you?" I asked.

The driver looked up in surprise as if seeing me for the first time.

"Oh! I'm sorry, sir. We were told nobody would be home. We're here to clean."

"Obviously," I said, gesturing to the logo on the van. "But why are you here to clean?"

She looked past me at the house with a confused expression, then looked down at a notebook she was holding.

"This is the right address, right? Number eighty-seven?" she asked.

"Yes, that's the right house number," I confirmed. "Who told you nobody would be home?"

"It was the nice lady who contacted us from Quinn & Wilkshire. She said a tenant recently vacated the property, and it needed to be cleaned top to bottom. She gave us a code to get in through the side door. Is that okay?"

Vacated the property? Had Kallie left the house for good? Did she go to a hotel?

My eyes widened, suddenly realizing how I might be able to find out where Kallie was.

"I'm sure everything is fine. You can go on ahead and do what you need to do. Thank you for your help," I said and rushed past the cleaning crew toward my car. Once inside, I pulled up my email on my phone and searched for the contract from Quinn & Wilkshire that Milo had forwarded to me three months earlier. After locating the PDF file, I found the logo, address, and telephone number for the PR firm typed across the top. Dialing the phone number, I impatiently tapped my thumb on the steering wheel as I waited for someone to pick up. After the third ring, a pleasant voice greeted me.

"Thank you for calling Quinn & Wilkshire. How may I direct your call?" she asked.

"Hello. My name is Sloan Atwood. I'm trying to reach Kalliope Benton Riley."

"I'm sorry, Mr. Atwood. Ms. Riley is currently out of the office on assignment. Would you like her voicemail?"

"I know she's on an assignment—I *am* the assignment. Unfortunately, I'm unable to get in touch with her at the moment."

"Oh, I see. Please hold for one moment." It seemed like I'd caught her off guard, so I waited patiently and listened to what sounded like clicking on a keyboard. A moment later, she returned. "Mr. Fitzgerald Quinn, the owner and senior partner, is available to speak with you. If you'd like, I can put you through to him."

Kallie's father. Fuck.

I had hoped to get some low-level employee to tell me where Kallie was. I didn't plan on having to talk to her father of all people. He didn't know me from Adam, and I didn't know how to explain what I wanted without sounding like a psychopath.

"That's fine. Put me through," I told the receptionist. I was placed on hold for only a few seconds before Kallie's father's voice came through the line.

"Mr. Atwood. Fitz Quinn here. How can I help you?"

"Hello, Mr. Quinn," I replied as respectfully as possible, then dove right in. No sense in beating around the bush. "I'm actually trying to locate Kallie. Have you heard from her by any chance?"

"Kallie? Um, yes. I'd heard there was a little problem

regarding your compatibility. I can assure you, Mr. Atwood. My partner, Devon, and I are on it. We'll have a replacement agent out to you within a few days."

"No, sir. I don't want a replacement. I'm perfectly fine with Kallie representing me. That's why I'm trying to reach her. I need to tell her that I want her to stay," I said, hoping beyond hope that I was able to keep any signs of pleading out of my voice.

"I'm not sure what the confusion is. I haven't spoken to Kallie directly. I just received a message stating that she would be on a plane to return today. I believe her flight leaves at five."

A knot formed in my throat, so big I could barely breathe around it. She was really going to leave. She was giving up on me—on *us*. I couldn't let that happen. Pulling the phone away from my ear, I looked at the time. It was going on three-thirty. The chances of me getting to her before the plane took off were slim to none, but I had to try.

"Thank you, Mr. Quinn. That's all I needed to know. And sir?"

"Yes?"

"I just wanted to say that you have one spectacular daughter."

Without another word, I ended the call, threw the car in reverse, and backed out of the driveway.

I raced through the streets to the nearest on-ramp for the I-405, then headed south toward the Los Angeles International Airport. Traffic wasn't too terribly bad for once. The fifteen-minute drive only ended up being thirty-five minutes. It could have been much worse, but I was still running out of time. I glanced at the clock on the dash as I pulled into a parking space in the short-term parking lot at the airport. It was after four. Most likely, Kallie's plane would begin boarding within the next thirty minutes.

Hurrying out of the car, I hit the button on the key fob to

lock the doors. As I ran across the lot toward the airport entrance, I realized I'd forgotten to grab the flowers I had purchased for Kallie but didn't want to waste time going back for them. Getting to her was more important right now.

I couldn't get past security without a plane ticket, so once inside, I went straight to the ticket counter. The line was four people deep, leaving me no choice but to wait. The seconds and minutes ticked by painfully slowly as I stared at the clock on the wall behind the counter. It reminded me of the old saying about a watched pot that would never boil. I shoved an impatient hand through my hair, wishing the line would move faster.

"Can I help you, sir?" said the attendant behind the counter when it was finally my turn. I glanced at her red and blue name tag with the heart logo. Her name was Judy, and she'd been with the airline company for sixteen years.

"Hello, Judy. I need to get on the next flight to Washington D.C."

"You don't have a ticket?"

"No."

"Let me see what we have available," she said and began typing on her keyboard. "It looks like there are still a few seats available on the five o'clock flight to Reagan National Airport, but I'm not sure if you'll make it to the gate in time. I can get you on the seven-ten flight tomorrow morn—"

"I'll take today's five o'clock flight. I'll run to the gate if I have to."

"Um, okay. Well, I'll need to see some identification," she eventually said. She eyed me strangely, almost as if she were sizing me up, while I pulled my license from my wallet. She took it from me, scrutinizing it carefully. I tapped an impatient foot, wanting to scream that I wasn't on the terrorist watch list. I was simply a man who needed to get to his girl.

"Oh my gosh! You're Sloan Atwood—as in *the* Sloan Atwood!" Judy said.

Dammit! I don't have time for this.

"That's me," I responded with a shrug, hoping the people standing nearby hadn't heard her.

"My husband is a huge fan of yours—well, he was. What happened to you was terrible," she prattled on. "We were all praying for you after your accident. I'm glad to see you looking so well."

"I appreciate that," I replied, desperately trying to keep the impatience out of my voice. "Look, I know I seem like I'm in a hurry—I am. You see, the woman who I'm supposed to spend my life with is getting on that plane. I need to get to her."

Her head snapped back, and her eyes were alight with excitement.

"Oh! You said you're supposed to spend your life with her—are you proposing to her here at the airport?" she asked, seeming giddy at the prospect. At this point, I would tell her anything she wanted to hear if it meant she would move faster.

"Yes, ma'am. That's the plan."

"Well, then we'll just have to make sure you make it to the gate in time." Without another word, Judy moved at lightning speed. In a matter of minutes, she began printing my boarding passes. As we waited for my required documents and receipt to spit out from the archaic dot matrix printing machine, she smiled and said, "I'll call the gate to let them know you're coming and ask them to give you a few extra minutes."

"You don't have to do that," I told her, but she waved me off and picked up the phone next to the computer. A few seconds later, she spoke into the receiver.

"Hi, Celia. This is Judy from ticketing. I just wanted to let you know that you'll have a passenger arriving a few minutes late to the gate. It's Sloan Atwood. I'm sure you've heard of him. He's the race car driver who had that awful accident last year."

She paused, nodding her head rapidly, while the person on the other end of the line spoke. "Oh, perfect! That works out then, doesn't it? He'll be there shortly. Oh, and I should tell you, he's going to propose to someone when he gets there! Can you believe it?"

She was practically squealing like a schoolgirl.

Shit.

The tickets finished printing, and she handed them over to me.

"Thank you," I said, eager to get away from the woman who had nothing but hearts in her eyes.

"Don't worry about rushing. The flight is delayed slightly due to a hazmat issue, so you should make it to the gate in plenty of time."

Not bothering to ask more specifics about the hazmat delay, I thanked her again and rushed to security, where I had to wait in yet another line. As I slowly made my way through the snaking rows of retractable belt stanchions, I had a minute to absorb what had just happened at the ticket counter and found myself chuckling over the irony.

Married? Right.

However, the more I toyed with the idea of marrying Kallie, the better it sounded. Hadn't I just been thinking about spending forever with her? That's what marriage meant after all. Perhaps this was fate's way of giving me a nudge. The rational part of me erred on the side of caution. A lifetime was a long time. There were so many things Kallie and I had yet to learn about each other. Still, despite the unknowns, a lifetime with her felt right—like it was just the way things were meant to be.

After I got through security, I followed the signs to my assigned gate number. When I reached it, I didn't even have to search for Kallie. Just like the first day I saw her on the beach, she stood out among the ordinary, and I felt her gravity pulling me like an invisible magnet.

Slowly, I put one foot in front of the other and studied her. Her golden hair was pulled back into a ponytail, the red and blue extensions still in place. She was looking down at a magazine on her lap, her beautiful face focused on whatever text she was reading. My breath caught in my throat. The idea that I might have lost her—that I might lose her still—caused all the air to steal from my lungs.

As if she felt the pull, too, she slowly turned to face me. I couldn't tell if she was sad or happy to see me. She shook her head as if to stop me from coming any further, but I didn't stop walking until I reached the end of the row of chairs on which she sat. Only then did I pause. She stared at me with stormy green eyes for a long while, her expression distant and untouchable, as if she were trying to hide the feelings she was trying to sort out.

Emotion welled up inside me, erupting from a place I didn't know existed. My words—everything I'd practiced in my head during the drive to the airport—got caught in my throat as I stared at her. Instead of trying to say everything I was feeling, I said the only thing that seemed to matter.

"I love you, Kallie. Please don't go."

28

Kallie

I gasped. It felt like the ground had quite literally fallen out from beneath my feet. I couldn't speak. A shiver raced down my spine, and energy crashed through the air like a thunderbolt. I knew I had to say something one way or the other, but fear of getting the words wrong rendered me speechless.

Sloan stood only a few feet away from me, his eyes searching mine. His blue gaze was piercing and devastating, just as it was on the day we first met. He was a force of nature, and he was here—for me. Something profound twisted in my heart. My love for him was bigger than anything else I'd ever felt. It was intense and potent—just like he was. As I stared into his expressive eyes, I wanted nothing more than to leap into his arms. However, before I did that, I had to be sure his declaration of love wasn't just in response to mine.

"Sloan, what are you doing here?" I asked once I could find my voice.

"I'm here because I couldn't handle the thought of you leaving."

"But you should be on your way to San Antonio."

Moving over to sit in the empty seat beside me, he took my hand.

"I'm not going to San Antonio, Kallie."

I had to fight every bone in my body to stop myself from reaching up to touch his face. Whenever he was around, I was unable to resist being close to him. But after the emotional and physical strain of the past few weeks, I hesitated. Although he was right next to me, he seemed so far out of reach.

"What do you mean you aren't going?"

"I mean, I quit. I'm giving up racing. You were right—the risk to my body is too great. But it's more than that. It's about you, too. I feel like every turn I've made since before my accident has sent me the wrong direction on a one-way road. I kept trying to dodge the oncoming traffic instead of going the way everyone else was. But then you came along, and you made me realize there was more than one way to travel. I—"

Whatever else he was about to say was interrupted by a loud voice coming over the gate's intercom system.

"Ladies and gentlemen, we apologize for the delay. The captain just informed us that we should be able to begin boarding in about fifteen minutes. As a reminder, those with disabilities and people with small children will be allowed to board first."

"It's a good thing for the flight delay," Sloan said. "I wouldn't have made it here in time if not for that. The lady at the ticket counter said it was a hazmat issue. I wonder what that's all about."

"Poop on the tarmac," I replied, only to receive the most bewildered expression I'd ever seen on Sloan's face.

"I'm sorry?"

"Apparently, when the service guys were emptying the waste tanks from the previous flight, the hose outside the plane broke. So, that means poop on the tarmac—literally. They had to call hazmat to clean it up before we could board. Shit happens, you know?" I said with an ironic smile to try and lighten the somber mood. I felt uncharacteristically nervous because I didn't know why Sloan was here. I wanted to know, yet I didn't at the same time.

Sloan returned my smile, but it didn't quite meet his eyes. He looked out through the floor-to-ceiling glass windows at the plane. When he spoke, his voice was quiet, and I had to strain to hear him.

"You were really going to leave."

Overcome with sadness, I dropped my head and pulled my hand from his.

"Yes. And I still am, Sloan. I just think it's for the best. I can't come between you and racing. I know how much you love it. It would be wrong for me to make you choose. Please don't quit because of me."

"That's just it—I *am* quitting because of you, but it's not because of anything you did or said. It's because of how I feel about you. Kallie, I—" Once again, his words were cut off when his cellphone began to ring. Reaching around to pull it from his back pocket, he glanced at the screen and frowned. "Shit. It's Milo. Kallie, I'm sorry. I need to answer this."

I pursed my lips, trying to hide my irritation over Milo's interruption. I was on pins and needles. I wanted to finish hearing what Sloan had to say. However, this just further proved why I needed to leave—racing would always come first.

"It's fine. Do what you need to do," I waved off as casually as I could to mask the sting.

"Just give me two minutes. I have to do something I should've done a long time ago." Turning back to his phone, he slid his finger across the screen and brought the phone to his ear. "This is Atwood."

"Where the hell are you? You were supposed to leave hours ago," Milo barked. Despite the busy airport, I could hear him loud and clear. He was yelling, and he sounded furious.

"I'm not going to San Antonio, Milo," Sloan told him.

"What do you mean you're not going? The whole crew is packed and waiting—"

"I quit. I'm sorry it's so last minute, but it is what it is. I'll call Tyler and explain."

I stared at Sloan with incredulity. He truly was going to quit. It wasn't just a line he was giving to appease me. Still, guilt clawed at my chest. I had meant what I said—I didn't want him to give up what he loved on account of me.

"Explain? You'll have to do more than explain! The reps at Kapton are going to lose their goddamn minds!" I heard Milo booming, forcing Sloan to pull the phone slightly away from his ear. "Do you know how much money has gone into this? I haven't been busting my ass to get you here for nothing. Do you think I work for free?"

"Well, it looks like you did this time. But don't worry about your precious money. If you have anything out of pocket, I'll reimburse you. I would say I'm sorry that you'll miss your payout for this race, but I'm not. There will be others. I just won't be the driver. You're fired, Milo."

"You can't fire me!"

"I just did," Sloan stated matter-of-factly.

"Does this have anything to do with the blonde bitch?"

"Man, you really are a dick. Don't call me again. And if you even think about smearing my name or Kallie's, I'll have to inform the International Racing Association about the little baggie of pills you gave me. I don't think they'll look favorably on an agent handing out illegally-obtained oxy like it's candy."

"You wouldn't dare. Nobody would believe you, and it would be your word against mine."

"You sure about that? Your fingerprints are all over the bag," Sloan pointed out, then angled his head to toss me a wink. "Your clients will start dropping like flies once word gets out."

"Why, you son of a—"

"Goodbye, Milo." Sloan ended the call with a satisfied smirk and turned back to me. "God, that felt good. I should have cut him loose years ago. He's such an asshole."

"You know, my fingerprints are on the bag, too," I reminded him.

"I know, but Milo doesn't know that," he said with a shrug before giving me a sexy, lopsided grin. "So, where were we?"

"You were talking about giving up racing, and I said I didn't want you to do it for the wrong reasons."

"Kallie, you aren't the wrong reason."

"What about Tyler? I mean, there's so much at stake. If you want to pull out of racing in the MILL because of your hip, that's one thing. But I can't be the reason Tyler's wife doesn't get the treatment she needs."

"I've thought about that. A while back, I briefly spoke to Cooper about doing a fundraiser. I know Rochele was looking into it, but I don't know how far she got. The more I think about doing a benefit, the more I think we'd be able to pull in a ton of cash if we got all of the top drivers involved—maybe do a silent auction or something like that. Serious fans would pay a mint for a signed helmet worn during a prominent race. We might even be able to raise more money than I'd be able to win in the MILL. I won't just leave Tyler high and dry. I know he was counting on me, and I won't let him down."

"That might solve the problem with Tyler, but that still leaves one huge unanswered question. Are you really going to be able to give up racing for good? You're forgetting that I saw you on the track. The way your spirit came alive was like magic

—like seeing a caged bird set free to fly. What are you going to do without it?"

"I thought about that, too," he told me and then paused. A faraway look spread across his face for a moment before he focused on me once more. "I went to the cemetery after I left your house earlier today."

"The cemetery?" I asked with surprise.

"Yeah... I felt the need to visit my parents' gravesites. I didn't realize how much soul-searching one can do in a place like that. If I did, I might have gone there long before today."

"What prompted you to go there?"

"I needed to make amends. I've finally come to understand why my mom did what she did. She really loved my father. After he was gone, she gave all that love to me. When she thought she would lose me too, it was just too much for her to handle. I know that with certainty now. I never really comprehended the depths of that love until I met you. When I thought I might lose you, I finally understood what it meant to feel like I couldn't live without somebody. Everything just seemed to make sense after that, and I realized I'd been too hard on my mom."

"Sloan, I—"

"Wait. Let me finish," he said and held up a hand to silence me. "I also talked to her and my dad about life without racing. Neither of them would have approved of what I was doing. You were right about that, too—I was killing myself. I'd blurred the line between perseverance and foolishness. So, I asked my dad what he thought about me possibly getting into consulting or coaching, and the strangest thing happened. Your universe, the one you love to talk about, spoke to me. I *can* go on without racing. I thought about working with Wings Halfway House like you suggested, possibly starting my own racing school, looking for a job as a crew chief, and everything else in between—

but I don't want to do any of those things if you aren't with me."

My heart began pounding rapidly. I loved Sloan, but I was terrified to hope. I studied his face, desperately trying to read his expression. I couldn't tell if he was happy, sad, or relieved to have shared all of that with me.

"What are you trying to say, Sloan?"

"I'm saying you made me a believer in romance—and I believe in us. It isn't racing I need. It's you and only you."

I squeezed my eyes closed, trying to sort the multiple emotions that ravaged my thoughts. When I opened them again, I noticed a bunch of people with their focus trained on Sloan and me.

"Why does it seem like everyone is staring at us?"

Sloan's gaze scanned the small crowd waiting at the gate.

"I don't think everyone is, but I'm pretty sure the airline employees behind the desk are. There's kind of a funny story behind that."

I raised my eyebrows.

"Oh?"

He grinned sheepishly and shrugged.

"Yeah... So, when I was rushing to get a plane ticket so I could catch you in time, the woman who was taking care of me was moving at a snail's pace. I tried to hurry her along by telling her I needed to get to the woman I wanted to spend my life with. She got all excited and sort of assumed that meant I was going to propose."

My eyes widened in surprise.

"Sort of assumed? And you didn't correct her?"

"As I said, she was moving too slow, and I had to speed her along. How was I supposed to know she was going to call the gate and tell them I was going to propose to you?"

"Wait, are you telling me the reason people are staring is that they're waiting for a marriage proposal?"

"Maybe. What do you say, Rainbow Brite? Want to get hitched?"

I would have laughed at the idea, but there was nothing humorous about his expression.

"You're serious right now?"

"I can be if you want me to be. But I will say, I thought if I were going to propose to you, it would be someplace better. We're in an airport, for crying out loud—I can do better than this. I just want you to know how serious I am about you—about us. I love you so damn much it hurts. I was a fool not to realize it before today," he admitted, his voice raw with emotion. "I know you have a life in D.C., and I'm not asking you to give that up. The reality is, there's nothing for me here. I can pack up and go wherever you are if that's what it takes. Did you really mean what you said? Do you love me?"

"I meant every word. I do love you, Sloan—but I wasn't thinking marriage. It was more like... I don't know. Take me slow dancing on the beach, make love to me under the stars, and discover each other over time. I never want to get divorced, and I don't think this sort of thing should be rushed."

"I didn't come here to propose to you, so don't feel rushed. But once I started thinking about it, I couldn't shake the feeling that it just seemed right," he explained. "I didn't plan on falling in love with you, just as I don't think you planned on falling for me. But once we met, the gravitational pull was undeniable. I've never felt anything like it before. What we have is rare and beautiful."

He sat a foot away from me, his eyes searching mine. I understood what he was saying. I felt the same way. As I processed the emotion swirling in his endless blues, I saw something in our future that would go on forever. It was all I could do not to reach into my carry-on bag and pull out my tarot deck. Official proposal or not, I just needed a sign—

anything that would allow me to leap into his arms and tell him I would be his partner in life forever.

"Now boarding Group C," said a woman's voice through the overhead speaker.

"That's me," I said, wishing I could buy more time.

"It's me too."

I looked around. There was only a smattering of people nearby since two-thirds of the passengers were already on the plane, but it seemed as if every single person in the immediate area had their eyes trained on Sloan and me.

"Should we board?" I asked, more to myself than to him. I was so flustered, and I felt as if every thought in my head was given a voice before I could think it through. "I mean, you could come home with me and meet my parents. Maybe we could talk more about his then—when we don't have so many people looking at us."

I watched him curiously as he shifted from his seat to kneel on the floor in front of me. I didn't panic because he wasn't on one knee. He just seemed to want to be in my direct line of sight so he could have my undivided attention. He reached up and took my chin in between his fingers.

"Kallie?" The questioning tone of his voice was low and husky. Goosebumps pebbled over my skin.

"Yes?" I whispered.

"I know we have a lot to learn about each other. I have no doubt that I want to marry you one day. You're my checkered flag, baby. I want to wake up to rainbow hair spread across the pillow next to me every single damn day for the rest of my life —but I also don't want to skip the steps in between. I want to meet your family and see your home in D.C. I want to learn your favorite songs, favorite foods, and maybe even try Tofurky one day—no promises on that, though," he added with a wink before turning serious again. "But I do promise to give you the sun, the moon, and every one of the millions of stars in the sky. Will you give me the chance to make good on that promise?"

Tears began to well hot in my eyes and threatened to fall. He could be all mine if I allowed it. He could be mine forever. I reached up to trace the lines of his face with my finger, moving over his strong jaw and chiseled cheekbones, pausing only to cup the side of his head. The potent way he was looking at me made my words catch in my throat, and that's when I saw it—my Don Lockwood. Sloan gazed at me just like Don Lockwood had beheld Kathy Seldon in *Singin' In The Rain*. Maybe life could be like it was in the movies, after all. There was no doubt I wanted to spend my life with him—but he was right about the steps in between, and I didn't want to miss a single one.

"Sloan, I don't need you to promise me the moon and the stars—I just want you to promise to watch them with me. Always."

"What do you say we start by jumping on that plane? I bet the sunset will be beautiful above the clouds."

I grinned. "I think that's the perfect place to start."

Sloan got to his feet, gripped the sides of my shoulders, and pulled me up so he could wrap his strong arms tight around me. He rained kisses on my cheeks, forehead, and nose. Tears leaked down my face as I fiercely clung to him. My heart wanted to explode with love. The past three months had been a complete whirlwind, with our relationship moving at breakneck speed. We'd been living in the fast lane, and I didn't know how we'd gotten to this point. All I knew was that I was looking forward to finally slowing down to enjoy the road ahead.

The gypsy had been wrong when she said my eagerness to express my emotions would be my downfall. Yes, I was a Gemini, but she failed to predict I would partner with a Taurus. While the two paired together might look like total opposites at first, Geminis and Tauruses were a dynamic match when the planets aligned in their favor—and that was precisely what had happened. What I shared with Sloan was more than just a fierce physical attraction. We had so much to offer one another as long as we never stopped believing in *us*.

I pulled back to share my thoughts with Sloan, but paused when I heard clapping coming from somewhere behind me. Blinking my tears away, I slowly turned my head to see three airline employees looking at us with wide smiles. When the other bystanders turned to see what they were clapping at, Sloan shrugged sheepishly.

"Should we tell them we aren't really engaged?" he whispered.

"Nah. No need to tell them. I have a feeling we will be soon enough."

Sloan beamed, then stepped back to pick up my carry-on bag. Taking my hand, he looked down at me with eyes brighter than the clearest blue sky.

"Come on, Rainbow Brite. We've got a sunset to watch."

Thank you for reading *Endurance*!
I hope you enjoyed Kallie & Sloan's story! If you enjoyed this book, you might like *The Stone Series*. It's my first book series and is still my number one bestseller.

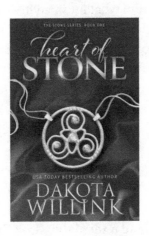

Bound by need. Entwined in secrets...

Krystina

I had dreams and aspirations, none of which included a man by my side. Been there, done that. Then I forgot my cellphone, and all of my carefully laid plans went to hell.

He wasn't supposed to be there when I fell. I wasn't supposed to get lost in a sea of sapphire blue when he helped me up. And he wasn't supposed to be Alexander Stone, the New York billionaire real estate tycoon.

I saw the dark promises in his eyes when he looked at me. But the shadows of my past haunted me, making me afraid to explore the possibilities I could never before have imagined.

Alexander

I was used to getting what I wanted. I understood the value of finesse and patience to achieve the desired result. But a chance run-in with Krystina Cole quickly turned my world upside down.

She was strong, determined, devastatingly beautiful—and stubborn as hell. Her quick wit and firecracker attitude was the complete opposite of what I wanted in a woman. But I still wanted to claim her. Tame her. Make her mine.

And I always get what I want.

Heart of Stone is the first book in Krystina & Alexander's epic love story. It's the beginning of the steamy and unforgettable series by *USA Today* Bestselling Author Dakota Willink.

"Fans of Fifty Shades and Crossfire will devour this series!" ~ *After Fifty Shades Book Blog*

"Heart wrenching and undeniably sexy! This series is going to my TBR again and again!" ~ *Not Your Moms Romance Blog*

One-click HEART OF STONE!

If you loved *Untouched* check out a some of the other books in my catalogue!

The Stone Series
If you haven't read my books, *The Stone Series* is my first book series and is still my number one bestseller. This sexy, billionaire romance was literally my whole life for over three years. It's a complete trilogy and it's available on all platforms!

The Sound of Silence

Meet Gianna and Derek in this an emotionally gripping, dark romantic thriller that is guaranteed to keep you on the edge of your seat! This book is not for the faint-hearted. Plus, Krystina Cole from *The Stone Series* has a cameo appearance!

For more titles, please visit www.dakotawillink.com.

SUBSCRIBE TO DAKOTA'S NEWSLETTER

My newsletter goes out twice a month (sometimes less). It's packed with new content, sales on signed paperbacks and Angel Book Boxes from my online store, and giveaways. Don't miss out! I value your email address and promise to NEVER spam you.

SUBSCRIBE HERE: https://dakotawillink.com/subscribe

BOOKS & BOXED WINE CONFESSIONS

Want fun stuff and sneak peek excerpts from Dakota?
Join Books & Boxed Wine Confessions and get the inside scoop!
Fans in this interactive reader Facebook group are the first to know the latest news!

JOIN HERE: https://www.facebook.com/groups/
1635080436793794

MUSIC PLAYLIST

Thank you to the musical talents who influenced and inspired *Endurance*. Their creativity helped me bring this story to life.

"Leaving on a Jetplane" by Peter, Paul & Mary
"Ventura Highway" by America
"Marry Me" by Train
"Luminous" by Alice & the Glass Lake
"I Want You to Want Me" by Cheap Trick
"Don't Stop Believin'" by Journey
"The Distance" by Cake
"Boys of Summer" by The Ataris
"Fade Into You" by Mazzy Star
"Highway to Hell" by AC/DC
"Exodus" by Ruelle
"21 Guns" by Green Day
"Last One to Know" by Leah Noble
"Drive" by Halsey

LISTEN ON SPOTIFY

ABOUT THE AUTHOR

Dakota Willink is an award-winning *USA Today* Bestselling Author from New York. She loves writing about damaged heroes who fall in love with sassy and independent females. Her books are character-driven, emotional, and sexy, yet written with a flare that keeps them real. With a wide range of publications, Dakota's imagination is constantly spinning new ideas.

Dakota often says she survived her first publishing with coffee and wine. She's an unabashed *Star Wars* fanatic and still dreams of getting her letter from Hogwarts one day. Her daily routines usually include rocking Lululemon yoga pants, putting on lipstick, and obsessing over Excel spreadsheets. Two spoiled Cavaliers are her furry writing companions who bring her regular smiles. She enjoys traveling with her husband and debating social and economic issues with her politically savvy Generation Z son and daughter.

Dakota's favorite book genres include contemporary or dark romance, political & psychological thrillers, and autobiographies.

AWARDS, ACCOLADES, AND OTHER PROJECTS

The Stone Series is Dakota's first published book series. It has been recognized for various awards and bestseller lists, including *USA Today* and the *Readers' Favorite* 2017 Gold Medal in Romance, and has since been translated into multiple languages internationally.

The *Fade Into You* series (formally known as the *Cadence* duet) was a finalist in the *HEAR Now Festival Independent Audiobook Awards*.

In addition, Dakota has written under the alternate pen name, Marie Christy. Under this name, she has written and published a children's book for charity titled, *And I Smile*.

Also writing as Marie Christy, she was a contributor to the Blunder Woman Productions project, *Nevertheless We Persisted: Me Too*, a 2019 *Audie Award Finalist* and *Earphones Awards Winner*. This project inspired Dakota to write *The Sound of Silence*, a dark romantic suspense novel that tackles the realities of domestic abuse.

Dakota Willink is the founder of Dragonfly Ink Publishing, whose mission is to promote a common passion for reading by partnering with like-minded authors and industry professionals. Through this company, Dakota created the *Love & Lace Inkorporated* Magazine and the *Leave Me Breathless World*, hosted ALLURE Audiobook Con, and sponsored various charity anthologies.

Printed in the USA
CPSIA information can be obtained
at www.ICGtesting.com
LVHW050006141223
766467LV00040B/898

9 781954 817067